JACK CALDER

The Fracture of the Veil: Book Two of the Veil Saga

This book was professionally typeset on Reedsy.
Find out more at reedsy.com

Contents

1

Fog, Messages, and the Disbanded (Brentford, England 1899)

A hard winter fog rolled in from the Thames that night, thick enough to swallow the sound of carriage wheels on Brentford's streets. The fog turned gas lamps into dim halos and make a man question whether the ground beneath his boots was truly solid. December had come with a vengeance, bringing frost that clung to the cobblestones and made each step crack faintly under my weight.

I walked from Brentford Dock through streets that appeared more ghost town than living city. The warehouses loomed dark and silent on either side, their brick facades slick with condensation. Coal smoke mixed with the river smell, that combination of industrial waste and low tide that marked London's western reaches. The Grand Union Canal lay somewhere to my left, invisible in the murk, but I could hear water lapping against stone and the occasional groan of a barge settling against its moorings.

Brook Road South appeared out of the fog like something conjured. The street was residential here, narrow houses pressed together with their windows shuttered against the cold. A dog barked somewhere, muffled by the weather. A woman's voice called out briefly, then silence returned.

The Griffin stood at the junction with Braemar Road, a corner pub with a distinctive tower-like structure that caught what little light escaped the gas lamps. The building itself was Fuller's, built some fifteen years earlier with that solid Victorian confidence that declared permanence. The polygonal corner treatment gave it an unusual profile, angular and severe, like something cut from different geometric shapes and forced together.

Above the entrance, carved into the stonework, a griffin watched the street with blank eyes. The brewery's symbol. Fuller's had owned the orchard that once stood here, and the pub bore their mark like a brand. The creature looked pale and stiff in the icy gloom, frost gathering along its wings and beak.

The pub's windows glowed with warm amber light that made the cold outside feel sharper by contrast. Smoke from the hearth drifted through the glass in slow curls, and the silhouettes of patrons leaned toward the fire the way men do when they cannot remember the last time their bones felt warm. I stood outside for a moment, letting the cold settle deeper into my coat. The fog pressed close, patient and hungry.

Then I pushed open the door and stepped inside.

The world changed. Heat hit me first, the blessed shock of warmth after the brutal cold of the streets. The fire snapped loudly in its grate, battling the winter air that crept in each time the door opened. The smell was thick and immediate: coal smoke, wet wool, spilled ale, tobacco, and beneath it all the yeasty scent of bread from the kitchen. The smell soaked into wood and never quite left.

The interior was all dark wood and brass fittings. An L-shaped bar sat to the back of the room. Behind it, bottles gleamed on shelves, and the brass taps caught the firelight. There were various tables tucked into corners and some benches running along the walls where working men could sit and nurse their pints in relative privacy.

Coats steamed slowly where they hung near the hearth, dripping condensation onto the floorboards. A few men stood at the bar with their hands wrapped around pints. Others sat hunched over tables, speaking in low voices that mixed with the crackle of the fire and created a background hum that was almost alive.

Gas lamps hung from chains, their mantles glowing steady and warm. The whole place was like a refuge, a pocket of civilization carved out of the winter darkness. A place where a man could forget, for an hour or two, that the world outside was cold and hostile.

I chose a corner table away from the draft, settling into a chair that creaked under my weight. The wood was worn smooth by use, and someone had carved initials into the armrest. J.M. 1887. I wondered who J.M. had been and whether he was still alive.

I pulled off my gloves and rubbed warmth back into my fingers. Despite never aging, my hands looked old in the candlelight, calloused from work that spanned centuries. I let the heat from the candle on the table soak into my skin. The flame bent each time a gust rattled the windowpanes, dancing and recovering, dancing and recovering.

Around me, the pub conducted its evening business. A group of dockworkers occupied a table near the fire, their faces red with ale and heat. They spoke loudly about wages and foremen and which tavern girl would look their way. Near the window, an older man sat alone with his pipe and his thoughts, staring into nothing. Two younger men played cards at a side table, slapping down their hands with theatrical flourishes. They went about their business, drinking and laughing and arguing, secure in the delusion that the world was safe and reasonable and governed by natural laws.

I envied them their ignorance.

Lucan arrived a few minutes later. He stepped in from the cold with frost on his coat and tension in his jaw. As he entered, he scanned the room, found me, and made his way through the press of bodies. He moved like a soldier, economical and aware, always conscious of exits and potential threats.

He looked more troubled than when I'd last seen him. It had been three years, perhaps four. He had not aged in the hundreds of years I had known him, not in the way mortal men do, but he had a look of strain and a tiredness that comes with the weight of eternity. He shook the chill off like a man returning from a long march rather than a short walk through Brentford's streets.

"You look frozen," I said as he sat.

"Frozen and tired." He pulled off his gloves with stiff fingers. "And neither seems to be improving."

I flagged the barman, a thick-armed man with a scarred face and the look of someone who'd seen his share of trouble. I ordered two pints of mild along with a bottle of whiskey. The prices were chalked on a board behind the bar: twopence for mild, threepence for bitter, sixpence for a measure of spirits. Working man's rates.

When the drinks arrived, Lucan held his glass close, letting the heat seep into his fingers before taking a drink. He closed his eyes briefly, savoring the warmth.

"Thank you," he said quietly. "I had almost forgotten what warmth felt like."

"You wrote as if the matter was urgent."

"It is. And growing worse." He set down his glass and leaned forward, lowering his voice. "Three deaths in Brentford. All near the river. All drained of blood. Have you heard anything? I know you live just across the river."

Around us, the pub noise continued. Someone laughed, high and a little tipsy. The fire popped as a log shifted. The dockworkers started an argument about football, voices rising.

"No, but I have been travelling. When?" I asked.

"First one was six weeks ago. A dockworker, found behind one of the warehouses near Brunel's old dock. Second was a prostitute, three weeks later. Third was just five days ago. A merchant's son."

"That last one will cause trouble."

"It already has. The police are asking questions. The father has money and connections. He's demanding answers." Lucan drank again, deeper this time. "But the police won't find anything useful. They're looking for a human killer. They don't understand what they're hunting."

"And you do?"

"Not entirely. That's why I need help."

Before he could continue, the door opened again. A sharp gust of winter air rushed in, carrying fog and the faint smell of the river. Two figures emerged from the doorway, both brushing frost from their coats as they stepped inside. The other patrons barely glanced at them. Just more cold souls seeking warmth and ale.

But I looked. Old instinct. Always note who enters a room.

The woman entered first. Tall, more than five and a half feet, with dark hair damp from the fog and pulled back in a severe style that emphasized the sharp angles of her face. Beautiful in a predator sort of way. She moved with economy, no wasted motion, scanning the room with green eyes that missed nothing. Her coat was well-made but practical, designed for movement rather than fashion. She carried herself like someone who knew how to handle trouble. There was something in the way she assessed the room, not the casual glance of someone seeking a seat, but the calculated sweep of someone cataloging exits, threats, and tactical advantages. It reminded me of a sniper selecting a position.

Behind her came a man with the unmistakable bearing of an American. Thin, broad shouldered and corded muscle. He had a swagger that warned of danger, wearing a coat with the collar turned up against the cold. He stomped frost from his boots before scanning the room like a soldier entering unfamiliar ground. His face was weathered, his jaw strong, his eyes the pale blue of winter ice. His right hand stayed near his coat's opening, hovering over what I suspected was a weapon. Even in an ordinary pub, his body was coiled, ready.

Lucan rose, lifting his hand in greeting. They spotted him and made their way through the tables.

"James, this is Corisande Valencourt," Lucan said as they approached.

She extended her hand. Her grip was firm, her palm rough. The hand of someone who'd trained with weapons. "A pleasure," she said, "and please, Cori is fine." Her accent was educated, the Queen's English spoken with a cadence that said she didn't spend much time in aristocratic circles. "I have heard your name for years."

Her green eyes held mine for a moment longer than courtesy required, and I had the distinct impression I was being weighed and measured against some internal standard. Whatever her conclusion, she gave no indication.

"Only the flattering stories, I hope."

She smiled faintly. "Flattering stories are rarely the ones worth telling."

The American offered his hand next. "Ezekiel Whitmore. Call me Zeke."

His grip was crushing, the handshake of someone who'd grown up in a place where physical strength mattered. "Lucan tells me you're the real deal," he said, his Southern drawl warm and genuine. "Hope he ain't overselling, because we surely need someone who knows their business."

"We shall see."

They settled around the table. The barmaid appeared, a tired-looking woman with graying hair and knowing eyes. She took their orders without writing anything down. Two more pints, another whiskey. She returned quickly, collected her coin, and disappeared back into the crowd.

Cori held her hands near the candle, letting the warmth touch her fingers. Zeke wasted no time pouring himself a generous shot of whiskey. He downed it with a satisfied nod and immediately poured another. "Now that's proper," he said. "English winter'll freeze a man's soul."

For a moment, we sat in silence. The pub noise swirled around us, a cocoon of ordinary human activity that seemed surreal given what we were about to discuss. The fire cracked. Someone dropped a glass and cursed. The dockworkers' argument about football escalated into friendly shoving.

Lucan leaned forward again. When he spoke, his voice was barely above a murmur.

"The Watch is gone. Rome dissolved it in September. Pope Leo signed the papers himself. After twenty-two hundred years, they decided we were no longer necessary."

Cori's jaw tightened, but she said nothing.

Zeke muttered something that sounded like a Texas curse, low and creative.

"It only lasted this long because of people like you and your dedication to the original mission," I said.

Lucan's expression hardened slightly. "Our mission doesn't end because we have no bureaucracy to support us. The Watch has been slowly dying for years and a few of us saw it coming." He spread his hands to include Zeke and Cori. "For the last two centuries most of the few new members that have been admitted have been different. Many have shown signs of aging, and their powers are weaker. But we're not here to mourn the past."

Lucan pulled a notebook from his coat. The leather was worn smooth, the pages dog-eared. "We've chosen to carry this work forward, with or without the Vatican's blessing. Which brings me to you, James. I need your experience on this."

He opened the notebook to a marked page. The candlelight caught sketches and notes, all in Lucan's precise handwriting. Maps of streets. Drawings of footprints. Dates and times.

"This is no common predator," Lucan continued. "We've been tracking it for six weeks. It hunts at night, obviously. Prefers victims who won't be missed quickly. Dockworkers, prostitutes, vagrants. People the authorities don't care about."

"Until it killed the merchant's son," Cori said quietly. "A miscalculation. Which suggests either growing confidence or deteriorating control."

"Exactly. That was a mistake. Too visible. Too important. Now there's pressure to solve the case, which means more police presence, which makes investigation harder. It's reminiscent of a vampire, but I don't think it is."

"What makes you think it's not a vampire?" I asked.

Lucan turned to a page showing sketches of wounds. Two puncture marks, precise and clean. "The wounds. A vampire feeds messily when hungry, carefully when cautious, but it's never precise. These wounds are surgical. Perfect punctures, exactly the right depth and placement to drain a body in minutes."

"Could be an old one," Zeke suggested. "Vampire with some real control and finesse."

"I considered that. But there's more." Lucan flipped to another page. A symbol, roughly drawn but clear. A circle with three intersecting lines, each ending in a different shape. Square, triangle, spiral.

I felt something cold rise in my chest. I'd seen that symbol before. Long ago, in a different century, in a city that no longer existed.

"That was found near the third body," Lucan said. "Scratched into the wall of the alley. Fresh. Probably done the same night."

I reached for the notebook, studying the drawing more closely. The proportions were different from what I remembered, but the basic structure was unmistakable. I leaned in and studied it closely.

"This looks familiar," I said.

Cori leaned forward, her focus sharpening. "You've seen this before?"

"Something like it. Different configuration, but the same principle. We called it a binding mark. Used in ritual magic to contain or control supernatural entities."

"Control specifically how?" she asked. Her tone was precise, demanding exactness rather than generalities.

"That depends on the ritual. Could be summoning. Could be banishing. Could be binding a creature to a specific task." I looked at Lucan. "If someone's using binding marks, they're working with real knowledge. Not the superstitious nonsense most people think is magic."

Zeke leaned back in his chair, the wood creaking. "So, we got something powerful killin' folks in Brentford, leavin' mystical signs at murder scenes, and Rome disbands us right when it starts up?" He shook his head. "That stinks worse than a Texas slaughterhouse. Someone knew this was comin'."

"You think Rome knows," Cori said. It wasn't a question. Her voice held the cool certainty of someone who'd already reached that conclusion and was waiting for others to catch up.

"Rome always knows more than they're tellin'," Zeke said, bitterness creeping into his drawl. "They decided we were more trouble than we're worth, and whatever's happenin' in Brentford ain't their problem anymore."

Lucan closed the notebook and tucked it away. "Which brings us back to my question. Will you help?"

The fire popped loudly in its grate. Outside, the fog pressed against the windows like something trying to get in. The pub seemed suddenly smaller, the warmth less comforting. Somewhere in this city, something was hunting. Something that combined the efficiency of a predator with the knowledge of a sorcerer. And we were four people with no support and no authority to stop it.

I looked at my old friend. We'd fought together in Damascus, back when the world was younger and the threats more straightforward. He stood by me when I decided to leave the Watch after Arnaut disappeared. He was the only member of the Watch that I still spoke with, and the only one I have trusted for over 400 years.

"You know I will," I said.

I motioned to Cori and then Zeke, "I assume you're part of this as well?"

"Hell yeah." Zeke's response was immediate and fierce. "Been at this near 50 years. Ain't about to let some papal decree tell me when I'm done."

Cori's smile was cold and elegant, her green eyes sparkling in the candle-light. "I didn't come to London for the weather, Mr. Crable." She lifted her glass in a salute. "Something this interesting deserves proper attention."

I found myself noticing the precise way she moved, the controlled economy of every gesture. When she lifted her glass, there was no wasted motion, no unconscious flourish. Everything deliberate. It was oddly compelling.

Lucan smiled, though it didn't reach his eyes. "Good. We need your experience, James. You've seen more than any of us, and this thing," he tapped the notebook, "this requires someone who studied runes and binding marks."

"This thing is smart," he continued, his voice taking on the tone of a commander briefing his troops. "It varies its hunting grounds. It never uses the same approach twice. It leaves no witnesses and no clear pattern except the bodies themselves."

"And the symbols," I added.

"And the symbols. Which suggests purpose beyond simple feeding." Lucan drank the last of his whiskey. "One person couldn't track it properly. Two might get lucky. But four of us, working together, we have a chance."

"What's the plan?" I asked.

Lucan pulled out a larger map, unfolding it on the table. It showed Brentford and the surrounding areas, the Thames a thick blue line running through the center. Red marks indicated the three murder sites. They formed a rough pattern along the river's edge.

"I've been mapping the kills," Lucan said, tracing the marks with his finger. "Trying to predict where it might hunt next. There's an area near the docks, here, that fits the pattern. Old warehouses, minimal foot traffic at night, easy access to the river."

"You think it uses the river," Cori said.

"For movement, perhaps. Or escape. The fog's been heavy all month, and the water muffles sound. It's perfect hunting ground."

I studied the map. The marked areas clustered near the industrial heart of Brentford, where Brunel's old dock connected the Thames to the railway network. Warehouses and loading yards, mostly empty at night. Dark alleys between buildings. Plenty of shadows for something to hide.

"When do we start?" I asked.

Lucan's tone shifted, becoming more commanding. "Tomorrow night. Meet here at dusk, he pointed to a spot on the map in the dockyard. "Bring whatever weapons you have." He looked at each of us in turn, making it clear this wasn't a suggestion. "And be ready for anything."

"We went out two nights ago," Cori said quietly. Her fingers traced the rim of her glass, then she seemed to catch herself and stopped, her hand going still. "The frost showed prints for a few minutes before the fog erased them. We found tracks near one of the warehouses. Human-shaped, but wrong. The stride was too long. The depth too even."

"Each print was exactly the same depth," she added, her analytical mind clearly still working through the details. "No variation for weight shift or gait. It appeared to glide rather than walk."

The words hung in the air between us. Around us, the pub continued its oblivious business. Men drank and laughed and argued about things that didn't matter. They had no idea what walked in their streets at night. No concept of the darkness that lived alongside their ordinary lives.

We sat in silence for a while, each lost in our own thoughts. The fire burned lower. The candle on our table guttered and reformed. Outside, the December night deepened, and the fog grew thicker.

Finally, Lucan stood. "Tomorrow at dusk. Don't be late."

We left separately, a precaution from old habits. Cori went first, pulling her coat tight against the cold and disappearing into the fog. As she passed, she caught my eye briefly, and something unspoken passed between us, an acknowledgment, perhaps, or a challenge. Then she was gone.

Zeke followed a few minutes later, clapping Lucan on the shoulder with enough force to make a mortal man stagger. "Tomorrow then," he drawled. "Time to show this thing what real hunters look like." His broad shoulders hunched against the winter air as he pushed through the door with characteristic directness.

Lucan stood and we clasped hands. "It's good to see you old friend." And with that he turned and walked out.

I was last, stepping out into a night that had grown even colder. The fog was so thick now that I could barely see the building across the street. The gas lamps were just dim suggestions of light, barely strong enough to illuminate their own posts.

The cold hit me like a physical blow. My breath rose in thin plumes, lost as soon as the fog closed around them. Ice crunched under my boots. Somewhere in the distance, a dog howled, the sound lonely and haunting.

I stepped out from the Griffin's warm haze and turned east along Brentford High Street, the cobbles slick. Past the shuttered shopfronts and the silent wharves of the Thames, I kept to the road that bent toward Kew Bridge. The gas lamps threw weak halos against the fog, and the river's dark breath followed me as I crossed. Beyond the span, the lanes narrowed, leading me through quiet cottages and the shadowed edge of the gardens. The world was hushed, every hearth-bound family tucked away from the chill, leaving only my footsteps to mark the way back toward Kew.

I thought about what Lucan had shown us. Three deaths. Bodies drained of blood with surgical precision. Binding marks scratched into walls. Something tall and fast that moved through the fog like it was made of it.

And all of it happening after Rome disbanded the Watch.

The timing was wrong. Too convenient. Too neat. Like someone had been waiting for exactly this moment, when we were scattered and disorganized and without resources.

But who? And why Brentford? I thought about Kew Gardens and the Green Man and tried to find a connection.

The questions followed me through the fog, unanswered and troubling.

I reached my house, a block from the gardens, its brick front softened in the summer by ivy but now browned by the winter cold. The glow of a gaslight spilled from the fanlight above the door. Inside, I lit the lamp in the hall and let the familiar warmth wash over me. The polished oak floor gleamed beneath a Persian runner, and the scent of cedar drifted faintly from the paneled study to the left. Through the doorway I glimpsed my shelves lined with books, a heavy desk scattered with papers, and the quiet promise of work yet to be done.

I opened a secure trunk marked with sigils and examined its contents. Priceless and dangerous items I'd collected over centuries. I removed my old sword. The sigils on the scabbard glinted in the lamp light.

I drew it carefully. The blade was marked with more runes and sigils, and sharper than when it was newly forged. I carried this since I was a newly admitted member of the Watch. Now the Watch was gone.

I cleaned the blade and checked for any imperfections I already knew wouldn't be there.

Tomorrow night, we'd hunt.

Four members of a disbanded order, without authority, tracking something that had already killed three people and would certainly kill more if we failed.

I smiled grimly in the lamplight. This was familiar ground. Despite the time that had passed, this was what I knew.

I thought about my new companions. Lucan, steady as always. Zeke, all swagger and instinct. And Cori, precise, controlled, with those calculating green eyes that seemed to see straight through pretense to the truth beneath. It had been a long time since I'd worked with anyone who moved with such lethal grace.

I lay down on the narrow bed and closed my eyes, but sleep was slow coming. My mind kept returning to the symbol Lucan had shown us. The binding mark. This was no amateur conjurer we were dealing with. Lucan was right to seek my help.

If someone was using binding marks in Brentford, they were playing with forces they didn't understand. Or worse, they understood perfectly and didn't care about the consequences.

Either way, it needed to stop.

Outside, the fog pressed against the window. The temperature dropped further. Frost formed on the glass in delicate patterns, beautiful and foreboding.

Somewhere in this city, something was waking up. Getting ready to hunt. Choosing its next victim from among the thousands of souls who had no idea danger walked among them.

Tomorrow night, we'd be waiting.

None of us would need to do this. Immortal members of the watch had lifetimes to accumulate wealth and comfort. We did it because someone needed to stand against the dark.

That was a mission I could get behind.

I drifted into restless sleep, dreaming of fog and blood and symbols drawn in darkness. Dreaming of the work that never ended, no matter what Rome decreed or the world believed.

The night deepened. The fog thickened. And in the darkness beyond my window, something moved through Brentford's streets, hunting.

2

Tremors, Data, and the Warning (Ohio, Present)

Grant Park felt steady again.

I noticed it the moment my boots hit frozen grass. The steadiness made me uneasy. The pressure that had lived at the base of my skull since the attack last summer was gone. No tightening behind the eyes. No crawling warning along my arms. The anchor beneath the park rested into itself, holding shape the way it was meant to.

Stable.

After everything that had happened here, stability seemed temporary.

Winter had stripped the park down to essentials. Bare trees and hard ground, with nothing to hide behind. Sound carried farther in the cold, each step crisp and deliberate. The sky threatened snow without yet committing to it.

As I followed the familiar path toward the old oaks, my eyes traced what most people would never notice.

Copper-threaded sigils had been etched into the bases of three lampposts. Subtle. Integrated into city maintenance markings. Charlie's work. Each one anchored to a sensor buried below the frost line, feeding constant readings into a system he had insisted we make permanent.

Not a prototype anymore. After Grant Park, none of us were interested in being surprised again.

Those sensors didn't watch for monsters. They watched for strain. Microvariations in pressure. Resonance shifts. The early signs that reality was being asked to do more than it could tolerate.

We had installed them so the park would never scream again before anyone was listening.

On top of that, David had been talking long before the attack on Grant Park about expanding his cybersecurity business into the data analytics market. Broader visibility. Infrastructure already in place. Systems that could see patterns instead of reacting to outcomes. Before the attack, it sounded like ambition.

Afterward, it sounded like necessity.

I had agreed to help finance the acquisition because I was done relying on luck. Because I had spent centuries learning what happens when you wait for problems to announce themselves.

The closing was days away. David and I would be in Tel Aviv to finish it in person.

After that, if something shifted, we would know.

I reached the shallow hollow where the Wendigo slept and knelt, pressing my palm to the frozen ground.

The response came immediately. Not sound or vibration, but a presence. Deep. Settled. Whole.

The land held itself. The guardian beneath it slept the way something sleeps when it expects to wake again. No desperation. No clinging. Just rest.

Then something brushed against it. It wasn't force, but contact. It was deliberate, like the area was being probed.

The Wendigo stirred beneath the soil, like a dog that twitches in its sleep. I straightened slowly and the air above the hollow shifted just enough to notice. It didn't tear so much as parted and the Veil slid aside like a heavy curtain. Layers separating just enough to allow passage before settling again and something stepped through.

I recognized it immediately. A trow.

The old stories placed them in the north of Scotland, along coasts and caves. In barrows and places where stone met water. They were blamed for missing livestock, spoiled food, sudden illness. Folklore flattened them into goblins because people preferred monsters that could be dismissed.

In truth, trows were watchers. They lingered at edges. Surveyed places where reality behaved strangely. They weren't destroyers. They were indicators.

When one appeared, it meant something else was paying attention.

This one fit the legends too well to be coincidence.

Small and hunched, almost human until the second look corrected the mistake. Skin dark and rough like wet stone. A hooked nose jutted sharply from a narrow face. Large black eyes reflected light without warmth or depth. Eyes that never quite blinked.

Its hands sealed it. Long fingers stretched too far, faint webbing visible between them. They flexed constantly, testing distance and air.

It took one step forward.

Then it saw me and its grin slipped before it could stop it.

"Weel now," it rasped, vowels dragged long and low. "That wisnae pairt o' the reckonin'. Didnae think tae find you here."

It spoke in an old Orcadian Scots dialect.

"You sound a long way from home," I said.

Its eyes stayed on me longer than they should have.

"Ye werenae in the projection," it said. "Nae listed. Nae flagged."

"And yet," I replied, "here I am."

Its fingers stilled. The webbing tightened, then eased.

"This grund wis marked quiet," it said. "Healin'. Nae active meddlin'."

"Lists get old," I said. "Especially when people stop correcting them."

Its gaze slid toward the hollow, then back to me, sharper now.

"This anchor's mair hale than forecast," it muttered. "A fair bit mair."

"That happens when you take care of things," I said. "Which brings us to why you're here."

Its head tilted, curiosity thinning into caution.

"I'm no here tae harm," it assured me. "Only tae ken."

"Know what?"

"That strain laid elsewhere still travels," it said. "That even stitched grund still answers."

"You're surveying?" I asked.

"Aye," it replied. "As we aye dae."

"And you're far from the places your kind usually favors."

Its mouth curled.

"We gang whaur we're permitit."

That landed wrong.

"By whom?" I asked.

It hesitated. Just long enough to matter.

"The Architect," it said. "He plans. We tak the measure."

No reverence. No fear. Just process.

"Your kind have never been good at understanding consequence," I said. "You pull at threads without caring what comes undone."

"Ye cling tae things meant tae rot," it snapped. "Decay's pairt o' the makkin'."

"Not when it's forced."

The air behind it tightened and the opening was done waiting.

The trow let out a soft, humorless chuckle. "He'll hae his way," it said. "He aye does."

The pull came hard. Space folded inward as the opening closed, the trow's form breaking apart as if the world itself rejected it.

"This wis naught but a survey," it snarled. "The design's already set."

Then it was gone. The opening sealed seamlessly.

Grey grit scattered across the frost and vanished as the park settled back into quiet and the feeling of calm stability returned. Which meant the trow had not come because this place was weak. It had come because something elsewhere was pressing hard enough to make even well-tended ground worth testing.

It was then that my phone vibrated in my pocket. Charlie.

Get to my place ASAP. We'll talk then.

I turned away from the hollow and headed for the street at a brisk pace. A sense of unease was building inside me.

Charlie opened the door before I raised my hand to knock.

"You picked a bad time for a quiet morning," he said. "Come inside."

The living room had become a command center. Screens lined the walls. Cables crossed the floor. Sigil-etched components were wired into modern circuitry with precision.

Erin sat at the table, eyes locked on her laptop.

"The park sensors tripped," Charlie said immediately. "Not hard, but just enough that I couldn't ignore it."

Erin nodded. "The data shows a short, but powerful anomaly."

"That's why we came straight here," Charlie said. "Those sensors were built to catch strain before it tears."

I moved closer to the displays.

"When did it start?" I asked.

"Less than an hour ago," Erin said. "No buildup. It just appeared."

"That makes sense. I was in the park when it happened," I said.

Both of them turned.

"The Veil opened. Something came through," I told them.

Charlie's jaw tightened. "What kind of something?"

"A trow," I said.

Erin frowned. "I'm sorry, a what?"

"Trow," I repeated. "Northern folklore. Scotland. Orkney. Most people call them goblins, which is wrong."

Charlie leaned closer. "Well then what are they actually?"

"They are watchers drawn to chaos," I said. "They show up where strain is building."

Erin's hands stilled. "You mean it was scouting?"

"Yeah," I said. "And it was surprised to find me."

"It spoke?" Erin asked, surprised.

"Yes," I replied. "And it said it was permitted to be there."

Charlie exhaled slowly. "That sounds ominous."

"Agreed," I said. "It also named whoever is giving permission."

Erin looked up. "Who?"

"The Architect."

Silence blanketed the room.

Erin broke it. "Is this Arnaut?"

Charlie shook his head. "Doubt it. This feels bigger. Arnaut spent months setting up Grant Park. He put in everything he had to destabilize one site."

"So even if he's involved," Erin said.

"He's not the whole picture," Charlie finished.

I nodded. "He may be a piece. But this is larger than one person."

Erin turned her laptop so we could see it. "That's not the only problem."

She stacked datasets with precision. I could see data labels on her dashboard: seismic, atmospheric, electromagnetic, transportation, weather, and others. She was nothing, if not thorough.

A world map filled the screen.

Points appeared. Then more.

I recognized several immediately.

"These aren't random," I said with growing concern.

"No," Erin replied. "But they do recur."

"They're near guardian sites," I said. "Some directly. Others close enough that the distinction barely matters."

Charlie stared at the screen. "Are you saying the Veil structure itself is under pressure?"

"Yes," I said. "Someone is seeing how much can be strained at once."

Erin leaned back and waved her hand in front of the map on her computer. "We cannot handle this alone."

"No," Charlie said quietly. "We barely protected one park."

She looked at me. "Crable, we're going to need help."

"I'll reach out to Eliyahu," I said. "I also have a friend who owes me one."

"I'd love to meet a friend who owes you a debt," said Charlie. "Who is it?"

"A very old friend and someone you haven't met. Lucan Colonna."

Erin tilted her head. "Who is he?"

"He joined the Watch centuries before I did," I said. "He kept going when Rome walked away. Kept working with a small circle of friends."

"Older than you?" Charlie asked and gave a low whistle.

"Yes," I replied. "And we need that knowledge."

Charlie nodded once. "Keep us posted. We'll hold down the fort from here."

"I will," I said.

I stood, feeling the familiar weight of command settling onto shoulders that had carried it before. The quiet suburban life was again over for now.

"One more thing," I said. "Everything we've discussed stays between us until we know more. We don't know who we can trust yet, who might be part of the group causing this. We move carefully. We verify everything."

"We got it," Charlie said. "Not our first rodeo. Ours just has a demon bull, a possessed clown, and one magical cowboy in desperate need of therapy."

They both nodded, understanding the implications.

I left them to their work and drove home through streets that looked peaceful and safe. Families bundled in coats heading to indoor activities. Dogs being walked quickly, their owners eager to get back inside. Normal suburban life continuing, oblivious to the fact that reality's borders were being systematically attacked across the globe.

I got home and had a sense I was being again pulled into something I had left behind long ago. I poured a glass of wine and sat at my desk, thinking about old friends. I hadn't seen Lucan in decades.

My text to him needed to be carefully worded. Informative enough that he'd understand the urgency, vague enough that it wouldn't reveal too much if intercepted. Given the likely scale and resources of what we were picking up, you can't be too careful.

After several drafts, I settled on something simple, but with a sense of urgency only he would understand:

Lucan, I trust you are well. There are some events in the works that I could really use your expertise on. Similar to old problems we dealt with together, but broader scale and with a short timeframe to respond. Would value your perspective. Think Brentford on a larger scale. We should talk soon. Best, James

I hit send and sat back, wondering if he was off on some adventure of his own, quietly keeping the world safe. Hoping maybe, just maybe, we weren't as alone in this fight as it seemed.

My phone buzzed thirty minutes later. A reply from Lucan, just as carefully worded:

James, that's worrisome. Been tracking disturbances across Europe. More widespread than I initially thought. We have our hands full here, but we may be dealing with the same issues. We should meet. I'm in London. Does your travel agent still work in Kew?

My "travel agent" in Kew was a reference to the portal between my home there and the one in my basement. He could be here in seconds rather than hours if he used it.

I responded:

The agent is still active. Open all hours so feel free to contact when you are ready to travel. Time is of the essence. It will be good to see you. Been too long.

The message flashed with a thumbs up emoji. This was good. We weren't alone.

I next reached out to Rabbi Eliyahu. Rabbi Eliyahu Ben Ami leads the Shomrei ha Adama ha Nitzchit, the ancient order known as the Keepers of the Eternal Earth. They are the keepers of the original guardian, an earth golem that lives below Jerusalem. If anyone would be picking up these disturbances, it would be him.

I texted:

Rabbi, our friend in the park continues to heal. However, there appears to be something probing, but it's not local. It seems he has enemies far and wide. Are you aware of this?

Three dots appeared immediately.

Baruch HaShem. I am glad our friend is getting better. Your note is quite concerning. My fellow Keepers and I are trying to assess anomalies that appear to be local to us. I was going to seek your help, but the issue makes it impossible for me to travel. Can you come to Jerusalem?

Yes, they were investigating. Yes, we should coordinate.

It doesn't sound like I have much choice, but luckily I'll be in Tel Aviv in a few days anyway. I'll coordinate here and get back to you. Keep me informed if there are any changes on your end, and I'll do the same.

By the time I went to bed, the outline of a response was taking shape. We had monitoring data. We had the beginnings of a network. What we needed now was David's acquisition to provide the infrastructure, coordination to provide the manpower, and a better understanding of who we were fighting and what they hoped to accomplish.

I set my alarm for six, though I usually never needed one. The meeting with David was at eight, and I needed time to prepare. There was an urgency to this now that didn't exist before.

I lay in bed thinking about the interference patterns Charlie had shown me. About forty anchor points under attack across the globe. About a group with the resources to coordinate at scale. About the mysterious Architect.

Someone out there had been watching. Learning. Planning. And now they were moving, systematically attacking anchor points with knowledge and precision that came from centuries of training. I was sure Arnaut had a hand in this.

He had allies, but so did we. I just hoped we weren't too late.

I didn't have answers yet. But I would find them.

Because the alternative was watching the world learn firsthand what happened when the monsters stopped being myths and the borders stopped holding them back.

And I'd spent too many centuries protecting humanity's ignorance to let that happen now.

3

Portals, Arrivals, and the Reunion (Ohio, Present)

The text came through in the early afternoon.

In Kew. Using the agent. Arrival imminent. Don't shoot. – L

I read it twice, then set the phone down slowly.

The "agent" was code for the portal between my homes in Kew and Centerville. You can never be too careful, and talking about magic over open comms is something I try to avoid.

I was sitting at my desk with a glass of wine and maps spread across the surface. Old habits from centuries of planning campaigns. When you know something is coming, rest becomes elusive.

Grant Park lingered at the edge of my thoughts. The way the Veil had parted that morning. Clean. Controlled. Like someone was using it as a door. That took a level of understanding and skill I didn't truly understand, and that worried me.

I stood and headed downstairs. The basement lab welcomed me with its familiar, collected quiet. A welcome comfort, surrounded by items collected over many lifetimes.

The portal sat between two standing stones I'd taken from a Neolithic site in northern Scotland centuries ago. Tools now, not curiosities. Engineered and refined over generations.

The stones vibrated softly. The sigils carved into the floor responded in sequence, lighting one by one. Lucan had activated the portal on the other side.

The air between the stones rippled, then flattened into a clean vertical aperture.

My Kew office resolved on the other side. A brick wall, my bookshelves, and the familiar disorder.

Lucan stepped through. He moved quickly but not comfortably, boots striking the concrete hard as he caught himself on the nearest stone. His face was pale, jaw tight. He exhaled slowly and coughed, as if his body was still catching up to this reality. Transit sickness. An unfortunate side effect of using the portal. It still beat seven hours in the air and airline meals.

He lifted his head and met my eyes.

"James."

"Lucan." I smiled warmly.

Relief passed between us without ceremony. Then the portal flared again.

A large figure emerged mid-stride and immediately lost the argument with gravity, landing on hands and knees with a sharp exhale.

"Well," the man said, voice thick with a southern drawl, "that was profoundly unpleasant."

I stared for half a second, then smiled.

"Zeke?"

He looked up, eyes bloodshot but alert, and grinned.

"Afternoon, hoss."

Lucan stepped aside. "He insisted."

"I didn't insist," Zeke said calmly. "I was strongly encouraged."

I stepped forward and pulled him to his feet.

"I was not expecting you," I said honestly.

Zeke straightened, rolled his shoulders once, and smiled wider.

"Good," he said. "Then this is a pleasant surprise all around."

And it was.

Lucan bringing Zeke meant he understood the scale of what was unfolding. Meant he was not gambling on optimism.

The portal collapsed cleanly behind them.

Zeke leaned against my workbench and took a careful breath.

"I need bourbon," he said. "Food. Possibly water. In that order."

"You're in the right house," I said.

His eyes flicked to a chunk of obsidian on the bench and he withdrew his hand slightly.

"And I'm making a personal decision not to touch anything in this room." He said as he took in his surroundings.

"Wise," I said.

Lucan exhaled slowly, tension easing from his shoulders.

"You brought help," I stated.

He met my gaze and shrugged. "You asked for allies."

I nodded once. "Thank you."

Upstairs, things improved rapidly.

Zeke showered and returned looking far more human. Lucan took the guest room nearest the back of the house by instinct. I pulled together some food and retrieved a bottle of bourbon from the shelf.

When I set the bottle on the table, Zeke stopped mid-step.

He leaned forward slightly, eyes narrowing as he read the label, then let out a low, appreciative whistle.

"Well now," he said. "that's not a casual decision."

Lucan glanced at the bottle. "Is it special?"

Zeke looked at him as if he had just asked whether gravity was optional.

"Twenty-three year Pappy Van Winkle," he said. "That's not bourbon. It's a life event."

I poured three glasses.

"How do you take it?" I asked.

"Neat," Zeke said immediately. "Please don't insult it with ice, water, or good intentions."

I slid the glass toward him.

He lifted it, inhaled once, then took a slow sip. His eyes closed.

"James," he said quietly, "whatever horrible thing we're about to deal with, this almost makes it worth it."

Lucan accepted his glass next, tasting it thoughtfully. "A good drink always works for taking the edge off," he said.

Zeke nodded. "Hoss, if this ever stops working, civilization has already collapsed and we're all lying to ourselves."

Lucan moved to the window and pulled a cigarette from a silver case.

Muratti. Same brand since the Great War.

"Mind if I smoke?" he asked.

I shook my head and grabbed an ashtray for him.

He lit the cigarette and exhaled slowly against the glass.

He turned back to me. "You look tired."

"So do you."

"Fair."

He took another drag. "Tell me what you saw."

I told him.

About the park. About the trow. About how the creature said it had *permission*. About the Architect.

"The Architect," he repeated. "That's new."

"Not a name you've heard?"

"No," he said. "Not that I can recall anyway."

Zeke nodded from the couch. "Sounds like a Bond villain. Maybe he'll tell us his plan when we meet."

Lucan listened as I explained the data my friends had been gathering. Both the patterns, and the pressure points.

"This is larger than one man," I said. "Arnaut may be involved, but this goes beyond him."

Lucan nodded slowly. "Then you were right to call."

We made small talk for a bit after that and caught up, then freshened up and headed to dinner.

Lucan took a long drag. "We have been seeing disturbances in Europe," he said. "More breaches, more strange behavior, more things acting as though they have permission. I'm tired of arriving late."

His voice was flat, but the anger underneath it was unmistakable.

I didn't speak. There was nothing useful to say.

Lucan's hand tightened around the cigarette.

"This does not feel like Arnaut," he said finally.

"No," I agreed. "Arnaut was behind the attack here, but he spent months setting up to destabilize one site. This feels bigger than one man."

Lucan nodded once.

"So, what do you need from me?" he asked.

"Your knowledge," I said. "Your experience. And your eyes in Europe. We're building something here, but we need to coordinate and expand it. We need to stop reacting because we were caught off guard."

Lucan studied my face.

"You sound certain," he said.

"I'm certain about one thing," I replied. "We cannot do this alone."

He let the silence hang for a moment, then nodded.

"All right," he said. "What is the plan?"

"Tonight," I replied. "we're meeting some friends for dinner and I want them to brief you on what they've found and you can tell us what you have seen. We start putting pieces together."

"Tonight," Zeke called from the armchair. "I was hoping for at least six hours of shut eye before we dove back into the apocalypse."

"You can sleep in the car," I said.

Zeke sighed like a man suffering deep injustice. "I can sleep anywhere, hoss. Don't mean I want to."

But he was already standing, setting down his glass and eyeing the bottle with visible regret.

I sent a text.

Old friends arrived. Meet us at the Oakwood Club at eight. Private room.

The response came immediately.

That was fast. You don't mess around.

I typed back.

Nope. See you at eight.

My favorite spot in Dayton for a good meal was The Oakwood Club. It occupied a brick builindg on Far Hills that had started life as a grocery store in 1919, but now sat in a neighborhood of old money and deliberate quiet.

The restaurant fit right in.

Dark wood and red leather defined the interior. Low amber lighting glowed over comfortable booths and a long bar that carried the weight of generations of quiet deals and strong cocktails. The bartender knew your drink by your second visit. The waitstaff knew when to hover and when to vanish.

It was a place where Dayton went when it wanted a perfect steak and conversation that stayed in the booth where it was spoken.

The host nodded as we entered.

"Good evening, Mr. Crable. Your private dining room is ready. One of your guests has already arrived."

We found Charlie seated at a table set for eight, a basket of bread untouched in front of him. He stood when we entered, and I noticed him take in Lucan and Zeke with curiosity. After all, most people didn't meet immortals every day.

"Charlie Mitchell," I said, making introductions. "This is Lucan Colonna and Zeke Whitmore."

Charlie shook hands with both of them.

Lucan's handshake was warm and controlled. Zeke's was firm enough to make Charlie's eyebrows lift, which said something since Charlie had the firmest handshake I know.

"Pleasure to meet you both," Charlie said, sitting back down. "Jimmy has told me you have been active in Europe."

Lucan gave a small nod. "As much as one can be."

Zeke settled into a chair that creaked under his weight.

"Hopefully he only told you the successful parts," Zeke said, drawl easy and friendly.

"Some of the successful parts," I replied.

A waitress stepped in, professional and efficient. She scanned the table, three men who looked like they had slept poorly for centuries, and one engineer with the posture of a man about to present a thesis to a firing squad.

"Good evening, gentlemen. Can I start you with drinks?"

Charlie lifted his beer. "Another when you get a chance, please."

Zeke leaned back slightly and offered the waitress a smile that had probably gotten him both out of and in to trouble in equal amounts.

"Ma'am," he said, voice warm as honey, "if you got a bourbon that pairs well with cold nights and worse news, I will trust whatever you choose."

She paused, just long enough to show she was not immune.

"And if I choose wrong?" she asked with a slight smile.

Zeke put a hand to his chest. "Then I will bravely suffer through it and spare the rest of y'all the trauma."

She looked him over once, quick and practiced.

"Aren't you the gentleman. That's either charming or dangerous," she said.

"Why not both?" Zeke replied.

Charlie coughed, trying not to laugh.

Lucan, to my surprise, looked amused.

The waitress's mouth twitched. "All right. I will bring something smooth. But if you start confessing your secrets to me, I'm charging extra."

Zeke cast his arms wide. "Ma'am, I do not have secrets. I have stories."

She shook her head, smiling now despite herself, and turned to Lucan. "And for you?"

"A Negroni," Lucan said. "Dry gin, if you have it."

She looked at me.

"And you, Mr. Crable."

"Rye old fashioned," I said. "Light on the sugar."

She left with a noticeable glance over her shoulder at Zeke.

Zeke watched her go and said to no one in particular. "I like this place."

Charlie smiled and shook his head at Zeke. He slid a pen from his jacket pocket.

Lucan looked to where the waitress exited and then to Zeke, "We aren't here for the scenery."

"That's where you're wrong," Zeke said. "We can be here for two things."

Before Lucan could respond, the door opened again.

Erin and Casey came in together, followed by David. Erin looked focused, while Casey looked excited, cheeks pink from cold air and motion. David looked both tired and nervous, with his usual wrinkled clothes and his phone clutched so tightly you would think he was holding a live grenade.

Casey spotted Zeke immediately. Her eyes lit up like she had found something she had not known she was looking for.

Zeke stood, polite as a Southern preacher, and tipped his head slightly.

"Well, hello," he leaned into his drawl. "You must be the trouble James keeps talkin' 'bout."

Casey laughed. "Oh, I am definitely the trouble."

"Good," Zeke said. "It's always a relief to meet honest people."

Casey looked at him like he was a new favorite song.

Erin shook hands with Lucan and Zeke, efficient and direct.

"Welcome," she said to Lucan. "Crable told us you have been dealing with Europe."

Lucan nodded once. "And it's worse than I hoped."

David sat down heavily.

"Sorry I'm late," he said. "Just got off a call with Tel Aviv. The acquisition is finalized. Papers signed. We fly out in three days."

Charlie's pen paused.

"Finalized," he repeated.

David nodded. "Signed. Done."

Erin's attention sharpened.

"That changes everything," she said.

Menus arrived. Orders were placed, and conversation flowed around the table as people settled.

The waitress returned with drinks.

"Four Roses Single Barrel," she said, placing a glass in front of Zeke. "Careful. It has a way of making men linger longer than they planned." Her eyes watched him long enough to notice, but short enough to not make it awkward.

Zeke raised it to the light like a jeweler appraising a diamond and beamed his most charming smile.

"Ma'am," he said, "your taste is impeccable."

She arched an eyebrow. "Not always."

Zeke leaned forward slightly. "Then I suppose we both have a weakness for the wrong decisions."

Casey covered her mouth with her hand, clearly delighted.

The waitress shook her head, but she was smiling. "Try not to flirt your way into more trouble than you can afford."

Zeke smiled back and winked. "Ma'am, I can afford a whole lot."

She walked away, and Casey leaned toward him.

"You talk like that all the time?" she asked.

"Only when I'm bein' polite," Zeke said.

Casey laughed again, completely taken.

Charlie pushed a napkin toward Lucan and started drawing.

"This is what we have been working on," he said. "Veil integrity, geometry, signal mapping, and so on. After the attack at Grant Park, we built and installed permanent sensors. Those sensors tripped today. That was our first alert."

Lucan leaned forward, attention fixed on Charlie.

"You built permanent sensors into a guardian site?" he asked.

Charlie nodded. "They don't detect creatures. They detect strain. We look for microvariations and resonance shifts. The early signs that reality is being asked to do more than it can tolerate."

Lucan's gaze flicked toward me briefly, then back to Charlie. "That is... smart. I can't believe we haven't thought to do this."

"It's necessary," Erin said. "The anomaly today was short but powerful. Enough to confirm the park is being tested."

Lucan's eyes narrowed. "Tested."

"Yeah," I said. "A trow stepped through. Called it a survey."

Zeke's brows rose. "A survey. Sounds like a construction site."

"Not far off, but I'm betting more on a demolition site" I replied.

Charlie continued drawing his intersecting lines and highlighting the nodes where they crossed.

"The Veil is like a membrane," he said. "Weak points follow patterns. Pressure follows geometry. Erin pulled anomalies from multiple public datasets and the points cluster. They recur."

Lucan watched the lines like they were scripture.

"And you believe it's global," he said.

"Absolutely," Charlie replied. "We have points lighting up across continents. It does not look like a single rupture. It looks like pressure applied at multiple nodes."

I leaned in. "Many of those nodes are near guardian sites."

Zeke squinted at the napkin. "Looks like a spider web."

"That's not a bad way to think about it," Charlie said. "If I can map the web and track changes in amplitude, I can predict where the next breaches might form before they happen."

Zeke leaned back. "You had me at predict. I like my apocalypses scheduled."

Lucan's fingers hovered over the napkin.

"And the sigils," he asked. "How do they factor in."

Charlie drew a hexagon and added symbols inside it.

"They aren't just symbols," he said. "They describe how the boundary holds. Rabbi Eliyahu has been helping me learn how to interpret the logic. When I overlay sigil structure with sensor data, patterns emerge."

Lucan's interest sharpened.

"You're blending guardian principles with modern engineering," he said.

That surprised Charlie. "Yes. Exactly."

Lucan pulled out his own pen and added marks around Charlie's hexagon, flowing script that looked Arabic but was not quite.

"These are seal marks," Lucan said. "Guardian work. Old."

Charlie's eyes widened. "You can read the symbols?"

"Recognize more than read," Lucan said. "But the structure is familiar."

Zeke held up his hand. "Y'all lost me again."

Charlie grabbed a fresh napkin.

"Reality is a sheet," he said, folding it. "The Veil is a seam. Stitches hold the seam. Guardians reinforce the stitches. Someone is pressing the seam in multiple places and seeing what gives."

Zeke nodded slowly. "Now I get it. Somebody is pokin' holes in the fabric and hopin' our pants fall down."

Casey laughed so hard she nearly spilled her drink. "That's the worst metaphor I have ever heard."

"It's accurate," Zeke said, pleased with himself.

David leaned forward, tapping the table once. "And now we'll have the tools to see it better."

Erin nodded. "Real time monitoring. Better filtering that includes more feeds. We can finally scale the models."

David swallowed, then looked at Erin with more nervousness than usual. His hands shook and he placed them on the table to stable them.

"Which brings me to something we need to discuss," he said. "Erin, we need to ask you something."

Casey glanced between them. "Katz, you look like you're about to confess to a crime. What's going on?"

David took a breath and took a long drink from his glass. He set the glass back down and looked up at Erin, his discomfort apparent.

"This company we're buying needs someone running it," he said. "Someone who can navigate boards and also understand what we're dealing with."

Erin's expression shifted, cautious now. "David."

"No, let me finish. You have a reputation in the analytics community," he said. "Strategic thinking. Crisis work. But you're buried in projects beneath your skill set. This company needs a CEO. Someone who can run operations while I focus on the cyber side."

The table went quiet.

"You're offering me CEO?" Erin asked with surprise.

"Yes," David replied. "Full authority. Equity of course. James and I discussed it. We agree."

Erin looked at him, then at me.

"You're serious?" she asked, still in a bit of shock.

"Completely," I said. "We need someone who can run the business while we handle field work. You're the best person for it."

Erin leaned back, processing. You could see the model building behind her eyes.

Finally, she said, "I'm expensive."

"I know," David said. "We planned for that."

"I mean executive compensation," she said. "Real authority. Full ability to make necessary changes."

"Done," David said without hesitation. "That's why we want *you*."

Erin took a slow sip of wine and set the glass down.

"Then yes," she said. "I'll do it."

Casey grabbed Erin's arm. "Holy shit! Erin, that's amazing."

Zeke raised his bourbon. "Hell yeah. Nothing like a battlefield promotion."

David let out a breath like someone had lifted a building off his chest.

"Thank you," he said. "Seriously."

"Thank me after I deal with your board," Erin said, but she was smiling now.

Lucan raised his Negroni. "To new leadership, and better odds than we have had lately."

"I'll drink to that," Zeke said, and emptied his glass. "Hell, I'll drink to anything."

Casey lifted her margarita. "I guess we're going to the Med. When do we leave? I guess I need to shop!"

"Three days," David said. "Time to coordinate logistics, brief the board, and let Erin start transitioning."

"We aren't flying commercial," I said. "The clock is against us. Last thing we need is a delay. I will charter us a flight."

Food arrived. Steam rose from steaks and pasta. The smell of garlic and charred meat filled the room. It was grounding and real.

Around the table, the mood shifted. Still serious, but lighter. Like maybe assembling the right people in the right room at the right time mattered.

Zeke made Casey laugh again, this time with a story that started with an imp in Budapest and ended with a priest who never forgave him. Casey watched him like he was the most entertaining thing in the room. Which, to be fair, he often was.

Charlie and Lucan leaned over another napkin, comparing marks and structures. Erin was already rearranging David's corporate hierarchy in her head, probably in color coded tiers.

Under the warm lights of the Oakwood Club, with good food and better company, it seemed like we might pull this off.

Which probably meant we would not. But I had learned a long time ago that you do not fight because you think you will win. You fight because the alternative is unacceptable.

Looking around the table, at the old warrior, the new allies, the brilliant minds now aligned, I knew one thing for certain: we would find the answers, or we would die trying. The alternative was still, and always, unacceptable.

4

Flames, Betrayal, and the Butterfly (Granada, Spain, 1492)

Granada always felt older than the stones it was built from.

I arrived just after dawn. I rode through the foothills of the Sierra Nevada on a borrowed mule that had seen better years. The beast picked its way along muddy ruts while morning mist clung to the valley floor. Above us, the rooftops of the Albaicín caught the first light, terracotta tiles still damp from night dew, whitewashed walls blushing faint gold in the thin winter sun. The narrow streets twisted upward in tight spirals, houses leaning so close their upper floors nearly touched. It created a labyrinth that had swallowed armies and kept secrets for a thousand years.

Woodsmoke drifted from morning fires. The air carried the sharp sweetness of oranges ripening in hidden courtyards. There was also the mineral bite of mountain water running through ancient acequias, the Moorish canals that still threaded through the city like arteries. A rooster crowed somewhere above me. A dog barked and was silenced. The city was waking.

I chose my arrival time deliberately. Dawn meant fewer eyes, fewer questions. I'd been careful for forty-three years, ever since Jerusalem, ever since the portal swallowed Arnaut and I walked away from the Watch, unable to serve an institution that I didn't believe in anymore.

They'd been hunting me since. Desertion carried a death sentence, and the Watch had long memories.

From the Plaza Larga, I stopped to study the Alhambra perched on its red ridge across the valley. Even at this distance, it looked both magnificent and tired, a palace that had housed poets, mathematicians, and astronomers now reduced to a Christian fortress watching over a conquered people. The Nasrid kingdom had fallen mere months ago. Isabella and Ferdinand had claimed the city in January. In March, they'd issued the Alhambra Decree, expelling all Jews from Spain by summer's end. The Muslims had been promised freedom of religion in the surrender terms, but everyone knew those promises were fragile as morning mist. No one believed that freedom would last.

The changes were already beginning. I could see where a few minarets had been topped with crosses, converting prayer towers into bells that rang for a different faith. Some Arabic script had been chiseled from the most prominent archways, replaced with Latin verses. But Granada remained overwhelmingly Muslim, the city was too vast, too deeply Islamic, for the conquerors to remake quickly. Most minarets still called the faithful to prayer five times daily. Most courtyards still held fountains carved with Quranic verses. Most doors still bore Arabic blessings for those who entered. The bones underneath weren't just Moorish; they were the living body, still breathing despite the new Christian banners flying from the Alhambra's towers.

This was why I had come. Not for the politics or the religion, though both hung over Granada like a pall. I'd come because the Keepers had sent word.

The message had arrived to me months ago. The Keepers in Jerusalem, the Shomrei ha'Adamah ha'Nitzchit, had ways of communicating across vast distances. Perhaps through other guardians. Perhaps through methods older than either Islam or Christianity.

The message had been clear: a manuscript existed in Granada. A treatise written by a Nasrid mystic-scholar who'd believed geometry could explain the ordering of creation itself, mathematics woven with spiritual philosophy.

The Keepers wanted it preserved. They'd identified someone in Granada who held the manuscript, a caretaker who understood its value but could no longer protect it. The Crown was systematically destroying anything that didn't align with Christian doctrine. The manuscript would burn unless someone retrieved it.

Someone like me. Someone who understood the Veil, who could recognize the truth hidden in geometric proofs and mathematical ratios. And someone that the Keepers could count on for both strength and secrecy.

These manuscripts never named the Veil directly, but the years of study since Jerusalem had taught me that the old mystics, the real ones, saw the same underlying structures. Different vocabulary, different symbols, but describing the same truth. Their geometries held insights sharper than any priest's doctrine or alchemist's formula.

If the manuscript existed, I needed to see it. Needed to preserve it. And needed to keep it from the flames to be cared for by the Keepers.

Because understanding the Veil's structure was the only way I would ever find out what happened to Arnaut. Where that portal had taken him. Whether he was alive or dead or something worse.

The mule snorted and stamped, shaking me from my thoughts. I urged it forward into the Albaicín proper.

The streets narrowed further as we climbed. Whitewashed walls rose on either side, broken by heavy wooden doors studded with iron. Most doors were closed. Those few people in the streets moved quickly, heads down, carrying bread or water jugs. Muslim women in their modest dress, men in traditional robes and turbans, moved with the wariness of people who'd learned overnight that their world had changed. No one made eye contact. The morning held the silence of a city that had learned to be quiet.

I passed a small plaza where a fountain trickled, its basin carved with Arabic calligraphy, still intact here, unlike the damaged fountain I saw earlier. The geometric patterns in the tilework were pristine, unmolested. An old woman in hijab filled a clay jar at the fountain. When she saw me, a Christian stranger, she grabbed her jar and hurried away without a word.

Fear lived here, you could smell it under the oranges and woodsmoke. The fear of a Muslim city under new Christian rule, waiting to see if the promises made would be promises kept.

By midmorning, I found the Madrasa of Granada tucked between the clustered houses near the silk market. The façade was restrained, but the doorway itself told another story, stucco carved in flowing arabesques, Quranic inscriptions running like lace across the arch, and painted woodwork catching the morning light. It was a threshold meant to announce learning and devotion, a jewel set discreetly into the city's fabric. I tied the mule to a post and knocked.

The door opened a crack. A thin man with ink-stained fingers studied me through the gap. His eyes were sharp, intelligent, and deeply cautious.

"I'm looking for the Shaykh al-Madrasa," I said in Spanish.

He said nothing, waiting.

I switched to Arabic. "The Shomrei ha'Adamah ha'Nitzchit sent me. About a manuscript."

Recognition flashed in his eyes. Relief, perhaps. Or maybe just resignation that the moment he'd been expecting had finally arrived. He looked past me, checking the street, then stepped aside.

"Quickly."

I entered and he shut the door immediately, dropping a heavy bar across it.

Outside, Granada choked under conquest and fear. Inside the madrasa, silence fell like a blessing. The air cooled and stilled. Shafts of light fell through high windows, glancing off tiles patterned in stars and polygons that seemed to stretch into infinity. Carved stucco rippled across the upper walls in patterns so intricate they appeared to move; lacework of plaster and geometry, a testament to Nasrid artisanship.

You could sense this was home to knowledge and learning, in the weight of the air, in the way sound dampened and focused. This space had been built for thinking, for study, for work that required silence and time.

The caretaker locked the door and turned to me. Up close, I could see he was older than I had first thought, perhaps sixty, though his dark eyes held a younger sharpness. His robes were simple brown wool, patched at the elbows. A scholar's clothes, worn for comfort rather than appearance.

"You traveled far, Señor Crable," he said. His Spanish carried the lilting cadence of Arabic underneath, words shaped by a different tongue. "The times are dangerous for strangers."

"The Keepers said you were expecting me."

He nodded slowly, studying my face. "They sent word through their networks. Told me a man would come who understood what this manuscript truly represents."

He gestured toward a corridor leading deeper into the madrasa.

"The manuscript is safe, but I cannot protect it much longer. The Crown grows more zealous, not less. They have taken or burned most of what we had. This survived only through luck and their ignorance."

"Then we shouldn't waste time," I said.

He studied my face for a long moment. Then his expression softened.

"Then perhaps you may find what you seek." He paused. "Though I wonder if you seek only a manuscript, Señor Crable. Or if you seek answers to older questions."

I said nothing. Let him read what he would.

He nodded to himself, as if I'd confirmed something. Then he gestured toward a corridor leading deeper into the madrasa.

"Come."

We walked through halls where sunlight fell through mashrabiya screens, wooden lattices that broke the light into geometric patterns on the floor. The air smelled of old paper and stone that had been cool for centuries. Our footsteps echoed softly. Somewhere above us, I heard the flutter of wings, birds nesting in the eaves.

The caretaker led me to a small study chamber at the back of the building. He produced a heavy iron key and unlocked a wooden door bound with bronze fittings gone green with age.

The room inside was barely larger than a cell. A single high window. Stone walls. A low table in the center covered with a worn rug. And on that table, wrapped in faded linen and tied with red cord, a manuscript.

"When the soldiers came the first time," the caretaker said quietly, "they burned most of what we had. Anything not scripture or practical language guides went into the fire. Philosophy, mathematics, poetry, most of it consumed." He moved to the table and rested one ink-stained hand on the wrapped manuscript. "I had this one hidden away, and they didn't bother to check everywhere."

A faint, bitter smile touched his weathered face. "Their ignorance bought us time. But ignorance is not safety. Eventually, someone will look closer. Someone will decide that all of this must burn."

He looked at me directly. "The Keepers asked me to preserve this until someone came who could protect it better than I can and deliver it into their safe hands. You understand what this is, yes?"

I approached the table slowly, feeling the weight of what the Keepers had arranged. This wasn't chance. They'd identified the manuscript, recognized its value, and sent me specifically to retrieve it. They were always adding to their network of preserved knowledge. Too often it was insurance against the Church's systematic destruction of anything that contradicted their narrow doctrine.

"Yes," I said. "I understand what it represents."

"Then take it." He pushed the wrapped manuscript toward me. "The Keepers' wisdom extends beyond what any of us can see. If they sent you, there is purpose in it. Let that be enough."

I knelt beside the table and carefully untied the red cord. The linen fell away.

The manuscript was perhaps fifty pages, bound in old leather that had cracked and faded to brown. The pages were heavy parchment, the kind that would last centuries if kept dry and safe. The ink had browned but remained clear, the handwriting precise and deliberate, the work of someone who understood that what they wrote might outlive kingdoms.

I opened to the first page and read the title written in careful Arabic: On the Proportions of the Spheres and the Mathematics of Unity.

Below it, in smaller script: By Abd al-Wahid ibn Sahl al-Gharnati, in the year 788 of the Hijra.

I did the conversion in my head. 1386. Just over a century ago. Written in the waning years of the Nasrid kingdom, when Granada's scholars must have sensed the twilight approaching.

The pages that followed were extraordinary. Geometric diagrams filled the margins, circles within circles, ratios that approached but never quite reached completion, grids containing symbolic notation I recognized from hermetic texts I'd studied decades ago. The scholar had used mathematics as a form of prayer, mapping divine order through geometry.

But it was more than that. As I turned the pages, I began to see connections. The ratios here, the way certain shapes reinforced each other, the mathematical relationships between geometric forms, they echoed what the Keepers had shown me in Jerusalem. Different vocabulary, different symbols, but describing the same underlying structure.

The Veil. He was describing the Veil without knowing what he described.

"Thank you, I will keep this safe," I whispered.

"Knowledge is always worth preserving, even if we don't understand it. Even if it survives in margins and hidden rooms. In the memories of old men and the curiosity of strangers..." he looked at me directly. "...for one day it may be understood and bring light to those who live in the dark."

Before I could respond, a shout cut through the madrasa's silence.

Sharp. Distressed. Then another.

The caretaker's face went still. We both listened.

More shouts from outside. Running feet. A woman's scream that ended abruptly.

"Soldiers," the caretaker murmured. "They've come to the Albaicín." His hands were shaking as he moved to the window. "They search for Moriscos, Muslims accused of secret practices, or simply people the Crown wants gone. Sometimes the accusation itself is enough."

I stood and moved beside him. Through the high window, I could see smoke rising from somewhere deeper in the quarter. Not the white woodsmoke of morning fires. Black smoke. Burning oil or pitch.

"How often does this happen?" I asked.

"More and more." His voice was tight. "The surrender terms promised freedom of worship. But already they find excuses. They take men, women, families. Sometimes the families simply disappear, and sometimes worse." He turned from the window. "You should leave, Señor Crable. Finish quickly and go. Christian strangers caught in a roundup ask questions the soldiers don't want to answer."

I looked at the manuscript on the table and hesitated for a moment, pondering what secrets it contained.

But the screaming outside was getting louder.

I carefully wrapped the manuscript and tucked it into my pack. The caretaker watched but said nothing. Maybe he'd known from the start. Maybe the manuscript was always meant to leave this place, carried by someone who could understand and preserve it.

"I'll keep it safe," I said.

"I know." He moved to the door. "There's a back way. Through the courtyard and into an alley that leads to the silk market. Go now."

He led me through narrow corridors I hadn't seen on the way in, past storage rooms filled with broken furniture and stacked clay jars. We emerged into a small courtyard open to the sky. A pomegranate tree grew in the center, bare branches reaching upward. The ground was paved with ancient tiles, most cracked or missing.

Cold wind hit us, carrying the smell of smoke and something worse underneath. Burning wood, yes. But also burning fabric. Burning flesh.

A narrow wooden gate stood in the far wall. The caretaker unlocked it and pushed it open to reveal an alley barely wide enough for two men to pass. Morning sunlight fell in a thin stripe down the center.

"Follow the alley to the left," he said. "It will take you past the old hammam and down to the market. From there you can find the main road out of the quarter."

I shouldered my bag and stepped toward the gate.

Then stopped.

Two streets over, the screaming had changed. Not panic now. Terror. The raw sound of people who knew they were going to die and couldn't stop it.

And underneath that, something else. A pressure in the air. A wrongness that prickled instincts honed over centuries of hunting things that didn't belong.

I'd felt this before. Corrupted magic left a signature, a taint in the air like spoiled meat or poisoned water. Not quite supernatural, still human at its core, but twisted. Bent toward purposes that warped the user as much as the target.

The caretaker saw my face change. "Don't," he said quietly. "There are dozens of soldiers. You're one man. You'll die trying to help, and the manuscript will burn with you."

He was right. Tactically, strategically, in every practical sense, he was right.

But I kept hearing that scream. Kept feeling the corrupted magic signature getting stronger.

I'd watched Arnaut walk into a portal to save people and I hadn't acted quickly enough. I wouldn't make that mistake again.

The book was important, but what was the point of all that knowledge if I walked away from people screaming for help?

"I'm sorry," I said to the caretaker. "I have to see."

"You'll die," he repeated.

"Maybe." I handed him my bag. "If I don't come back, get the manuscript to Córdoba. There's a Jewish scholar named Levi ben Samuel who'll know what to do with it."

The caretaker took the bag reluctantly. "You're a fool."

"Been called worse."

I turned and ran toward the screaming.

The alley twisted and climbed, forcing me to slow at corners where the walls pressed close enough to touch both sides. Laundry hung overhead, drying in the cool morning air. A black cat scattered from my path. Somewhere a baby cried, the sound muffled behind thick walls.

The smoke got thicker as I climbed. The corrupted magic signature grew stronger, making my teeth ache and my vision sharpen in the wrong ways. This wasn't a trace or a residue. Someone was actively using corrupted magic, and recently. Within the hour. Maybe within minutes.

I emerged into a small plaza where the streets opened enough for ten people to stand together comfortably. Under normal circumstances, it would be a neighborhood gathering place, a well in the center, stone benches along the walls, a few stunted trees providing shade in summer.

Now it was a killing ground.

Twenty, maybe twenty-five Muslim families were pressed against the far wall, men in traditional robes and turbans, women in hijabs clutching children, elderly who could barely stand. They held each other, belongings scattered on the cobblestones. Cloth bundles torn open. Pottery smashed. A child's wooden toy horse lying broken near the well.

Soldiers formed a loose cordon around them. Not the polished troops you'd see in Seville or Madrid. These were regional forces, poorly uniformed, weapons maintained but not pristine. Hired muscle more than professional army. Men who took this work because it paid and asked no questions about the orders.

Eight soldiers that I could see.

The families weren't fighting. They were begging. An old man on his knees, hands raised, pleading in Castilian Spanish. A woman holding two children, trying to shield them with her body. A young man, maybe twenty, standing in front of his pregnant wife, unarmed but defiant.

This was no ordinary roundup. The fear was too thick, too overwhelming. These families knew they weren't being relocated. They knew what was coming.

And then the soldiers parted, and she stepped into view.

Young. Perhaps twenty, though something about her made age difficult to judge. Black hair braided severely down her back, not a strand out of place. Skin pale despite the Andalusian sun, like something that avoided daylight by choice. Eyes so dark they swallowed light rather than reflect it.

She wore a long charcoal coat that moved around her like wings when she walked, fastened with silver clasps shaped like butterflies. The coat was stitched with symbols I recognized, not royal insignia, not military marks. Witchcraft sigils. The kind used in the Alpujarras mountains to ward, to track, to bind. Or to kill.

The corrupted magic radiated from her like heat from a forge. Even though she hadn't released it yet, it was coiled and ready. A snake waiting to strike.

She surveyed the cowering families with a calm that made my blood cold. No anger. No passion. Just the clinical assessment of a predator selecting prey.

"We have orders," she said. Her voice was clear without being loud, a voice that expected to be obeyed. "Seditious households are to be relocated. Resistance will be treated as treason against the Crown."

"We follow the surrender terms!" the old man cried. He was still on his knees, tears streaming down his weathered face. "We are leaving the city!"

"You practice your old faith too openly," Dina said flatly. "Witnesses have testified. Your household has been judged."

"Lies! Who testified? Show us!"

The woman tilted her head, studying him the way a child might study an insect before pulling off its wings.

"You ask for mercy from a God who abandoned you," she said softly. "How quaint."

She raised her hand. Shadow gathered around her fingers, coalescing into something sharp and cruel.

The old man had time to scream once before the magic struck him. His body convulsed, back arching, mouth open in silent agony. Dark veins spread across his skin like ink in water. Then he collapsed, eyes still open, still seeing, but empty.

Dead. Just like that. No trial. No chance. Just gone.

The families shrieked. A woman threw herself over the body, sobbing. Children cried. The young man in front of his pregnant wife went pale and began to shake.

She lowered her hand and studied her work dispassionately.

"That," she said, "is what happens to those who question my justice."

A soldier stepped forward to grab the young man, emboldened by the demonstration of power.

I covered the distance in four strides and caught the soldier's wrist before his hand reached the man's shoulder.

Silence crashed over the plaza.

Every head turned. The soldier stared at my hand gripping his wrist, then at my face, confusion and anger mixing. The families froze. The other soldiers reached for weapons but didn't draw, uncertain what they were seeing.

And the woman in the charcoal coat turned to face me slowly, deliberately, the way a predator turns when something unexpected enters its territory.

"Let go," the soldier said. His voice shook.

"You just watched her murder an unarmed man," I said, keeping my voice even despite the rage building in my chest. "These people aren't soldiers. They're not criminals. They're terrified."

The soldier tried to pull free. I didn't let go.

"I said let go!"

"No."

The woman took a single step forward. The shadows near her feet deepened and thickened, spreading like oil across the cobblestones.

"How fascinating," she said, and there was genuine interest in her voice now. Predatory interest. "You interrupt an execution. Either you're supremely confident in your abilities, or supremely stupid."

"Neither," I said. "Just tired of watching people die for no reason."

"No reason?" She smiled, and it was the coldest thing I'd ever seen. "They're heretics. Enemies of the state. Pollutants in a kingdom that needs purity. That seems like reason enough."

"You don't believe that."

Her smile widened. "Perhaps not. What I believe is currently aligned with what the Crown believes. That is sufficient enough."

She took another step. Power coiled around her like smoke, visible now to anyone with eyes to see. Several soldiers backed away instinctively, recognizing the presence of something beyond their understanding.

"You stand in my way," she said.

"I stand between murder and innocent people."

"Innocent?" She laughed, sharp and bitter. "There's no such thing. Everyone's guilty of something. These people are guilty of existing in a world that doesn't want them. I'm guilty of being the tool that removes them. And you..." Her eyes narrowed, studying me with predatory focus. "You're guilty of thinking your interference matters."

We stood three paces apart now. Close enough that I could see the dark veins creeping up her neck, disappearing under her collar. Close enough to see how her eyes weren't quite human anymore, too dark, too deep, like looking into wells that had no bottom.

I had seen this magic before, at Anglesey, but I hadn't seen it so ingrained in a person.

She studied me with an intensity that made my skin crawl. Not looking at my face, but looking deeper. Sensing.

"You have power," she said quietly. "I can feel it. Old power. Disciplined." Her eyes narrowed. "Church magic. The Vatican has chosen you."

Several of the soldiers stepped back at that word. Even regional conscripts knew enough not to question Rome.

"I was," I confirmed. "Not anymore."

She absorbed this information, her expression unreadable. Then she glanced at the families pressed against the wall, at the soldiers standing uncertain, at me blocking her path.

"Your name," she said. "Tell me."

"James Crable."

She tasted the name silently, the way some practitioners tested a name's weight and shape in their mind. Old magic, that. Knowing someone's true name gave you power over them, or so the theory went. I'd never found it to work in practice, but people still tried.

"I am Dina Gallardo."

The families shuddered. The nearest woman whispered something that sounded like a prayer against evil. Someone else murmured words that carried through the plaza like a curse.

La Mariposa Negra.

The Black Butterfly.

I'd heard the name. Rumors mostly, whispered in taverns and market-places across Castile. A witch who hunted rebels in the mountains. A woman who didn't age. A weapon used by the Crown to keep the conquered people terrified and compliant.

"Let them go," I said quietly.

Dina looked at me for a long moment. Her eyes were cold, absolutely focused. Then she looked past me at the families.

She raised her hand. Shadows gathered around her fingers, visible now, dark tendrils of power that made the air taste like copper and ash.

I responded with my own motion without thinking. Reached for my magic, the disciplines I'd learned over the centuries. Clean, pure, refined through study and practice until it responded to will alone.

Light gathered in my palm. Faint. Subtle. But there.

We stood three paces apart now, power coiled, neither of us moving.

The soldiers had backed away, giving us space. Even the families had gone quiet despite their grief, sensing they were witnessing something beyond their understanding.

The witch's eyes locked on mine and searched my soul. In them I saw nothing human. Just calculation. Assessment.

She was measuring me. Deciding if I was threat or opportunity.

Then, unexpectedly, she lowered her hand. A slight uncertainty flickered briefly in her demeanor. The shadows dispersed, pulling back like a tide.

"Release them," she said.

Her soldiers stared. "Lady Gallardo, the orders..."

"Are mine to interpret." Her voice was silk over steel. "I said release them."

The soldiers hesitated another heartbeat, confused by the reversal. Then they began backing away, lowering weapons, opening the cordon.

The families didn't move at first, couldn't believe what was happening.

"Go," she said, still not looking at them. Her eyes stayed on me. "Before the demonstration of mercy expires."

That broke the spell. The families scattered. Some ran immediately, heading for alleys and side streets. Others grabbed what belongings they could carry, moving as fast as age and burden allowed. The woman over the old man's body had to be pulled away by younger hands, still sobbing. The pregnant woman's husband pulled her away, glancing back at me with an expression I couldn't read.

Within a minute, the plaza was empty except for Dina, her soldiers, the old man's corpse, and me.

She watched the last family disappear around a corner. Then she turned back to me, and the smile that crossed her face was predatory satisfaction.

"Do you know why I let them go?" she asked.

"Mercy?" I said, though I doubted it.

She laughed. The sound was genuine amusement. "Mercy. How delightfully naive. No, Señor Crable. I let them go because you're far more interesting than they are."

She began to circle me slowly, studying me from different angles like an artist examining a sculpture.

"You have power. Old power, refined power. Church training but no longer Church bound. That makes you either a deserter or something worse." She paused. "The Holy See hunts deserters. Yet here you are, alive, free, intervening in Crown business. Which means you're skilled enough to evade them. Skilled enough to survive."

"Or just someone with a conscience."

"My point," she said, stopping directly in front of me again, "is that useful tools should not be discarded lightly. Those families?" She waved dismissively toward where they'd fled. "Insignificant. Replaceable. Their deaths would have satisfied today's quota and nothing more. Besides, they won't be hard to find if they stay."

She leaned closer, voice dropping to something almost intimate.

"But you. Powerful, experienced, with no loyalty to the institutions that created you. That's rare. That's valuable. And I've learned that the truly intelligent predator doesn't kill everything that crosses her path. Some things are worth cultivating."

"I'm not interested in whatever you're offering."

"Not yet," she agreed easily. "But perhaps one day."

She gestured to herself, the motion elegant and mocking. I couldn't tell if she meant what she said, or if she was unsure whether she had the ability to defeat me.

"Consider today an investment. I spare the families. You remember that I could have killed you and didn't. And someday, when you need someone who understands what it means to survive outside the rules, to use power without apology, you'll remember *La Mariposa Negra*. We'll meet again, Señor Crable. And next time, you won't have families to defend. Just yourself. We'll see how your principles hold up then."

Then she walked away, her soldiers falling in behind her. They disappeared into the narrow streets of the Albaicín, leaving me alone in the plaza. Perhaps I should have ended her right then and there, but I had a mission, and a cold, honest truth, I didn't know if I could. La Mariposa Negra, I would not forget her.

I stood there for a long moment, heart still racing, magic still humming under my skin. The old man's body lay where it had fallen, eyes still open, still staring at nothing.

A merchant leaned out from behind a door where he'd been hiding. He was old, face creased like worn leather, eyes wide with terror.

I looked at the empty street where she'd vanished.

She was completely and utterly corrupted. That was clear from the casual murder, the predatory intelligence, the utter lack of remorse. The darkness in her wasn't just real, it had consumed everything else. And it gave her real power. I could feel it wash through me.

I thought of Arnaut. Of the portal. Of the years spent searching for answers about corruption and the Veil.

Maybe this was an answer I hadn't expected. Not about redemption, there was no redemption in what I'd just witnessed. But about how completely corruption could consume someone. How it could take whatever humanity remained and twist it into pure calculation.

Dina Gallardo wasn't a victim anymore. She was a weapon. One that thought, planned, and killed with absolute precision.

And she'd marked me as something worth keeping alive.

That should have been comforting. Instead, it made my skin crawl.

I retrieved my bag from the madrasa, the caretaker was relieved to see me alive, and left Granada by the northern road before I attracted any more attention. The sun was higher now, warming the air, but I felt cold.

The old man's face stayed with me. The way he'd died. Casually. Effortlessly. A demonstration of power meant to terrorize the survivors.

And Dina's smile afterward. Satisfied. Amused. Completely unmoved.

As the miles passed and Granada shrank behind me into memory and mist,

I kept thinking about what she'd become. About the corruption that had eaten away everything human and left only predatory intelligence and ruthless self-interest.

She was right about one thing: we would meet again. She'd made sure of it. Marked me as a useful tool, something to cultivate for future use.

The question was whether I'd be ready when that meeting came.

Because La Mariposa Negra was more dangerous than any creature I'd hunted during my time in the Watch. Not only because of her power, though that was considerable, but because she thought. Planned. Manipulated. Killed with no hesitation.

She was calculated cruelty.

The road north stretched ahead, winding through Castile. Behind me, Granada burned its heretics and buried its secrets.

And somewhere in that ancient city, a woman with dark eyes and darker magic smiled, satisfied with the day's work.

One old man dead. Families terrorized. And tucked against my side, wrapped in linen, a manuscript that promised answers about a loss that now felt even heavier.

<h1 style="text-align:center">5</h1>

Arrival, Ambition, and the Warning (Tel Aviv, Present)

The chartered Gulfstream touched down at Ben Gurion in the midafternoon.

We had left Ohio sixteen hours earlier. Direct flight, no connections, and no chance for fate to intervene at a baggage carousel or gate change. Time mattered more than cost now, and I had enough money to make that problem disappear.

Seven people in a pressurized tube, each keeping themselves occupied in various ways. Lucan and Zeke took the front seats and spent most of the flight in quiet observation. Charlie buried himself in models and code. Casey slept with earbuds in, waking only for water. David worked through acquisition documents with the focus of someone who preferred contracts to meetings. Erin sat across from me, already wearing the CEO job she didn't officially have yet.

The plane rolled to a stop near the private terminal. Through the glass I saw Emetrix's Tel Aviv team waiting with tablets. Ten minutes later we were in three SUVs, moving north as the city woke up around us.

Tel Aviv takes you in quickly. Highway, interchanges, then streets that shifted from glass offices to older stone and small shops crowding together. Traffic built in layers. Buses, taxis, scooters cutting through gaps that weren't really gaps. Horns were frequently used as punctuation.

Young and impatient. The city wore its ambition openly.

January air off the Mediterranean carried a cool edge. Not Ohio cold, but enough to keep your jacket on. The light was softer than summer, the sun lower, everything washed in a pale gold that made the white buildings look even brighter.

Emetrix headquarters occupied two floors of a glass tower near Rothschild Boulevard. Open workspace spread beyond glass walls, clusters of desks, multiple monitors at each station, whiteboards covered in equations. The low noise of people thinking and the deeper hum of servers doing the same at higher speed.

The board meeting was a mere formality and took only forty minutes. Papers signed, funds transferred, authority granted. Erin was officially CEO. David looked like someone had slid a weight off his shoulders. Erin like she had been handed a puzzle she could not wait to solve.

"First thing I did was guide them toward environmental monitoring as a growth vertical," Erin told me afterward. "Gives us budget room for the tools we need. Makes our hiring decisions look reasonable."

"As long as they don't ask for full methodology," I said.

"They won't, they are all financiers, not technocrats. As long as the margins are healthy, no one will look twice."

Charlie had disappeared into a warren of meeting rooms with Emetrix engineers and scientists in tow. Within minutes, he had a small crowd around a whiteboard, the engineers' initial skepticism giving way to the focused excitement of people who'd just been handed the keys to a much more interesting universe. Several of the staff ran off, excited to get started immediately on his ideas and suggestions.

"I'll set up alerts," he said when I checked on him an hour later. His eyes were bright with the enthusiasm he got when someone finally understood his work. "We can get the sensor outputs online now according to the team. That will give us real time monitoring. I already have a link to their interface and dashboards, and set alerts for patterns outside of the norm. If anything spikes, we'll know immediately."

Casey claimed a corner with coffee and her laptop, catching up on the work she had ignored to make this trip.

Lucan and Zeke took a walk.

"We're going to look around while you handle business," Lucan said with Zeke in tow. "Text us when you're done."

By late afternoon, David had arranged lunch.

"There's a place near Shuk HaCarmel," he said. "My parents brought me there when I was eight. Been coming back ever since."

We met up with Lucan and Zeke and took two taxis. Traffic thickened as we headed to the crowded market. The buildings crowded in, balconies stacked three and four stories high, laundry hanging between them. The air picked up smells. Spices. Exhaust. Hot bread.

We got out two blocks from the market.

Shuk HaCarmel announced itself before you saw it. The noise came first, a wall of voices haggling and laughing and shouting prices in Hebrew and Arabic and Russian and English. The men in the stalls clearly targeting the obvious tourists to get them to sample their wares, or offering the best deals and calling everyone, "my friend."

Then the smell hit. Cumin and cardamom. Fresh bread from the Iraqi bakery. Grilled meat. Overripe fruit starting to turn in the cool air. Fish on ice, still showing this morning's catch. The sweet rot of produce past its prime mixed with jasmine from the flower stalls.

We walked into it.

The main corridor ran straight through the center, covered by a patchwork of tarps and corrugated metal that turned the sunlight into stripes. Stalls pressed against each other on both sides. Pyramids of oranges and pomegranates. Olives in five different brines, their smell sharp enough to taste. Nuts roasted in huge drums, vendors scooping them into paper cones while they were still hot. A spice merchant sat surrounded by burlap sacks, each one open to show turmeric, sumac, za'atar in shades of gold and green and rust.

People moved through the corridors in currents. Old women with rolling carts, testing every tomato before making a choice. Young couples holding hands, laughing at nothing. A boy running between stalls with a tray of coffee in small glasses, balancing it with the ease of someone who had been doing this since he could walk. A butcher called out the day's prices while his cleaver worked through a hanging lamb, each strike precise and final. The local Chabad offering to wrap the men in tefillin.

Zeke stopped at a stall selling dried fruit. The vendor, an old man with a face like leather left in the sun, offered him a sample.

"Hello my friend," he said in accented English. "These are the best dates in Tel Aviv. I give you good price."

Zeke took one, bit into it, and closed his eyes. "Sir, you ain't lying."

The vendor beamed and tried to sell him a kilo. Zeke laughed and bought half.

We passed a stall selling fresh juice. The vendor fed whole pomegranates into a press, seeds and all, the juice running dark red into plastic cups. The woman next to him sold halva in blocks, some marbled with chocolate, others studded with pistachios. She cut samples with a knife that had seen decades of use, offering them on the blade's flat edge.

Casey bought a cup of pomegranate juice and drank it in three long pulls, then made a face like she had discovered something holy.

"I'm moving here," she announced.

The noise wrapped in waves. Vendors shouting. Radios playing three different songs at once. Someone arguing about the price of eggplant with a passion usually reserved for blood feuds. A woman laughed, high and delighted, at something her friend said. A motorbike honked twice and threaded through the crowd anyway.

It smelled like outdoor markets I'd walked through across the world, but with its own accent. Zaatar and diesel. Coriander and cigarette smoke. The sea somewhere close, salt mixing with garbage and grilled lamb and the bright sharp scent of lemon cut fresh.

The restaurant sat in an alley next to the market's southern edge. Simple frontage, hand-painted sign in Hebrew, metal tables outside on the sidewalk. A small heater glowed near the door, more for morale than necessity.

A stunning woman with dark hair, almost black, and striking green eyes sat at the table alone.

For a second, fog, cobblestones, and a confused dockworker. Then the present reasserted itself. Sun on glass and the sharp brightness of Tel Aviv. The century had changed her clothes, but not the assessing stillness in her posture.

Corisande Valencourt looked up as we approached.

She had adjusted her style to the century, but not much else. Dark hair pulled back. Linen shirt, light trousers. The same calm posture. The same clear green eyes that didn't miss details and didn't waste time pretending they had.

"There you are," she said. "I was beginning to wonder if you got trapped in a boardroom."

"Haven't been trapped yet," I said.

"You just haven't met the right person to set it," she replied, her eyes narrowing suggesting both a promise and a dare.

Her smile was brief, but her eyes stayed on me a beat longer than necessary. Over 100 years since Brentford. She looked at me like it had been three days.

"Cori," I said, and let warmth into my voice.

"James."

As we all took to our seats, Lucan gestured around the table. "Cori, you know James. This is Erin Taylor, new CEO of Emetrix. David Katz, the new owner. Charlie Mitchell, our resident genius. And Casey Donohue, who worryingly, seems to like Zeke more than most people."

Handshakes went around.

"Congratulations," Cori said to Erin.

"Thank you. The real work starts tomorrow."

"It always does."

A waitress appeared. She greeted David in Hebrew, kissed him on both cheeks, said something that made him laugh.

"What did she say?" Casey asked.

"She asked if you could handle spice. Their zhug will put hair on your chest."

Casey's eyes lit up. "I want extra."

The waitress turned to the rest of us. Her gaze flicked over the group, then paused on Zeke for a fraction longer than necessary.

Zeke noticed. Of course he did.

"Ma'am," he said, voice smooth and polite, "before you decide I'm trouble, I want to clarify something."

Her eyebrow rose. "Oh?"

"I've got a generous tolerance for trouble."

She blinked once, then smiled that showed more challenge than interest. "Have you met an Israeli woman before? We're more trouble than most men can handle. What do you want, charming trouble?"

"Something strong. Something that will make me believe I slept last night."

She glanced at his face, saw the faint paleness. "You traveled poorly."

Zeke nodded. "I traveled like a man who made questionable choices with questionable company, and then had to live with them."

Casey made a small sound of delight.

The waitress's mouth twitched. "Arak?"

"I'll try anything, ma'am. Can I get that neat?"

"No ice?"

Zeke put a hand to his heart. "Ice is for injuries. This is for moral support and tolerance around this lot."

She laughed, soft. "I will bring you something that does not embarrass you in front of your friends."

"That's awful kindly of you," he smiled. "I have a reputation to keep up."

She looked at me and rolled her eyes, then walked away. Casey leaned toward him.

"Is there anyone you don't flirt with?" Casey laughed and gave Zeke a feigned exasperated look.

Zeke looked thoughtful. "No ma'am, I'm just extremely polite."

Casey grinned. "I think I'm going to enjoy you."

"Shucks, that's the nicest threat I've heard in a while," Zeke replied, turning up his drawl to eleven.

Food came quickly.

Small bowls of salad, cucumbers and tomatoes chopped fine. Hummus that looked plain until you tasted it, sharp with lemon and tahini, olive oil pooling in the center. Pickled vegetables. Olives cured two different ways. Zhug, green and unapologetic.

The pita came straight from the oven, still puffed, hot enough that tearing it released steam.

Casey went straight for the hummus and added a heroic spoonful of zhug. She took a bite and closed her eyes.

"I take back every joke I ever made about David's taste."

"You made jokes?" David asked.

"Oh don't worry Katz, never to your face," she said without looking up from the food.

"Good policy," Erin murmured.

Then the malawach arrived. Layers of dough fried until the outside shattered when you touched it. Bowls of grated tomato and hard-boiled egg followed.

"You tear it," David said. "Dip it. Build a sandwich. There's no wrong answer."

I pulled off a piece. The outside cracked, flaky and golden. Cori reached for the same section at the same time.

We both stopped.

She gestured for me to take it. "You're buying lunch. You first."

"I'll consider this a return on investment," I said.

Her eyes crinkled. "Did you trade your sword for accountancy since I last saw you?"

"Hardly, I can barely balance my life's ledgers."

Cori leaned slightly closer. "Noted."

Her voice was quiet, but intense.

More plates came. Grilled lamb, charred outside and pink in the middle. Shakshuka in a cast iron pan, eggs poached in spiced tomato sauce still bubbling.

We ate without ceremony. Plates moved. Conversations overlapped.

Lucan told a story about Vienna that involved three different safe houses and a creature that should not have existed outside of Alpine folklore. Zeke added details Lucan had left out, most of them making Lucan look far more heroic than he would admit to.

Erin listened while managing three different email threads on her phone. Casey watched everyone with the focus of someone collecting stories for later.

David ordered more pita while Zeke caught the waitress's eye again when she returned with another glass of arak. He raised the glass in salute.

The afternoon stretched, the light softening to a honeyed gold. The market noise rolled around us like surf. Vendors calling. Scooters honking. Someone singing in Arabic from a radio two stalls over. Life happening at volume.

For a moment, it seemed normal. Just people eating good food in a city that was abuzz with activity. No guardians, no corrupted magic, and no pressure building under the skin of reality.

Just lunch.

Then Charlie's phone emitted a harsh, pulsating chirp, an alarm designed to slice through any background noise.

Charlie pulled it out, frowned, went very still.

"What is it?" Erin asked.

Charlie's fingers moved across the screen. His face changed.

"The sensor network I integrated this morning. Jerusalem just spiked." He turned the phone so we could see. The graph showed a clean baseline, then a sharp vertical line. "That's not drift. That's active. Someone's doing something right now."

The table went quiet.

Lucan leaned in. "How strong?"

"Strong enough that the system flagged it priority one," Charlie said. "This isn't background noise. This is someone actively working magic."

My phone buzzed. Rabbi Eliyahu.

I answered immediately. "Rabbi."

"James." His voice was steady but tight. "The golem heard a cry this morning. From Ein Lavan. The Shedim there. A sharp burst of fear, then silence. I sent two of my people to investigate."

The noise of the market faded.

"When?" I asked.

"They left three hours ago. We've had no contact since."

I let the weight settle onto my shoulders. Not fear, but command.

"We'll leave right now."

"Good. This doesn't feel like a simple breach, James. It's strong, very strong. I will be waiting for you."

He hung up.

I set the phone down.

"Jerusalem," I said.

Erin was already pulling out her tablet. "I'll stay here. Coordinate data, sync with whatever the Rabbi sends. You need me working the problem, not standing in a valley."

David nodded. "Same. I'll handle logistics and make your requests sound reasonable to people with budgets."

"I'm coming," Lucan said immediately.

"Same," Zeke said. "If something wants to test the world, I'm happy to give it a failing grade."

Cori watched me for a beat. "I can't let you boys have all the fun."

I caught the waitress's eye and signaled for the check. She brought it quickly, which is not something that often happens in Tel Aviv.

Zeke gave her a look that was equal parts regret and promise. "Ma'am, I want you to know I'm leavin' against my will."

She smiled. "You will be far safer than if you stayed, I can promise you."

Zeke pointed at her like she had scored a hit. "It takes more than that to scare me."

She waved him off, amused. "That's because you haven't met my boyfriend."

Zeke stood and gave her a small nod. "Yes ma'am. Consider me properly warned."

Outside, the light had shifted toward late afternoon. The market hummed behind us. People buying fruit and bread. Couples arguing about nothing important. A city moving forward because it could not imagine a reason not to.

Cori fell into step beside me as we headed toward the cars.

"Do you know what we're walking into?" she asked quietly.

"No idea," I said. "But it can't be good if Eliyahu's that worried."

We got into two cars. Tel Aviv shrank behind us in mirrors, bright and coastal.

The road climbed into the hills. The sea disappeared. Stone and history waited ahead.

And somewhere under Jerusalem, whatever had decided to start testing the boundary was about to learn something important.

We were paying attention now. And we were coming.

6

Threats, Spirits, and the Return (Jerusalem, Present)

Jerusalem rose before us in slow, deliberate layers. The car climbed the Mount of Olives along a narrow road carved between stone terraces and ancient olive trees, the branches twisted out over the lane. The Old City lay across the valley, its walls pale in the afternoon sun, its towers and rooftops pressed tightly together. The Dome of the Rock shone like a coin. The wind carried dust, olive leaves, and faint incense drifting from one of the churches behind us.

Charlie leaned forward in his seat and stared.

"This city is stunning," he said.

"It hasn't changed in centuries," Cori answered quietly. "I'm in awe every time I visit."

Lucan watched the slope intently. Zeke tapped his thumb on the doorframe, restless but attentive.

Our driver navigated between slow-moving buses and clusters of pilgrims before turning onto a smaller lane. The Keeper compound lay ahead, sealed behind a low stone wall. It resembled an old religious school, modest and unremarkable. A courtyard opened inside, with a single olive tree raising its branches to the fading sun.

Rabbi Eliyahu waited near the trunk. He wore a tailored black suit and a white dress shirt, the kind of formal simplicity common among modern Orthodox rabbis, the brim of his hat shadowing his eyes. His beard carried more gray now, and his shoulders carried the weight of the unslept hours. He had not slept since sunrise.

He stepped forward as we approached.

"James," he said. "Thank you for coming. All of you."

Charlie shifted uneasily. "What happened here?"

Eliyahu took a slow breath. "The Shedim at Ein Lavan cried out this morning. A sharp burst of fear. Our golem heard it through the stone of the lower chambers. It carried the warning up to us. Then everything fell silent. The Shedim. The valley. The resonance that runs under this ridge. And two of my people are missing."

Lucan frowned. "Missing?"

"They went into the valley to look for the source of the disturbance," Eliyahu said. "They haven't returned and we have been unable to contact them."

Zeke shook his head. "Can they protect themselves?"

Eliyahu looked at me. "They are scholars. I am worried."

He led us into the building. The hallway was cool and lit by narrow windows. Shelves lined the walls of the chamber he brought us into. Scrolls and books lay stacked in uneven piles. It smelled of parchment.

Eliyahu unwrapped a cracked manuscript and spread it across the table.

"Ein Lavan is old," he said. "The Shedim there is older. It has no interest in men. It only stirs when the land is disturbed."

Zeke leaned closer. "What exactly is a Shedim?"

"A spirit bound to place," Eliyahu said. "Not an angel. Not a mortal. Something that remembers the oldest shapes of the earth. Springs. Caverns. Ruins. They walk unseen. They think. They choose. Some have turned violent. Some are peaceful. Most don't care about our affairs unless we intrude too deeply."

Charlie glanced at the manuscript. "And this one? The one at Ein Lavan?"

"It has lived quietly for generations," Eliyahu said. "It's part of the natural balance in this area. It does not harm."

He paused.

"Unless it's harmed first."

Lucan's voice dropped. "Do you think someone attempted to bind it?"

"There are stories here," Eliyahu said, tapping the parchment, "of ancient men who tried to capture Shedim. Some believed that if they could force a spirit to bend, its strength would become theirs. Most died. A few vanished. All caused pain in the land they touched."

He folded the manuscript.

"I ask that you go to Ein Lavan. You're better equipped for what may be there. If the Shedim is bound, free it. Bring my people home."

Charlie opened his mouth, closed it, then asked, "What about me?"

"I would like you to stay here," Eliyahu said. "I want to hear about your methods, which James has told me about. There is much we can show you also."

Charlie nodded slowly, already glancing at the manuscripts on the shelves with the eagerness of a child.

We stepped into the courtyard again. The olive tree cast long shadows across the stones. The wind shifted, bringing the muted sound of traffic from somewhere below.

Charlie walked us to the gate.

"Message me the moment you see anything," he said. "I will watch for changes here and coordinate with Erin and David. See if they can pick anything up."

"We will," Cori said.

Zeke clapped him briefly on the shoulder. "Keep the fort from falling."

"I'll do my best," Charlie responded. "Have fun storming the castle."

Cori looked at him, confused.

"Sorry," Charlie said. "I've spent too much time with Jimmy here."

I chuckled and slapped his arm. "We'll need a miracle."

Charlie groaned and headed back.

We entered the waiting car. The driver nodded and began the descent into the southern neighborhoods. The road wound past pine trees and cypress groves until the buildings thinned and the land opened into rolling hills. He turned toward the Jerusalem Zoo, then onto a rough access road that ended at a dusty parking area high above a valley.

A sign marked the path to Ein Lavan. Two old stone pools glimmered faintly far below, shaded by fig and pomegranate trees. The air was cooler here. Still. Expectant.

We went down the steep zigzag steps. Gravel moved under our boots. The smell of the city faded until only the rustle of leaves and the sound of water remained.

Halfway down, Zeke stiffened.

"You feel that?" he asked.

I did. A faint pressure at the back of the skull. It felt like something under the earth noticed us.

Lucan touched the wall and closed his eyes. "Something is pulling the valley tight. The ground feels held."

We reached the bottom.

The lower pool should have reflected the sky. Instead, its surface was heavy, like stretched glass.

Cori stopped suddenly.

"God," she whispered. "Look."

Two bodies lay near the waterline.

Or what was left of them.

Their clothing was scorched. Their limbs were twisted beyond any natural position. Their skin was blackened in places and peeled raw in others. Patches of stone beneath them were singed like something hot had flared outward. One man's arm had been broken in more than one place. The other had half his face burned away, teeth and bone exposed to the air.

Zeke swallowed hard behind me.

"That's not binding," he said softly. "That's rage."

Lucan turned his face away for a moment. Zeke stepped forward, jaw clenched, all humor gone.

"It took power to do that," he said. "A lot of it."

Cori crouched and examined what she could without touching.

"This is vicious," she said. "Something tore them apart and burned them.

This was not quick."

I looked at the scorched stone, then at the water.

The ground trembled beneath us. A low, mournful pulse.

The water rippled.

A shadow moved beneath the surface. A curled shape pressed tight, unable to rise. Pain evident.

The Shedim struggled beneath the water. Trapped and panicking.

Lucan took the entire scene in and whispered, "This is cruelty."

Cori scanned the terraces.

"Whoever did this is cruel," she said, "and possesses immense power."

I followed her gaze to the far terrace.

Between two fig trees, a figure stepped into view.

A woman stood motionless, watching us.

She did not speak.

She only smiled.

A black dress cinched about her waist with a belt that had a black butterfly for a buckle. The smell of burning flesh from a Granada plaza, centuries old, ghosted across my senses.

And in that moment, we knew exactly who had done this.

The woman didn't move from beneath the fig trees. She stood in a black dress that caught no light, the butterfly-shaped buckle at her waist.

I recognized her at once.

Granada. Centuries ago. Dina Gallardo. La Mariposa Negra.

Cori sensed the shift in me. She stepped closer. "You know her."

Dina smiled and spoke in her elegant Spanish accent. "I told you we would meet again, Señor Crable. May I call you James? I didn't expect it would be so long truthfully. Where have you been hiding?"

I tilted my head slightly to address Cori, "We've met."

Dina's smile grew, warm and wrong in a place filled with burned bodies. "Ah, you remember me. I am truly honored."

Zeke whispered, "She likes this."

Dina's eyes flicked toward him, as if only now noticing he existed. "More visitors. How delightful."

Lucan took a step forward, posture rigid. "What have you done?"

Dina followed his gesture to the scorched remains near the water. She regarded them with mild interest, like she was assessing misplaced furniture.

"These things happen. They walked into what I was doing. Unfortunate, but they should not have interrupted me."

Cori's voice sharpened. "Bitch."

"They interfered," Dina said calmly. "And interference can be dangerous."

Lucan's anger bled through his composure. "You burned them alive because they interrupted you?"

Dina shrugged. "Nothing can stand in the way of science and progress. There are sacrifices that must be made from time to time."

Zeke's fists tightened. "You killed them because they were inconvenient."

Dina smiled brightly. "Exactly. You understand!"

The Shedim pulsed beneath the water. A ripple of agony trembled through the valley. Dina looked down with fascination, like someone watching a laboratory reaction.

"They stepped into a delicate structure," she said. "I couldn't have them disrupt my work. They died. These things happen."

Zeke lunged forward without waiting for permission. He threw both hands outward in a burst of raw magic. A shotgun blast of force exploded from his palms, wide and uncontrolled.

Dina flicked two fingers.

The blast bent sideways in midair, curved back, and slammed into Zeke's chest. He hit the stone hard and gasped as his breath vanished.

Cori darted to him instantly. Her fingers glowed with a thin, focused line of healing magic. She pressed it against his ribs.

"Do not move."

Zeke wheezed. "That hurt."

Dina approached him by half a step, curious. "You poor thing. Let me fix that."

A thin ribbon of green light drifted from her hand and touched Zeke's chest. His ribs knitted themselves together with unnatural speed. Zeke scrambled away from her.

"Don't do that again," he said.

"Tsk, tsk. Where are your manners? You're welcome," Dina answered cheerfully.

Lucan set his hand against the terrace stone. Power rose from the ground in answer, a defensive shell forming around us. The air tightened and shimmered.

Dina looked at Lucan with mild amusement. "Oh. Protective wards. I am impressed."

Cori's eyes narrowed. She held her breath and released a needle-thin bolt of silver magic. It sliced through the air straight at Dina's throat.

Dina caught it between two fingers without looking away from me. The energy evaporated in a puff of smoke.

"You travel with talented friends, James. How charming."

Cori's curse was sharp.

Lucan expanded the ward, strengthening it, anchoring it into the terraces. I dropped beside him and pressed my hand against the stone. The old lines of the valley responded instantly. Heat rippled upward through the ward.

Zeke steadied himself, then slammed his palm into the ground, adding a surge of raw force. It rattled the stones and pushed outward in a heavy wave.

Dina raised an eyebrow, entertained. "Look at you. Coordinated. Like a little team."

Cori flicked another bolt of magic, a quick, slicing thread aimed at Dina's shoulder. It traveled so fast it was barely visible.

Dina leaned a fraction of an inch to the side. The bolt cut a fig leaf behind her.

"You have exquisite aim," Dina said. "Are we done yet?"

The ground trembled under us. The Shedim twisted beneath the water, then fell still, trembling like a wounded animal.

Dina's smile softened. "No matter. I already took what I needed."

Lucan flared with anger. "You drained it."

"Only the part I required," Dina said. "More would have broken it, and I may yet have need of it."

The valley air thickened. Frost formed in thin lines along the terrace stones.

Lucan braced. I braced with him.

Cori wove tight counterlines along the ward's outer edge. Zeke added force to the base of the structure.

All four of us held.

Dina looked delighted. "Save your energy."

She lowered her hand. The pressure dropped instantly. The cold evaporated.

"I am finished here," she said.

Cori lifted her hand for another shot.

Dina wagged a finger. "Do not be rude. I am leaving." She turned to me, "James, it was an absolute pleasure to see you again. Let's not wait centuries to meet again."

She turned her back to us and walked toward the path. Zeke moved to chase her.

"Don't," I said.

He froze.

Dina waved one hand lazily and a bright light flared in front of her. At the top of the terrace she paused, glanced over her shoulder, and gave me a wolf's smile.

"Until next time, James." She stepped into the portal and the light faded as quickly as it had arrived.

The valley seemed to pause momentarily and then returned to life.

The water sagged inward. The Shedim's presence steadied, trembling but free. The wind returned. Birds called from the hillside above.

Lucan knelt by the pool. "It seems terrified."

Cori stood beside the burned bodies. "We need to let Eliyahu know what happened here."

Zeke rolled his healed shoulder. "I have a rule against punching ladies, but next time I see her I'll make an exception."

Cori snorted. "Get in line."

I lowered my hand over the pool. The Shedim's shadow stirred weakly. It recognized a gentler touch. It drifted closer to the surface without thrashing.

I called Eliyahu and gave him the basics of what happened. Including the news of his two colleagues. We tended to the bodies so that when the Keepers came to collect them they didn't have to experience the full shock of the attack.

We searched the area and noticed sigil marks around the pool. They were indecipherable to us, so we took our phones out and snapped some images for Eliyahu and Charlie.

We worked in silence for a bit. Letting the weight of the evening settle on all of us.

Cori finally turned to me. "James. Who is she?"

I kept my eyes on the water. "A problem we cannot ignore."

7

Grief, Arak, and the Division (Jerusalem, Present)

Night had fully arrived in Jerusalem by the time we returned to the Keeper compound.

The city was quieter after dark, but never still. Lamps along the stone walls cast halos against the ancient edges. The olive tree in the courtyard moved in the cool night air, its leaves rustling against one another.

Rabbi Eliyahu met us at the gate. He stood very still, one hand resting on the stone archway as if drawing strength from it. The lines around his eyes had deepened since morning. Not weaker, just worn. He stood straight despite it. He had already received our call on the way back. We had given him the essentials.

"The bodies are being brought in through the lower path," he said quietly. "They will be tended properly."

"I am truly sorry for your loss," I said.

He nodded once and turned, guiding us inside.

The main hall smelled of parchment, candle wax, and stone that had absorbed centuries of prayer. Narrow windows admitted slivers of moonlight. The long table at the center was already occupied.

Charlie stood beside it, laptop open, cables snaking across the surface. Papers were scattered around him, half filled with equations and annotations.

A cup of tea sat untouched near his elbow.

When he saw us, he straightened immediately, eyes scanning faces, hands, posture.

"You all look exhausted," he said. "What happened down there?"

"A lot," Cori said, lowering herself into a chair.

Zeke stayed standing, rubbing the back of his neck. Lucan leaned against the wall, arms folded, unable to settle.

Eliyahu stepped closer. "Tell me what you found. What you felt."

No one spoke for a moment. The hall was still.

Cori's gaze shifted to me. She studied me, then spoke. "The woman in the valley. You knew her."

Zeke let out a slow breath. "I don't know where you met her, sir, but I'm surprised you lived to tell about it."

I rested my hand on the table. "Her name is Dina Gallardo. I crossed paths with her in Granada centuries ago. The locals called her La Mariposa Negra."

Eliyahu's expression tightened. "The Black Butterfly."

"Yes," I continued. "She served the Crown during the Inquisition. Powerful then. Corrupted now. Fully."

Lucan nodded grimly. "She was experimenting."

Eliyahu held out his hand. "The sigils."

Lucan passed him the phone. Eliyahu studied the images by candlelight. His fingers tightened.

"These aren't modern forms," he murmured.

"They felt wrong," Cori said.

"They were bent," Eliyahu replied. "First Geometry, malformed. Predatory."

Charlie frowned. "She's warping foundational structures."

"Yes," Eliyahu said. "And doing so deliberately."

Charlie's laptop chimed.

"That's Erin," he said, already moving.

The screen filled with Erin and David standing behind her. Both looked exhausted. Jackets still on. Hair pulled back hastily.

"We ran deeper queries," Erin said. "The spikes are not isolated."

A map appeared behind her. Points pulsed faintly.

"Jerusalem," she said. "France near Lombrives Cave. And Mawphlang in India."

"All Guardian adjacent," I said quietly.

Charlie nodded. "These aren't random."

No one spoke.

Lucan broke the silence. "We can't cover all of them."

Zeke exhaled. "So we split."

"I'll stay," Charlie said immediately. "With Eliyahu. Coordinate data, monitoring, and response."

Eliyahu inclined his head. "That would be wise."

Lucan looked to Zeke. "India."

Zeke smiled faintly. "I've packed for worse."

Cori turned to me. "The site in France is close to my home. I have been there, and I'm familiar with the old routes."

I nodded. "Then we move at first light."

The call ended. The plan was set.

Later, I stepped back into the Jerusalem night.

I found a hotel near the Old City and I went to my room to freshen up. Once settled, I checked in with Erin and David, and then headed out to meet Cori.

The winding alleys of the shuk were still busy when I stepped from the taxi into the night. The market was different after sunset, half shuttered, half alive, lanterns strung between metal awnings, their glow caught on drifting dust and the edges of fruit crates being hauled away.

Cool air rolled through the lanes carrying competing scents of spices, grilled meat, cardamom, baked bread, and something citrus bright from a stand still open two doors down. Conversations in Hebrew, English, and Arabic overlapped, rising and falling in the way only old markets manage.

Cori waited near a shuttered spice stall whose painted metal door showed a fading mural of blues and golds. She leaned against the wall, arms folded, eyes tracking the street. When she saw me, she pushed off the wall and smiled.

"Evening," I said as I approached.

"Is arak still respectable this late, or am I dragging you into sin?"

"There is never a bad time for arak, and I don't think God will judge after the day we had."

We slipped into the narrow artery of the market. Vendors were closing up, the clatter of shutters, the scrape of wooden crates, the rhythmic brush of brooms on stone. In the growing nightlife crowd, I could see people glancing at Cori, unsure of what to make of her. Beauty and danger in balance. She had survived lifetimes and moved like it, easy and aware.

We turned a corner and found the bar. It was unmarked and squeezed between a spice merchant and a locked fruit stall. A string of bulbs cast soft pools of yellow light across the open entrance. Inside, it was like stepping into a pocket tucked away from the world, warm wood, low lights, the faint burn of cigarette smoke.

Cori chose a table against the wall, as hidden as one can be in such a confined space. Her eyes tracked the room.

She ordered at the bar. Arak with mint for the both of us.

For a moment we drank in silence, letting the day settle, or trying to.

"France," she said finally. "Lombrives."

"Yes."

She swirled the glass, watching the ice shift in the cloudy liquid. Outside, a distant rise of laughter from another alley. Music from another bar could be heard over the crowd, people singing along in Arabic to Haim Moshe's *Linda Linda*.

Cori rested one elbow on the table. "We're heading into something old. Older than the Cathars. As old as the caves themselves."

"Older than us," I laughed.

She smiled. "That's saying something."

The arak burned in my throat, anise, lemon, and mint, clean and sharp.

"Do you ever think about the people you lose along the way," she asked, voice quieter now. "Not the enemies. The ones we carry."

"All the time."

She nodded, not surprised. "It catches up. Eventually."

"It does," I agreed. "But you keep moving anyway."

"Why?"

"Because stopping hurts more. I have disappeared from the world on more than one occasion, but I always find my way back. New friends, new experiences, and old obligations."

She lifted her glass and tapped it against mine. "To old ghosts. And to making them wait their turn."

I clinked mine gently. "To not letting the world fall apart."

We drank.

Her gaze drifted toward the doorway, staring off at nothing in particular. "You know," she said, "immortality sounded romantic once."

"It rarely is."

"Lonely. Mostly lonely."

I met her eyes. "But useful. You learn what survives. What about Lucan and Zeke? You have been working together a long time."

She smiled. "They are like brothers, but they have their own paths. You seem to have found true friendships. How do you deal with the fact it's so temporary for us?"

"It's not that I don't recognize it, I do. But I learned long ago that you cannot remove yourself from what makes us human. Sure, I have lost. But I have also gained more. Life is meant to be lived and experienced, and that's what I have tried to do."

"A warrior poet." She raised her glass to toast mine.

The lights outside flickered. The market morphed into its nighttime routine, less commerce, more secrets.

Cori leaned forward, forearms on the table. "I don't know what we're walking into back in France, and after today I don't like splitting up."

"Agreed, but I don't think we have an option. Time is running out and we're still responding. We need more information, and we need it fast."

She studied me for a moment. "You're right of course. I guess I'm just being a little nostalgic and rueful in my old age."

I laughed, looking at her. She had not aged the slightest in the century or so I have known her. "You know, you're practically a child compared to me."

"Zeke always tells me I have daddy issues." She gave me a wry, slightly dangerous smile.

"Great, so I'm walking into unknown dangers with a world-weary immortal woman with an Oedipus complex."

"It could be worse. You could be going with Zeke. I'm much better company, and less likely to get you into trouble." She looked down at her glass and tucked her hair behind her ear.

"I seem to recall a dock worker in Brentford who may beg to differ." I laughed.

"Yes, but he had it coming, and I was the epitome of restraint."

She raised her glass again. "To friends old and new."

"To the epitome of restraint," I teased.

We clinked glasses and drank.

We sat through another round and discussed France, our work in Ohio, and what had kept each other busy the last few decades. We moved between our current situation, what to expect, and our personal lives. We let the day's events recede, replaced by the city's night sounds, the burn of arak, and the easy, complicated comfort of her company.

We left the bar well after midnight. The market had mostly emptied, its alleys now broken into pockets of darkness between the last lit stalls. The scent of roasted nuts and spice still lingered. A cat darted between crates. A man laughed far down the lane, already drunk, or mostly there.

I walked the long route out of the shuk, letting the rhythm of my footsteps reset the world in my head. The night air was cool. The city below hummed.

Tomorrow we would split, Lucan and Zeke east, Cori and I west. And whatever waited under Lombrives, I hoped we were prepared.

The storm was building. And we were finally moving toward its center.

8

Fog, Sigils, and the Docklands (Brentford, 1899)

The night after our meeting at the Griffin, we returned to the docks.

By the time we reached the edge of the Brentford docklands, the fog had thickened into something that pressed close to the skin. It was a heavy river fog that rolled off the Thames, damp and cold, nothing like the soft mist of open country. It dulled sound and swallowed distance until the gas lamps along the road were pale smudges, their light barely reaching the cobbles beneath them.

Somewhere ahead, the Thames ebbed and flowed. The sound was low and rhythmic, water against stone and hull, the creak of ropes and timbers carried through the gray.

Lucan waited near the quay where stone met water, hands loose at his sides, posture easy. He stood. If the cold bothered him, he gave no sign. Lamplight caught the edges of his coat and left the rest in shadow.

A few steps away, Cori had her coat buttoned high against the cold. Moisture clung to her dark hair despite how tightly it was pinned back, a few strands already escaping. When she turned her head, her eyes caught the light, bright green against the gray.

A dockman noticed her.

He emerged from between two warehouses, boots scuffing stone, his breath sour with ale. Drunk enough to be both foolish and confident. He stepped into her path, grin lingering too long.

"Well now luv," he said, voice thick with a poor attempt at being casual. "Didn't expect to see a lady like you down here after dark."

She turned slowly, deliberately, and smiled at him. The expression was light, almost friendly, but her eyes stayed fixed on his. She opened her coat just enough to show the sword scabbard.

"Did you mean to say that out loud," she asked, "or is this the part where you pretend it sounded better in your head?"

The man laughed nervously, uncertain, glancing once over his shoulder looking for any kind of support. Then his eyes returned to Cori and widened as they fixed on the sword. "Just bein' friendly."

"I know," she said. "That's why I'm giving you a moment to reconsider."

She didn't raise her voice. She didn't move. She simply stood there, waiting, the smile still in place.

The grin slipped. His eyes flicked past her, taking in Lucan's stillness, then me, then Zeke appearing out of the fog behind us, his tall frame and broad shoulders filling the narrow lane. Fear sobered him fast. Instinct took over, the kind that kept dockworkers alive.

"Didn't mean nothin' by it," he muttered, stepping aside with a hurried, clumsy bow.

"I'm pleased to hear it," Cori said pleasantly. "Because I'd hate for this to be the most exciting thing that happens to you tonight."

Zeke tipped his hat as he passed and gave a wide, mischievous grin. "Evenin', hoss."

Cori turned back to Lucan, the smile already gone.

Zeke joined us, boots crunching on frost. His coat was dusted with moisture. "Fog's thick enough to lose a cathedral in," he said mildly.

Lucan nodded once. "It will make what we do more difficult."

"That's fine by me," Zeke replied. "If it ain't difficult, it ruins the fun."

We moved off the road and deeper into the service lanes between warehouses. The ground grew uneven, cobblestone giving way to packed earth and old planking darkened by years of water and wear. A loose shutter tapped softly against a wall. Farther off, a barge bell rang once and fell silent.

Lucan stopped beside a warehouse wall where the brickwork had slumped with age, mortar cracked and crumbling. He raised his lantern and angled it low.

"Here," he said.

At first, I saw nothing but stained brick and old mortar, darkened by soot and moisture. Then the light caught shallow grooves cut into the stone near the base of the wall. They weren't random scratches. The lines intersected at deliberate angles, uneven in depth, appearing as though whoever made them had rushed the job.

I crouched, cold biting through my coat. The cuts were rough, edges chipped instead of clean. I'd seen Keeper wards in Jerusalem with similar geometry, careful, balanced, made by people who understood what they were doing.

This wasn't that. Same foundation, wrong execution.

"Looks chiseled," I said. "Or something tried to tear the wall open."

Zeke leaned in, squinting. "Looks more like claw marks."

A cold certainty settled in my gut.

The geometry was familiar, but the additions were off. Sharp, hard-angled lines cut through the symmetry of the design. It made no sense.

Lucan said quietly, "I found others like this along the river."

Zeke frowned. "Looks like someone tried to copy something they half remembered."

"Or rushed," Cori added.

The air near the carving felt strained. Like a rope pulled too tight.

We moved on, following the line of warehouses toward the river bend. Lucan showed us another carving near a narrow passage where fog pooled low to the ground. Same rough cuts. Same impatient angles.

"See this?" Lucan traced the sigil with one finger. "See how they're all angled? Every one points east-southeast. Back across the river."

"Kew Gardens," I said, more to myself than my companions. The pit in my stomach deepened.

"Let me get a better look." Cori climbed one of the warehouses, her movements nearly silent despite the damp stone. From above, she guided us with quiet gestures, pointing out where the marks clustered near choke points, places where men and carts had to pass.

Zeke drifted toward the open lane, making himself visible. He whistled softly, a tune that was popular in American saloons. I stayed near Lucan at the warehouse corner, watching the ground and the water both. Above us, Cori's silhouette shifted along the roofline.

The first sign was not sound.

Smell.

Metallic. Sharp. Like blood on a butcher's floor.

Lucan inhaled once. "Did you see that?"

"I do," Cori called from above, voice low and steady.

Zeke stopped mid-step. "That ain't no person."

"No," she said. "Movement's off."

A tall silhouette formed near the mooring rings, darker than the surrounding black of night. Seven feet tall, hunched forward like a man carrying something heavy, but its arms hung too low, knuckles nearly scraping the stones. Its proportions were wrong enough to make my stomach tighten. The thing paused, head tilting.

Lucan didn't move.

The creature advanced, passing directly over one of the carved marks.

The air tightened, and not metaphorically. I felt it in my teeth, pressure behind my eyes. Magic soured my tongue.

It then faltered, sliding sideways like it was being pushed by an invisible current. Then it corrected course with unnatural smoothness.

"Now," Lucan said.

Zeke stepped into the lane and scuffed his boot on a plank. The sound carried farther than it should have. He followed with a low whistle, casual and unafraid.

The silhouette turned.

And began to move toward us.

It didn't charge. It stalked, crossing the open ground in long, even strides. Its feet struck stone without slipping despite the frost, each step placed with assurance that made my skin crawl.

Zeke backed away slowly, keeping himself square to it. "That's right. Come on, then."

The creature crossed another carved mark.

The air tightened sharply. My skin pricked. Something pulled at my senses.

Lucan shifted a single step, angling it's path without drawing its attention. He raised one hand slightly, fingers curling, and the fog thickened between the warehouses, growing heavier. The sound of the river dulled further.

The being corrected its course again, faster this time.

That was when Cori dropped.

She fell from above like a shadow, silent until the last instant. Her blade flashed once, bit deep into the creature's back. The steel struck something dense. She flinched as the impact shuddered up her arm.

The thing shrieked.

The sound was unnatural. Pressure released through a shape never meant to make sound at all. It reeked of pitch and burned hair.

It spun faster than anything that size should have been able to. An arm whipped out, joints bending at angles that made my stomach twist. Cori spun aside but not fast enough. Claws raked across her shoulder, tearing cloth and flesh, and she was thrown clear, skidding across the stones.

Before it could follow, Zeke hit it.

He came in like a locomotive, fist wrapped in force that cracked the air when it connected. The blow drove it into a stack of barrels. Wood exploded outward, iron bands snapping, scattering frozen grain like pale sand.

The creature rebounded immediately.

It seized Zeke by the coat and hurled him bodily into a warehouse wall. Brick shattered under the impact. Zeke hit hard, slumped for a heartbeat, then forced himself upright with a snarl.

"That," he said hoarsely, "was rude. Real rude."

I closed the distance and struck.

My blade bit deep, but the resistance was wrong. Fibrous. Dense. Like cutting into something woven rather than flesh. Dark fluid spilled and steamed in the cold, carrying that sharp metallic stink with an undertone of burned pitch.

It staggered, then straightened, correcting itself with eerie precision. Its eyes snapped to me, empty of fear, empty of rage. Just... focused.

Lucan spoke a single word, sharp and resonant.

The ground beneath it shuddered.

Not enough to knock it down, but enough to disrupt its footing. Frost cracked outward in jagged lines, and the thing faltered, claws scraping stone.

Cori was already back on her feet.

She moved low and fast, one hand pressed briefly to her bleeding shoulder as she muttered under her breath. The air around her shimmered, just enough to bend the lamplight, and she vanished.

The creature turned too late.

Her blade took it across the hamstring, severing something vital. It collapsed to one knee, limbs spasming.

It lashed out blindly. Claws raked Lucan's ribs as he closed in for the fight. He grunted, staggered, then pressed his palm to the air and spoke again, quieter this time.

The fog surged, wrapped around the thing's head and upper body, thick and choking. The pressure made my ears ring. It thrashed, movements growing erratic.

Zeke charged again, magic flaring openly now. "You picked the wrong damned dock!"

He struck it's chest with both hands, releasing the force he'd been holding back. The impact lifted it clear off the ground and slammed it into a warehouse wall hard enough to crack the brick.

It still tried to rise.

That was when I noticed the magic begin to fail.

It didn't explode so much as tear.

The pressure around the creature spiked wildly, then collapsed inward. Air rushed toward it, biting cold snapping against my face. I heard stone crack beneath my feet.

The carved marks along the quay answered.

They flared with light, sharp and white. Each rough line blazed. For a heartbeat, the geometry stood out starkly against the dark, every careless angle revealed.

Then they began to fade.

"Now!" Lucan shouted.

I drove my blade through the thing's chest and into the stone beneath it.

This time, the resistance shattered. Whatever had been holding the thing together gave way all at once. The blade slid through, chipping stone.

It convulsed violently, claws raking uselessly at the air.

The light in the carvings flared once more, brighter than before.

Then they went out.

The creature collapsed, weight going slack, limbs finally still.

For a long moment, none of us moved.

Cori wiped her blade clean, face pale but steady. Zeke leaned heavily against a crate, breathing hard. Lucan knelt, one hand pressed to his bleeding ribs, eyes fixed on the now-dark stone.

"Someone taught it that geometry," he said quietly. "It was poorly done, but it was projecting power from the multiple carvings." He looked up at me, and for the first time that night, I saw something like worry in his expression. "That worries me more than the thing itself."

The carvings were just carvings again. The magic imbued in them released, or destroyed. I couldn't tell which.

The Thames moved beside us, dark and indifferent.

Somewhere beyond the river, someone was carving doorways into reality.

And they were learning fast.

9

Lentils, Wine, and the Blanket (France, Present)

Snow covered the foothills in a clean, unbroken sheet as we drove north from Carcassonne. The road narrowed as it climbed, stone walls half buried beneath fresh drifts, bare trees arching overhead like ribs.

The tires crunched softly over packed ice. The countryside had gone quiet and still in the way that new snowfall always brings.

Cori drove with both hands on the wheel, steady and unhurried. She knew this road. Every curve, every place where ice might hide beneath the snow.

"This place has a way of shrinking your world," she said. "Stone, sky, and cold air."

"Sounds like a perfect place for someone who likes things simple and with a healthy dose of solitude."

She caught my gaze. "Simple? That's not quite me. And I'll admit, sometimes the solitude can be overwhelming."

"The Watch never prepared us for this life. And I would hardly call you simple, women never are," I teased.

Her smile was quick, teasing. "Tread lightly!"

The road climbed higher, pulling us away from the scattered lights of the city below. Carcassonne faded into a distant glow, then disappeared entirely as the last ridge rose between us and the valley. The air was sharper here.

Cleaner. Snow clung to the branches of pines and oaks alike, weighing them down until their silhouettes blurred together against the pale sky.

Cori eased off the accelerator as a narrow turn approached. The estate came into view gradually, not announced by gates or ornament, but by the subtle clearing of trees and the rise of old stone walls.

The chateau itself sat back from the road, built into the slope like it had grown there rather than been placed. Pale limestone, weathered and unadorned, its lines softened by centuries of wind and rain. Snow rested along the roofline and window ledges, untouched.

The car slowed as we approached.

"I never think of it as empty," she said quietly. "But winter reminds me how far removed it really is."

"It feels intentional. Like the land agreed to keep it hidden."

"That's exactly why I chose it. No neighbors to ask questions, so no need to move and hide over the years."

We turned off the road and followed the long, curving drive upward. Gravel crunched beneath the snow, the sound echoing faintly off the surrounding hills.

We parked near the side entrance. When the engine cut, the silence rushed in immediately. Even the wind seemed hesitant to intrude.

Cori stepped out first, boots sinking into the snow. She paused and drew a breath, letting it out slowly as she looked at the house.

I joined her, the cold biting through my coat. Snow drifted lightly now, not enough to obscure anything, just enough to soften the edges of the world.

The door opened with a soft protest of old hinges. Inside, the air was cold but dry, the smell of stone and wood. Cori set her bag down near the entry and switched on a single lamp. Light bloomed gently across the stone floor, revealing a space that was spacious without being grand.

She shrugged off her coat and hung it by the door.

"I'm glad you came," she said without turning. "Not just because of the caves."

"I know," I replied with more tiredness in my voice than I meant to convey. "I'm glad to be here."

She looked at me then, her expression thoughtful. "You carry Jerusalem heavily."

I nodded. I had nothing to offer as I was still processing it.

She gestured toward the kitchen with a tilt of her head. "Come. I'll make something warm."

I followed her deeper inside as she moved through the rooms in semi-darkness. The estate was lived in, not staged. Every choice spoke of long residence rather than possession.

As she gathered ingredients, I leaned against the stone wall near the counter, arms folded, watching her work. Her movements were quiet confidence, with sleeves rolled back and hair loosely pinned. There was no urgency in her motions. Only intention.

For a moment, neither of us spoke.

The snow continued to fall outside, steady and patient.

And for the first time since leaving Jerusalem, the world didn't feel like it was pressing in on me from all sides.

Cori moved through the kitchen with grace and efficiency.

She set a kettle on the stove, then assembled her ingredients with a military-like precision. A tin of salt. A crock of peppercorns. A jar of dried herbs. She paused at the pantry door, one hand resting on the latch, assessing what she needed.

"It always feels like the first few minutes are negotiation," she said.

"With the house?"

"With myself."

She pulled the pantry open.

I stayed where I was, shoulder against the stone wall near the counter, watching her work.

She took out vegetables and set them on the counter in a neat line. Onions. Garlic. A bundle of carrots that still had a little soil clinging to the roots. Her movements were economical, but not rushed. The quiet in the kitchen made every sound distinct. The soft thud of produce on wood. The scrape of a knife being drawn from a block.

"Fire?" she asked without looking up.

"I can."

She pointed with the knife toward the other room. "The hearth. If you don't mind."

I nodded and walked back through the corridor into the main sitting room. It was colder there. Stone held the chill like memory. The hearth was wide and old, ash swept clean, a small stack of split wood arranged beside it.

I knelt, laid kindling, stacked wood, and lit it. The first flame caught reluctantly, then strengthened, taking the dry edges of the kindling and climbing into the larger logs. The sound of it was small at first, just a faint crackle. Then it deepened, turning into something steadier, like breathing.

When I stood again, heat was already starting to push outward.

By the time I returned to the kitchen, Cori had chopped onions into a bowl and was slicing garlic thin, her fingers sure and controlled.

She set a heavy pot on the stove and poured oil into it. The flame hissed as it met metal. She dropped onions in and stirred slowly, letting them sweat rather than brown.

The smell rose quickly, sweet and sharp. It filled the kitchen with something alive.

"I've always loved simple meals," she said. "Something that does not require attention. Anyway, I want to talk."

"That sounds dangerous."

Her eyes flicked up, amused. "Not dangerous. Well, probably not dangerous." She shrugged.

I leaned back against the wall again. Heat from the hearth was beginning to creep into the edges of the room, softening the cold.

"What are we making?" I asked.

"Lentils. With vegetables. Herbs. A little wine if you behave."

"It's easy to behave before the wine flows. It's what happens after that can get messy."

She made a quiet sound that could have been laughter or skepticism.

She stirred, added garlic, then carrots and herbs. The scent shifted, deepening. Something earthy.

A few minutes passed in the rhythm of cooking, and then she spoke again.

"You never answered me."

"About what?"

"About the city. Jerusalem. Dina. You carry it heavily."

I didn't respond immediately. I watched her hands, watched the way she measured things by instinct rather than by cup.

"She killed two of Eliyahu's people."

"Yes." But there were questions and prodding in that simple answer.

"And she did it to make a point. Not because she needed to. Not because she was threatened. She wanted us to see it."

Cori's jaw tightened, but her hands stayed steady.

"She wanted you to see it."

That landed differently. I didn't like how accurate it was.

I exhaled slowly. "She said something in Granada. That day. That she spared people because I was more interesting."

"She said it again, in her way. She could have killed us. She chose not to."

"She was playing."

"Yes. And she appears to be very good at it."

The pot simmered softly.

For a moment, the only sound was the bubble of lentils and the crackle of the hearth in the other room.

Then Cori reached up to a high cabinet and took down a wooden box. She set it on the counter without ceremony, opened it, and removed a bottle.

Even in the dim kitchen light, it looked old. Glass darker with age. Label worn and fragile.

She angled it so I could see.

My breath caught before I could stop it. A bottle of 1947 Chateau Petrus.

"You've got to be kidding."

Cori looked at me, assessing my reaction. "Is that approval or complaint?"

Her eyes stayed on me, and now the amusement sharpened. "I bought two cases back in the fifties."

"That's one of the most legendary bottles of wine of all time. It's not something you open because you feel like having a nice dinner."

"No. It's something you open when you want to see if a man knows the difference between sophistication and performance.”

I blinked once. “That’s what this is?”

“A small experiment. Call it curiosity.”

“You’re testing me?”

“I prefer the word evaluating. Testing implies I have a preconceived outcome.”

I held up my hands slightly. “And here I thought you invited me for caves and danger.”

“Oh, that’s still true. But danger is predictable. Men are not.”

I laughed once, short and quiet. Turnaround is fair play.

Cori turned back to the pot, stirred, then said as if it were nothing, “I bought two cases in the early fifties. It seemed sensible at the time.”

I stared at her.

She glanced up, caught my expression, and let a smile show fully for the first time since the drive.

“Buying it was foresight. And I have waited long enough to use it properly.”

“And tonight is proper?” I asked.

Cori’s expression softened just slightly. “The house has been empty other than me for many years. I feel like I might not be able to carry on with that kind of isolation much longer. I am glad you’re here.”

She tapped the bottle lightly with a fingertip.

“And that earns a little ceremony.”

I didn’t argue.

She took out a corkscrew, old and well used, and set it into the cork with steady pressure. The cork gave with a soft, reluctant sigh. When she pulled it free, the sound was quiet but intimate, like a door opening in a house you thought was empty.

She poured a small amount into two glasses and handed one to me.

I held it up, watched the color catch the light. Deep. Brick edged. Alive.

Cori watched me over the rim of her own glass. “Well?”

I inhaled first. The scent was layered and startling. Fruit and earth and something I could not name, something that felt like time.

I took a sip.

For a moment, I forgot about Dina. About sigils. About the Veil tightening.

It was not just good. It was impossible.

I let the breath out slowly.

"Alright. You win. Let's do this right. Do you have a decanter? This needs to breathe."

Cori's eyebrow lifted. "I think we all need to breathe right now, not just the wine."

"You bought two cases. You waited seventy years. You opened one on a night like this. And you wanted to see if I would recognize it without trying to impress you."

Her smile widened like I had solved a puzzle.

"And yes. It's extraordinary."

"Good. Because if you had called it nice, I would have thrown you into the snow."

"I would have deserved it."

She raised her glass slightly. "To competence."

I lifted mine. "To breathing."

The food finished slowly. Cori poured lentils into bowls, set bread beside them, then sat across from me at a small table near the edge of the kitchen.

For a few minutes we ate without speaking. A quiet that didn't feel strained. The hearth's warmth had begun to reach even here.

Cori ate with the same controlled ease she did everything else. Halfway through the meal, she set her spoon down.

"You asked me something in Jerusalem."

"I ask a lot of things."

She looked at me steadily. "You asked if I ever feel alone."

I didn't move. I didn't deny it.

Cori leaned back in her chair slightly, eyes drifting toward the dark window where snow continued to fall, steady as breath.

"This house is large. It's quiet even when it's full. There are days when I can go from morning to night without hearing another voice."

"And?" I asked.

She looked back at me. "And sometimes it's a relief, and sometimes it's a prison."

"I understand. Live as long as we do and life can feel conflicted."

"You're probably right. But not always. Sometimes it's sanctuary. Sometimes it's control. And sometimes it's penance."

I watched her as she spoke, the way her fingers rested on the stem of the glass.

"But there are nights when the silence becomes... heavy."

I nodded once, because I understood that kind of silence too well.

"You're never lonely?" she asked.

I laughed softly. "Cori."

She waited.

I set my spoon down and rested my forearms on the table.

"I have been alone in ways that would sound melodramatic if I said them out loud. I have lived through centuries where I didn't allow myself to know anyone well enough to lose them."

Cori's gaze stayed on me, unblinking.

"And then you went and built a life in Ohio."

"Yes. Which is either growth or stupidity."

"Or courage."

I almost smiled. "That's generous."

"It's accurate."

The conversation slowed after that, turning more personal without either of us naming it as such. We talked about years that didn't matter to anyone else, decades spent moving, hiding, watching the world change while we stayed the same.

We talked about Lucan, about Zeke, about the strange comfort of familiarity when your timeline stretches too long for most friendships to survive.

We finished the meal. Cori cleared plates without fuss. I offered to help. She gave me a look that suggested I should sit down and stay quiet.

When the kitchen was clean and the last of the wine sat low in the bottle, Cori carried the glasses into the sitting room.

The hearth had taken properly now. Firelight moved across the stone walls and the heavy furniture, warming the room into something softer.

Cori sat on the couch first. Not formal. Not careful. Just tired.

I sat beside her, leaving space out of habit.

She looked at the space, then at me, and made a small sound of disapproval.

"I didn't invite you to perch."

"I am not perching."

"You're hovering." She stood and crossed the room to a chest near the window. She pulled out an oversized blanket, the kind meant for cold winter nights.

She returned and shook it out once.

Then she sat again and draped it over both of us without asking.

The warmth was immediate, shared.

She tucked the edge around her legs and leaned back, shoulder brushing mine.

"You see. Much more reasonable."

I glanced at her. "You're very authoritative for someone who claims to enjoy solitude."

Cori smiled, small and pleased. "I enjoy choosing when I break it. That's a woman's prerogative."

She lifted her glass again. "Drink up."

I did.

The fire cracked softly. Snow continued its patient fall outside.

Cori's head tipped back against the couch. Her eyes half closed.

"Have you been to Lombrives before?" she said.

"No."

"It's not just a cave. It's a place that remembers. The Cathars called those that lived in the cave system Perfect. Not because they were without flaw, but because they were devoted to purity and balance in a world that liked neither."

She turned her head slightly to look at me.

"You will meet something old there. Not human. Not quite spirit. Something tied to the land. Les Parfaits. The guardians."

I didn't interrupt. I let her speak.

"They aren't like the Shedim. Not bound in the same way. Not elemental.

They are woven into the place through faith and ritual and time. They keep the anchor stable because they believe stability is sacred."

"And you have tended them."

"For decades. This site is close to my home. Close enough that I can feel when the land shifts, even when I am not there."

She paused, and for the first time since we sat down, something tightened behind her eyes.

"What are you expecting tomorrow?" I asked.

Cori's smile returned, but it was thin. "I think we'll see what someone has been doing in the dark."

Outside, wind moved through the trees. The house creaked softly as it warmed.

Cori shifted slightly under the blanket, closer now. Her shoulder pressed more firmly into mine.

"You're tired."

"So are you."

"Yes."

She looked up at me, expression open, which seemed rare for her.

I let my head rest back against the couch and stayed where I was, under the blanket, the fire steady, the wine easing the edges of the day.

Cori's breathing slowed.

At some point, without either of us naming it, the conversation faded. The weight of Jerusalem loosened slightly.

And when sleep finally came, it came with an ease that I hadn't felt since we left Ohio. Tonight, for a few hours, we were simply two people trying not to be alone.

<h1 style="text-align:center">10</h1>

Compulsion, Stasis, and the Cave (France, Present)

I woke before dawn.

The house was still, wrapped in the silence that only comes after deep winter settles in. The fire had burned down to embers, a faint warmth lingering in the stone. Cori slept beside me on the couch, curled slightly toward the back cushions, the oversized blanket pulled up around her shoulders. Her breathing was slow and even.

I didn't move right away.

There was peace in seeing her like this. Unguarded. The control eased from her face by sleep. I stayed where I was, careful not to disturb her.

Eventually, I eased myself free, folding the blanket back around her and tucking it in more securely. She shifted once but did not wake.

In the kitchen, I stood at the window with a mug of coffee warming my hands, watching pale light creep across the snow-covered hills. The estate looked untouched. Clean, like the world had reset itself overnight.

By the time Cori joined me, dressed and alert again, the sun had climbed just enough to turn the frost on the trees into scattered diamonds.

"You should have woken me," she said lightly, though her eyes were softer than her words.

"You needed the rest. We both did."

She studied me for a moment, then nodded once. "Thank you."

The snow had stopped during the night, leaving the foothills hushed and bright beneath a low winter sky. Frost clung to every surface of rock and branch. The world felt sharpened.

Cori moved with purpose, pulling on boots and a practical coat that still allowed her to move, her hair braided back tight. Before we stepped outside, she paused long enough to retrieve her sword from the cabinet near the entry. The blade slid free with a quiet, familiar sound.

I grabbed mine from the pack I brought.

Steel seemed right in my hand. Honest. Simple. It sat alongside a familiar weight in my chest. The fact that I still wished it didn't have to.

The drive to Lombrives was short but winding, climbing through pine and bare oak, the road narrowing as it traced the contours of the land. The caves revealed themselves slowly, not dramatic, not imposing. Just a dark opening in pale stone, half veiled by frost and scrub.

"This place was never meant to announce itself," Cori said as she cut the engine. "The Cathars believed truth didn't need spectacle. It has stayed that way ever since."

We shouldered packs and crossed the threshold.

The temperature dropped immediately. My breath fogged in front of my face, and the sound of our boots changed from crunch to a muted scrape, the ground swallowing each step and returning it a half-second later as echo.

Lombrives opened inward rather than downward. The entrance corridor was wide enough for two people to walk abreast, but the ceiling lowered quickly, the limestone pressing close. Moisture clung to the walls in thin, slick sheets. It smelled of wet rock, old earth, and minerals that made the back of my throat tighten.

Water moved somewhere unseen. Slow. Patient. The drip of it was irregular, like a metronome that refused to settle into rhythm.

We descended carefully, boots finding purchase on worn steps carved centuries ago. Some were uneven, edges rounded by time and countless hands. The air carried faint traces of smoke long gone, a memory of fires lit by people who had come here with prayer on their lips and fear in their bones.

"This place was sacred long before the Cathars," Cori said quietly. "But they understood it. Or thought they did."

The passage widened, then split.

Cori didn't hesitate. She turned left, following a corridor that angled downward and away, her boots sure on stone that would have sent a normal person sliding.

"You can feel it," I said.

"Yes. It's closer."

The air changed before the chamber appeared.

Pressure gathered behind my eyes. Not pain, exactly. More like the mountain was leaning in, watching, and my body was reacting to it the way it reacted to storms or battlefields. My skin prickled. The hairs along my arms lifted.

A rhythm pulsed through the rock, low and steady, vibrating in bone rather than sound.

Then the light appeared.

Blue.

Clean. Intense. Alive.

It bled into the corridor ahead of us, like a light spilling through a crack in a door, but there was nothing natural about it. Too sharp. Too deliberate. It made the wet stone gleam like glass and turned the frost along the walls into scattered stars.

We stepped into the chamber and stopped.

The space was broad, circular, the ceiling high enough that darkness swallowed the top of it. Standing stones rose from the floor in a wide ring, arranged with ritual precision. The ground between them had been scraped clean of debris, prepared like an altar.

Sigils flared along the cave walls and across the bases of the large rock formations.

They were dazzling bright, like captured lightning or cold starlight.

They pulsed with power, steady and deliberate, lines precise and elegant, glowing luminous blue that reflected off wet stone and pooled in shallow water like spilled ink.

Energy rolled through them in visible waves, moving from stone to stone in a circuit that made my teeth ache.

"They're active," Cori said.

"Yes." Unease settled into my stomach.

The Parfaits stood within the ring.

They had once been beautiful.

Now they were wrong.

Not monstrous. A wrongness that unsettled the mind more than the body. Their forms flickered between solidity and transparency. Edges blurred, limbs elongating and snapping back into place as the sigils forced motion into shapes never meant to move this way. They appeared locked into the pulsing of the sigils.

Their faces shifted, expressions breaking and reforming.

They weren't hostile.

But their presence pressed outward in contained violence.

As we stepped closer, the sigils brightened in response.

The pulse intensified.

Cori's hand tightened on her sword. "They're aware."

The hum deepened.

And then the blast came.

Blue light surged outward in a concussive wave, raw and immediate. Not a warning. A command.

It hit the chamber like a hammer, air turning into force. The standing stones shuddered. Frost exploded off the walls in a white burst. A thin shower of grit and limestone dust rained down from above.

I reacted without thought.

I stepped forward and drove my palm into the ground, forcing my will outward in a tight arc.

The ward snapped into place around us, air hardening into a translucent barrier just as the energy hit.

The impact slammed into it like a physical blow.

The ward buckled.

For an instant it appeared like it would fold, like my magic would fracture under sheer weight, but I dug in and held. My arm went numb to the shoulder. Pain lanced behind my eyes.

Blue power washed over the barrier, splitting around us in screaming currents that rattled the cave and sent more dust cascading from the ceiling. Pressure crushed inward, teeth rattling, ears ringing, but none of it reached us directly.

Cori staggered once, caught herself with one boot sliding on wet ground, and braced a hand against the inner curve of the ward, eyes sharp.

"That was quick," she said through clenched teeth. There was approval in it, even if she would never call it that.

"I expected something. Just not this much."

The sigils pulsed again, brighter.

showered and Parfaits reacted.

They turned toward us as one.

Their movements were erratic, spasmodic, as though pulled by invisible lines to the beat of the pulsations. One raised an arm and the sigils answered immediately, power surging into it in a harsh feedback loop that made the air scream.

The Parfait's arm jerked higher than it should have, joint bending the wrong way, then snapping back into place.

"They're being driven," Cori said. "Forced into response."

Another pulse slammed into the ward.

Cracks of light rippled across its surface, spiderwebbing from the point where the wave struck hardest.

I could feel the strain in my chest now, like holding a door shut against a crowd that didn't get tired.

"This won't hold forever," I warned.

Cori's gaze tracked the circuit of the stones, the flow of power between them. She wasn't looking at the guardians.

She was looking at the mechanism.

"Then we end this quickly."

We moved together.

I released the ward in a controlled collapse, letting it fall inward rather than shatter outward. The moment it dropped, the chamber's pressure hit us full force. My lungs tightened.

Cori stepped first, blade in hand, walking carefully across the outer edge of the ring in a practiced precision. Her boots found dry ground, then slick, then dry again. She didn't slow.

I followed, keeping myself just outside her shoulder, extending thinner layers of warding forward like angled shields. Not enough to stop a full blast, but enough to redirect the worst of it away from her path.

The Parfaits lashed out.

Not with intent to kill, but with desperate force.

Waves of pressure hammered at us, chaotic rather than targeted. Bursts of corrupted geometry snapped into existence and dissolved, shapes too sharp to process clearly. The air itself seemed to fold and unfold in wrong angles, making the chamber feel briefly too small, then too large.

One of the Parfaits surged toward Cori, feet skimming the earth rather than stepping on it.

She met it head-on.

She didn't swing to cut.

She swung to anchor. She channeled power through her sword. Sigils along the blade flared white.

Her blade carved a line through the air, and magic followed it, bright and restrained, a binding pattern drawn with the authority of someone who had done this more times than she could count.

The Parfait hit the bind and convulsed, body snapping back like it was yanked by a chain.

Cori's face tightened. "That should hold."

I stepped in, laid my palm against the air beside the guardian, and reinforced her binding with a second layer, containment over suppression, forcing stasis without collapse.

The guardian stilled.

Not peaceful.

But contained.

A second Parfait moved, faster, and the sigils flared in response.

The blue circuit surged, and the chamber answered with another concussive wave.

Focused this time.

Aimed.

It slammed into my ribs like a fist. I staggered, boots sliding on wet stone, and for a moment I could sense the warding around my body thin.

Cori's head snapped toward me.

"I'm fine."

I wasn't.

The wave had done more than hit me.

It had cracked the rock formations near one of the standing stones. A sharp sound rang out, stone splitting, and a chunk of limestone broke free from the ceiling and fell.

Cori saw it a fraction of a second before it hit.

She shoved me sideways, hard.

The chunk of rock struck where my head had been, exploding into fragments that sprayed across the floor like shrapnel.

Pain flared along my shoulder where I hit the ground.

Cori didn't pause. She moved again, already intercepting the second guardian, blade low, body angled.

"Stay on your feet," she snapped.

"I'm trying." I forced myself up.

The third guardian turned toward us, and the sigils brightened.

I noticed the pattern immediately.

Recognition came like a knife to the gut.

The structure beneath the blue was unmistakable.

Not identical to Brentford, but disciplined. Cleaner. More refined. The same language, written by a hand that had practiced.

"These sigils," Cori said, breath tight. "Do they look familiar to you?"

I stared harder, forcing my eyes past the glow, past the pulsing circuit.

"They are. Cleaner than Brentford. More disciplined. But it's the same, perfected."

Her jaw tightened. "I thought so."

The guardians fought against the bindings with erratic surges, their bodies flickering as the sigils fed them more power. Each time we anchored one, the circuit compensated, pushing harder into the remaining ones, refusing to lose control.

It was exhausting.

Every bind took precision from Cori. Her magic was a scalpel here, not a hammer, and she refused to cut deeper than she had to.

I reinforced each bind, layering containment over suppression, forcing stasis without collapse.

The sigils fought us the entire time.

When Cori anchored the last Parfait, it spasmed violently, head jerking back, mouth opening in a silent scream. No sound came, but the air around it rippled.

Then it stilled.

Locked in shimmering suspension.

For a heartbeat, the chamber went quiet except for the hum of the active sigils. Then the circuit softened, the brightness dropping a fraction, like a hand easing pressure rather than releasing it.

Not destroyed.

Not even close.

Blue light continued to pulse, but steadier now, less violent than the first strikes.

Cori stood motionless, breathing hard, sword hanging loose in her hand.

I stepped closer to the nearest standing stone, careful, feeling the pressure of the sigils like heat against skin. I didn't touch it.

Not yet.

"This isn't just corruption," I said. "It's an override. Someone with extreme precision and knowledge did this."

Cori's eyes narrowed. "Meaning?"

"Meaning someone didn't poison the Parfaits," I replied. "They rewrote the rules the Parfaits live by. If these are related to Brentford, then whoever did this has been at it a long time. A very long time."

The blue circuit pulsed again.

Cori's grip tightened on her sword. She sheathed it and walked over to the sigils, studying them. She raised a hand close to the glow without quite touching it and spoke a few words under her breath, old syllables meant to test, not to challenge.

The sigils answered with a sharp crackle. A scatter of blue-white sparks jumped across the cave, snapping into the air like static. The nearest standing stone trembled, and one of the suspended Parfaits twitched against its bindings.

Cori withdrew her hand immediately.

"I can't fix this," she said, voice flat with certainty.

I inspected the circuit again, tracking the flow from sigil to sigil. "No. The craftsmanship and power is immense."

We moved carefully through the ring, checking the floor and the bases of the stones. Waxy residue. Bone powder worked into cracks. Stains that were too dark to be mud. None of it felt accidental.

When we were satisfied the bindings would hold as long as they could, we backed out of the chamber the way we had come, leaving the blue pulse behind us like a living thing we could not yet kill.

The drive back to the château was quiet.

Snow had begun falling again, light and steady, softening the tracks we left behind as we descended from the hills. The road wound back through bare trees and rock walls, the world narrowed once more to headlight glow and falling white.

Cori kept both hands steady, eyes forward, posture composed. It appeared that she was holding back. The caves were still on us, clinging in that subtle way certain places did. Not fear. Not shock.

Aftermath.

I watched the snow collect on the windshield, melt, and vanish. Over and over.

"They were never like that," she said at last.

"No."

"I have tended that site for decades. Through wars. Through shifts in the land. Through careless visitors and worse ones. I have never seen the Parfaits behave like frightened animals."

"They weren't frightened," I said. "They were being driven."

Her jaw tightened.

We said nothing more.

The château appeared through the snowfall exactly as it had before. Patient. Waiting.

Inside, the warmth came slowly. We set our boots by the door. Hung our coats without comment.

I poured us some wine while Cori stood at the window for a moment, watching the snow fill the tracks we had just made.

"We did what we could," I said quietly.

"Yes," she replied. "And now we live with what we couldn't." She didn't turn from the window. "We need to figure this out, and fast. I'm just not sure where to start."

I didn't have any answers.

She turned at last, her eyes were bloodshot and exhaustion lined her features. I knew that I probably looked worse.

We stood there in the kitchen in comfortable silence.

That was when my phone vibrated.

The phone rang while the house was still quiet.

I checked the screen once, then answered.

"James," Lucan said. His voice was steady, but tight. "We just left the grove."

I exhaled slowly. Cori looked up from where she sat, her attention fixed on my face.

"You both OK?" I asked.

"Yes. Shaken. Not hurt."

That was enough reassurance. I didn't press for more yet.

"We reached the grove before nightfall," he continued. "The guardian was active when we arrived."

Cori leaned forward slightly.

"How," she asked, not waiting for the phone.

Lucan paused, choosing words.

"Unstable. Not violent. Not passive either. Erratic."

I stayed silent.

"There were sigils in the grove we hadn't expected," Lucan went on. "Marks carved into stone. Deliberate. Old stone, but recent work."

That got my full attention.

"They weren't decorative. And they weren't subtle. They pulsed a bright blue and seemed to hold the guardian in a trance. Whatever put them there wanted it controlled. When we arrived it behaved erratically."

Zeke's voice came through faintly. "It was like watchin' a horse spooked by its own shadow."

Lucan ignored the interruption, but didn't disagree.

"We couldn't remove the marks. And we couldn't calm the guardian without restraining it. Temporary stasis was the only option."

Cori closed her eyes briefly.

"You did what you could," she said. "That mirrors exactly what we found in the cave."

"Yes," Lucan replied. "But it's not a solution. Just time."

I rubbed a hand across my face. He was putting words to the same thought that had been grinding at me since we left the chamber.

"You said you didn't wait to call."

"No. Because the grove wasn't the only reason."

There it was.

"I heard from Rome," he said. "An old friend that I trust."

Cori and I exchanged a look.

"He says there's activity inside the Vatican. Quiet. Internal. People asking about Watch rites that haven't been discussed openly in centuries."

The cold reached behind my ribs.

"And artifacts. Specifically ritual ones."

I didn't interrupt.

"There's talk of a ceremony being planned," Lucan said. "He says there is a small group that has been secretive and quietly researching the Vatican archives."

Zeke muttered something I couldn't make out.

I stared at the dark window.

"Does he know when?" I asked.

"Soon. Soon enough. We need to get there immediately. Maybe there are answers to our questions."

Cori spoke before I could.

"We'll pack tonight and meet you in Rome."

The line went quiet for a beat.

"This obviously isn't coincidence," Lucan said carefully. "But I don't know yet what it is."

"Hopefully there are answers in Rome," I replied. "See you there."

The call ended.

I set the phone down and sat back.

Outside, snow continued to fall, steady and soundless.

Cori didn't speak right away.

"I can't help but feel we're playing a game that has been going on far longer than we have been aware," she said finally.

"Yes."

"And we need to find a way to learn what the game is."

I looked at the fire, then back at her.

"All we can do is press on," I said.

We started packing for Rome and arranging transport, moving with the efficiency that comes when you're out of time and out of options.

11

Zealots, Fire, and the Corruption (Bram, France, 1210)

The Albigensian Crusade had stripped the Languedoc of its peace long before we reached Bram. It began as a holy mission, or so the Church claimed, to stamp out the Cathar heresy that had grown bold in the south. But by 1210 it had turned into something else entirely. Villages burned. Families vanished. Armies marched with God on their lips and blood on their boots. Simon de Montfort ruled the land with fire and iron, and the Church blessed every stroke of his sword.

The Watch rarely involved itself in the Church's politics. Heresy was a matter for priests and soldiers, not for us. But rumors spread of a Cathar mage who had taken refuge among the townsfolk. It was said that he was able to shield entire households, to twist light and confuse attackers. De Montfort asked the Vatican quietly for help. The Church sent Arnaut and me. We didn't know at the time that they had sent others.

We learned the truth when we reached the ridge above Bram.

The smell hit us first. Burning wood, burning thatch, burning flesh. Smoke rose from the low fields and drifted like gray curtains across the hills. The air was hot enough to prickle my skin, and the wind carried the faint cries of the terrified.

Arnaut listened, head tilted.

"That's not only the fire," he said. "There is something wrong in the air."

A second pulse ran through the earth. It shivered up my boots and rattled the small stones in the path.

"Yes," I said. "Someone is using power. A lot of it."

"But the cadence is off," Arnaut said. "It feels...twisted."

Another pulse followed, heavier and oily, leaving the scent of scorched pitch drifting through the air.

"Something dark," he added quietly.

We quickened our pace.

Bram came into view as the last light of the sun clung to the sky. The town was fortified by a low stone wall, half Roman in its foundation, with a wooden palisade rising behind it. A square gate tower guarded the entrance. The houses inside were tightly packed, whitewashed with timber beams, their clay roofs glowing orange from the reflected fire.

Tonight, the walls offered no protection. Flames roared across the rooftops. The gate had been smashed open. Smoke curled upward in thick, black columns. When the wind shifted, ash drifted toward us like dying snow.

Arnaut steadied himself. "This was no ordinary siege."

"No," I agreed.

We descended the slope quickly. As we approached, townsfolk fled through the broken gate. A woman clutched a crying infant to her chest. A man dragged an elderly neighbor, coughing violently as smoke billowed around him. Chickens scattered underfoot. A mule brayed in terror and bolted past us, reins dangling.

One fleeing villager, soot-streaked and wild-eyed, grabbed Arnaut's sleeve. "It came from the square," he gasped. "Devils!"

"Go," Arnaut told him. "Get clear of the flames. There are soldiers in the fields."

We entered the town.

The heat closed in around us immediately. Roof beams cracked. Shutters burned like torches. Lines of smoke rolled low where the wind trapped them between the houses. The smell was thick, choking, mixed with the sweet rot of burning thatch and the bitter tang of charred stone.

Beneath it all came the unmistakable vibrations of power. But something was wrong. Normal magic hummed like a taut string, clean and pure. This was thick, sluggish, like the air itself resisted it.

Oily.

Sickened.

We reached the square.

There, a man stood near the communal well, robes torn and scorched. His hands were raised, fingers trembling as he managed to conjure a fading shield of pale gold. The mage we were to seek out. Each time he tried to strengthen it, the barrier flickered like a dying lantern.

Facing him were two men.

Gerhard von Hohenfels. Marko Zoric.

I knew them both. So did Arnaut.

Gerhard was tall and broad through the chest, a man built like an oak. Marko was smaller, quick in the hands and sharp in the gaze. They were not wearing anything that marked them as members of the Watch, but they didn't need to. The Watch was small. We knew every face.

Arnaut stopped dead. "Gerhard? Marko? Here?"

"Why weren't we told?" I asked.

"Indeed," Arnaut whispered. "But someone sent them."

At that moment the Cathar mage hurled a desperate spell. A bolt of fire leapt from his palm, bright enough to cut through the haze.

Gerhard lifted his arm.

The fire wasn't deflected, but bent.

Like it hit a wall of thick oil in the air. The flame elongated, curled, and slithered away from Gerhard before dissipating into a puff of blackened smoke.

Marko's eyes gleamed. He stepped closer and flicked two fingers.

The smoke thickened, turning into a ribbon of dark vapor that wrapped around the mage's legs. The man stumbled backward, hacking violently as the greasy air entered his lungs.

Arnaut's face twisted. "What is that?"

"Not any magic I am aware of," I said.

The mage steadied himself and conjured another strike, this time a spear of light. It shot forward with surprising strength for a man so drained.

Gerhard inhaled sharply. The air around him warped, darkening slightly. When the spear hit him, it shattered into sparks that drifted downward like dead embers.

Arnaut whispered, "That's impossible."

"No," I said. "It's corruption."

He didn't argue.

The mage made a final attempt. He gathered what light he had left and cast a wide arc aimed at both Watchmen.

Marko stepped forward and whispered something.

The word wrong, like a stone sinking into mud.

The flames surrounding the square guttered inward, then surged violently. Smoke coiled around Marko's arm, clinging to him like a living thing.

He thrust his hand forward.

A viscous blast of blackened force slammed into the mage. The man was lifted off the ground, thrown hard against the edge of the well. The stones cracked. The mage crumpled.

Still alive.

Barely.

Gerhard closed the distance, raising both hands. More smoke leaked from his fingertips, darkening the air between them.

Arnaut lifted his hand instinctively. "Stop. You have him. Stop."

If they heard Arnaut, they ignored him.

The final blow came from Marko.

A slow gesture.

A soft word.

A ripple of angry magic that crawled across the ground.

When it reached the mage, his body jerked violently. His back arched. His mouth opened in a silent scream. Smoke burst from his chest.

Then he fell still.

Arnaut stared in horror. "This...is not who we are. This is slaughter."

"And they look satisfied," I whispered.

Satisfied was too kind a word. Gerhard seemed calm, but Marko wore the faintest smile.

Arnaut whispered, "James…how are they doing this?"

"I don't know," I said. "But our magic should not act like that. It feels wrong. Unclean."

Arnaut tore his gaze away from the dead mage to look at Gerhard and Marko. He steadied himself, breath thin.

"We have to confront them," he said.

"I know."

We stepped forward.

Gerhard finally noticed us. His expression was unreadable.

"Crable. Arnaut. You came."

Marko tilted his head slightly. "You are late. It's done."

Arnaut stepped forward slowly and carefully. "What have you done here?"

Gerhard gestured at the burning square. "What was necessary. The Cathar mage resisted. We removed him."

"And the town?" I asked.

Gerhard shrugged lightly. "Heretics. De Montfort would have finished them anyway."

Arnaut flinched.

This was a man who had seen war, but not like this. Not the deliberate burning of innocents in service of a target.

Marko stepped closer. "You must not cling to old ways. The Church has shown us more powerful methods. For the first time, we understand how to shape the deeper currents."

"What currents?" I asked.

Gerhard glanced at Marko. "You'll see. All in time. It's not our place to share."

Arnaut said sharply, "Whatever you are using…it's poison."

Marko smiled faintly. "Power often feels like poison before you learn to wield it."

Smoke curled lazily from his hand.

The magic itself seemed hungry.

Arnaut's jaw tightened. He could not tear his eyes from it. "That should not exist."

Yet there was fascination beneath his revulsion.

Gerhard looked at us with something like pity. "You will understand soon. This is only the beginning. There is a greater design at work."

"A design by whom?" I asked.

Marko's smile widened. "A mind greater than ours. A guiding hand. Perhaps our Lord and Savior himself. We simply serve its plan."

"The Church serves its plan," Gerhard corrected quietly. "And we serve the Church."

The ground trembled as a nearby roof collapsed in flames.

The confrontation had only just begun.

Gerhard took a single step toward us. It was calm, almost polite, but the air shifted with him. The smoke around his feet curled inward, drawn by whatever power he channeled.

"You have questions," he said. "This is not the place."

Arnaut stared at him. "This is exactly the place."

Marko's eyes flicked to the burning homes, the cowering villagers, the charred beams falling in showers of sparks. "The Church commanded the eradication of heresy. We acted with purpose."

"You butchered a town," Arnaut answered.

"De Montfort would have done the same," Gerhard replied. "We simply did it with greater precision."

His tone was steady. Too steady.

I moved between Arnaut and the corrupted Watchmen. "You two were not deployed with us. Who sent you?"

Marko smiled. "Rome. Who else."

Arnaut shook his head. "No. Rome does not sanction this. This is not the craft. This is something else."

"Rome has learned much," Marko said softly. "And we have been taught."

The ground beneath us vibrated again. Flames licked higher along one of the nearby houses. The roof gave way with a crash that sent sparks rolling across the square.

Gerhard lifted a hand in a quiet warning. "Do not get in our way. There is work left to do."

Arnaut looked ready to tear his throat out. His anger shook inside him like a kettle left too long on the fire, but his voice stayed cold. "What work?"

Marko turned his gaze toward the far end of the square. "Survivors."

I followed his eyes. A group of villagers huddled behind the ruin of a collapsed butcher stall, children curled beneath their aprons. Two men held axes defensively, trembling as flames circled behind them.

"You aren't touching them," I said.

Gerhard raised one brow. "They housed a mage."

"That does not damn them."

"Does it not? Marko asked. "The Church seems to believe otherwise."

Arnaut stepped forward. "Do not move another inch."

Gerhard's face softened into something like pity. "You two are loyal. Dedicated. But you're still clinging to sentiment. There is no place for that in the future."

"We choose what place we give it," I said.

Marko sighed. "Then this becomes more unpleasant than necessary."

The air thickened.

A slick pressure rose at my throat.

They were preparing to cast.

I dropped into a stance, feet braced against the scorched cobblestones. Beside me Arnaut did the same. The old forms of the craft rose naturally in us, clean and balanced. A thin blue shimmer formed at my palms.

Gerhard chuckled. "You are not ready."

Marko flicked his fingers.

A coil of black smoke shot across the square like a living whip. The sound it made was wrong. It slithered more than cracked, like something being dragged through oil.

Arnaut moved first. He spoke a single sharp word and swept his hand across his body. A clean arc of blue force sliced through the smoke coil. The whip disintegrated with a wet rip, scattering flecks of dark soot across the stones.

Marko gave a small nod. "Better than I expected."

Gerhard raised his arms.

The smoke thickened. It poured from his sleeves, from the ground, from the burning homes. It seemed like it was drawing the very corruption from the air. The smoke wrapped around him like a cloak, pulsing slowly.

I braced. "Arnaut. Center."

He nodded. He knew the old forms as well as I did. Together we pushed our palms outward. A dome of clear energy billowed outward, shimmering with heat as it met the oily darkness creeping toward us.

The clash cracked the air like a thunder strike.

The dome held.

Barely.

Black smoke splashed across its surface like tar thrown against glass. It hissed. It crawled. It ate at the edges.

Arnaut gritted his teeth. "This is... unnatural."

"Hold," I said.

The ground shuddered beneath our feet. Flames surged higher. Smoke whirled around us.

The villagers behind us screamed. A beam fell, crashing inches away from a child. I sent a pulse of clean force backward, lifting the burning wood aside without breaking our shield.

Gerhard watched all of it with curiosity. "You're strong, James. Arnaut as well. But too careful. Too bound by what you think magic should be."

Arnaut spat ash from his mouth. "Better careful than corrupted."

Marko flicked his wrist again. Another lash of dark magic shot forward. This time it struck the dome harder, splintering it with cracks of black light.

The dome faltered.

Arnaut swore. His voice was strained. "We are not going to hold this long."

I lowered my stance. "We don't need to win. We need to delay."

"Until what?" he snapped.

"Until they stop."

He stared at me, confused.

Because I saw something he did not. Gerhard and Marko were not trying to kill us.

Not yet.

They were testing us.

Gerhard lowered his hands slightly. "Enough, Marko. They see our strength."

Marko exhaled slowly and allowed the smoke around him to fall. The oily tendrils shrank back like worms avoiding sunlight.

Gerhard stepped forward, face calm. "We have work to report. De Montfort awaits his news. He will be pleased to hear the mage is dead."

Arnaut stiffened. "You're going to report to him directly."

"We serve the Church," Gerhard said. "And he is its hammer."

"You killed an entire town to reach one mage," Arnaut answered.

Gerhard shrugged. "The Church would have burned it all the same. We simply hastened the outcome."

Marko smiled, small and terrible. "We will report your presence as well. And speak highly."

I stepped forward. "We'll accompany you."

Gerhard paused. He considered this.

Marko nodded. "Yes. Come. The Church will want to debrief you."

Arnaut whispered under his breath, "We are walking into a den of zealots."

"Yes," I whispered back. "Better to see the serpent's head than its shadow."

We followed them out of the burning square. Behind us, Bram continued to fall apart, flames devouring the homes as terrified villagers fled or hid. The mage's corpse smoldered where he had fallen, a trail of black smoke rising from his chest. The corruption hesitant to leave him even in death.

Arnaut glanced at the body. His expression twisted. "This is wrong. All of it."

"Yes," I said. "And we need to know where it leads."

Gerhard and Marko led the way along the ruined main road toward the field where De Montfort's camp glowed with torchlight.

The further we walked, the more Arnaut's shoulders tightened. He was still breathing hard from the clash. Sweat stuck soot to his forehead. He looked shaken, angry, and something else. Something dangerous.

I caught his eye. "Don't let that magic near your thoughts."

He swallowed hard. "I will try. But it sings, James. Even in the air. Something in it... calls."

I gripped his arm firmly. "That's how corruption begins."

His jaw clenched. "Then watch me. If I falter..."

"You will not," I said. "I will not allow it."

Ahead of us, the Crusader banners flapped in the wind. Soldiers paced before the tents. The smell of roasting meat carried through the air, jarring against the smell of burning Bram behind us.

Arnaut straightened his shoulders. "Simon de Montfort waits inside."

"Yes."

"And we walk in with two men who just murdered a town."

"Yes."

Arnaut exhaled slowly. "This will not go well."

"No," I said. "It will not."

We stepped into the torchlit camp.

The meeting with de Montfort was about to begin.

De Montfort's camp sprawled across the hill like a metal and canvas city. Hundreds of torches flickered in the twilight, their light rippling across rows of tents, cookfires, and armored men wet from sweat and grime. The smell of horse dung mingled with roasting meat and the iron tang of sharpened steel.

As we entered the main lane, soldiers turned to stare. Some were grim faced, others curious, but all wary. Word had already traveled faster than we walked.

Something had happened in Bram. Something unnatural.

A group of knights moved aside to let Gerhard and Marko pass. They walked with the calm certainty of men stepping into applause. Arnaut and I followed close behind.

There were mutters as we walked.

"Those are the Church men."

"De Montfort wanted them."

"What did they do in that town?"

"Something foul. Something that smelled wrong."

Gerhard heard it all and did not slow.

The largest tent stood at the center of the camp. A scarlet banner hung before it, embroidered with a simple cross. Two guards flanked the entrance, helms shining in the torchlight. They studied us, eyes lingering a moment too long on the soot staining Arnaut and me.

Gerhard nodded at them. "We have news."

The guards stepped aside immediately.

Inside, the tent was lit by a dozen oil lamps. A large wooden table stood in the center, covered in maps, letters, and a half-drunk goblet of wine. The air was warm, heavy with the smell of sweat, damp wool, and burning tallow.

Simon de Montfort stood at the far end.

He was taller than I expected, lean and severe, with sharp cheekbones and a gaze that cut through the room with unsettling clarity. His blond hair was cropped close, his beard trimmed but wild around the mouth. Armor hung at his sides, its plates spattered with dried blood. Not all of it was from battle.

He looked up as we entered.

"Good," he said. "My men told me Bram burns. Tell me it was worth it."

Gerhard stepped forward. "The mage is dead."

Simon's eyes sharpened. "Describe it."

Marko bowed his head slightly. "He resisted. He attempted to shield the villagers and hide among them. We routed him. He no longer poses a threat."

Simon smiled. It was small and satisfied.

"God's work," he said. "Heretics cannot be allowed to wield sorcery. Rome sent you for a reason. The Cathars hide behind tricks and false power. You cut the serpent's head clean."

Gerhard nodded respectfully. "Our mission is to serve."

Simon's gaze moved to me, then to Arnaut. He studied us with the interest of a man sizing up new horses.

"And these two," he said. "More of Rome's specialists."

"Assistance," Gerhard said. "They arrived late, but they saw the action."

Arnaut's jaw tightened. He said nothing.

Simon approached slowly. He circled us like a hawk evaluating prey. "You fought alongside the mage?"

"No," I said. My voice remained steady. "We arrived as he fell."

"Then you saw his wickedness," Simon said. "Sorcery foul enough to defy the Church."

Arnaut stepped forward before I could stop him. "I saw a man defending innocents."

Simon's gaze snapped to him.

No one spoke.

The oil lamps crackled in the silence.

Slowly, Simon stepped closer until he stood right before Arnaut, their faces inches apart. His voice lowered.

"Defending innocents," he repeated. "Or hiding behind them. The heretics use the weak as shields. Mercy toward them is weakness."

"They were villagers," Arnaut said. "Children. Elders."

Simon's lip curled. "Spare me. The Church gains nothing by delay. Heresy spreads in the cracks allowed by softness."

He turned away, dismissing Arnaut entirely.

Gerhard and Marko exchanged a brief look of amusement.

Simon poured himself wine, then turned back, goblet in hand. "Tell me. What manner of attack did the mage use? Fire? Light? Tricks?"

Gerhard answered calmly. "He used fire and force. But he was out-matched."

"By your training," Simon said approvingly. "Rome has given you techniques beyond what my men could dream of. All for our holy mission."

My stomach tightened.

He had no idea what he praised.

Marko added, "There are deeper methods that guide us now. We are learning more each month."

Simon drank deeply. "Then teach my men."

Gerhard shook his head. "These teachings are for Rome's chosen."

Simon did not like that answer. His eyes flashed briefly before settling again. "Then you four are Rome's blessing upon this land. I want heresy scorched from every valley and hill. If it takes fire, so be it. If it takes steel, so be it. If it takes your gifts, all the better."

Arnaut bristled. "You did not see what they did."

Simon turned sharply. "I saw the flames from the ridge. That's enough."

He set down the goblet.

"I have another assignment for you," he said. "There are whispers of a Cathar stronghold to the south. Men claim another sorcerer is among them. You will go there. You will do what God requires."

Arnaut took half a step forward. "If God requires slaughter, then perhaps God is not the one giving the order."

Gerhard inhaled sharply at the boldness. Marko stiffened. The guard outside shifted, ready to intervene.

Simon did not raise his voice.

He walked to Arnaut again.

"You are very certain of your place," he said quietly.

"I know my duty," Arnaut answered.

"You do not know mine," Simon said. "Or Rome's. Or God's."

His eyes glinted, bright as steel catching fire.

"This crusade will not stop until the Cathars are ashes. You and your companions will aid that work. If you refuse, I will assume you have joined them."

Arnaut's fists clenched.

I stepped forward to speak, but Simon lifted a hand.

"I do not need your belief," he said. "I need your obedience."

Gerhard bowed his head. "We will obey."

Marko added, "Always."

Simon looked at the two of them with approval before turning his gaze back to me and Arnaut.

"You will all ride at dawn," he said. "I expect results."

He dismissed us with a flick of his hand.

Gerhard and Marko bowed again, then turned to leave the tent. Arnaut hesitated. His eyes lingered on Simon, filled with a kind of quiet disgust, but something else too. Something hollowing him out.

We stepped back into the cooler night air.

Behind us, Simon de Montfort's voice carried through the tent walls.

"Burn them all. Leave none."

Arnaut flinched. He looked down at his hands like they were foreign objects.

"James," he said softly. "We're walking into darkness."

"Yes."

"It's everywhere," he said. "The Church. The Watch. Even us."

I placed a hand on his shoulder. "Not us."

He lifted his head slowly. "I am not so sure."

Bram still burned behind us. Black smoke rose into the night, thick and oily. It drifted across the camp, casting shadows across the torches.

Gerhard and Marko walked ahead, silhouettes outlined by the flames. Their steps were confident. Eager.

Arnaut watched them go, his jaw tight. He looked toward the dark horizon, the glow of another town faint in the distance.

At dawn, we would ride south.

12

Security, Planning, and the Visitors (Rome, Present)

The safe house sat three blocks from the Tiber, tucked between a shuttered gelato shop and a building whose ground floor sold religious trinkets to tourists. Four stories of weathered brick, narrow windows, a door that appeared not to have been painted since the seventies. Unremarkable. Forgettable. Perfect.

Lucan had arranged it through channels that predated email by several centuries. Old favors. Quiet arrangements. Infrastructure that survived because it stayed invisible.

We arrived separately for maximum safety. Cori first, then me, then Lucan twenty minutes later. Zeke came last, carrying two bags of groceries and humming like a man without a care in the world. Anyone watching would have seen neighbors coming home for the evening.

The interior was sparse but functional. Two bedrooms, a kitchen with a table scarred by decades of use, a sitting room with furniture that had seen better days. The windows faced an interior courtyard where laundry hung between iron balconies and pigeons argued over crumbs.

Lucan set his bag down and locked the door behind him.

"Bishop Marco will be here in an hour," he said.

"He's sure he wasn't followed?" I asked.

"As sure as anyone can be." Lucan moved to the window and checked the courtyard below. "He's been careful. But careful only goes so far when you're operating inside the Vatican."

Cori sat at the kitchen table, already pulling out her tablet. "What do we know about him?"

"Bishop Marco Forino," Lucan said. "Fifty-eight. Career Vatican administrator. He worked in the Congregation for the Doctrine of the Faith for fifteen years before transferring to the Secret Archives three years ago."

"Why the transfer?" I asked.

"He requested it. Said he wanted to focus on historical preservation rather than doctrinal enforcement." Lucan's mouth curved slightly. "The truth is he saw things in the Congregation that troubled him. Questions being asked about old records. Requests for files that should have been sealed. He started asking his own questions, quietly, and someone noticed. The transfer was suggested. For his own good."

Zeke set down the groceries and started unpacking. Bread. Cheese. Wine. Salami. Olives. "So, we got ourselves a whistleblower with a Vatican security badge. That's better than I was expectin', I'll be honest."

"He's a man with a conscience who happens to work in a place where consciences can be dangerous," Lucan said. "I received a call from him while in India. He's been monitoring restricted vault access and found something that made him reach out."

"What kind of something?" Cori asked.

Lucan pulled out his phone and navigated to encrypted notes. "Three cardinals have been accessing materials in the deep vaults. Documents related to ancient ritual practices. Historical records of sacred objects used in... certain ceremonies."

He paused, choosing his words carefully.

"Marco mentioned one artifact specifically. Something with unusual access patterns. Multiple inquiries over the past year. Questions about its provenance, ceremonial use, current condition."

"What artifact?" I asked.

Lucan met my eyes. "A ceremonial nail. Iron. Four inches long. Kept in

Vault Seven beneath the main archives."

The room went quiet.

"The Nail," I said slowly. "From the True Cross."

"The same one used in Watch initiations for nearly two thousand years," Lucan confirmed. "Marco didn't fully understand its significance, but he knew enough Watch history to recognize the references in the research requests. He said the cardinals have been studying corruption integration protocols. How to introduce progressive degradation into sacred objects without destroying their ritual effectiveness."

Cori's hands stilled on the tablet. "They're experimenting on it."

"Have been for months, possibly years. And Marco believes they've succeeded. The Nail has been systematically corrupted. The corruption began centuries ago, which explains why it began to fail generations back. But there is renewed interest. It's like they know something new about the taint."

Zeke finished arranging food on the counter and poured four glasses of wine without asking. "Well now, that's about as cheerful as a funeral in the rain. So, we're fixin' to rob the Pope's basement to steal back a holy relic that was already compromised. And now some cardinals want to turn it even more evil. That 'bout right?"

"That's about it," Lucan said.

"Just makin' sure I understand the mission before I commit to grand larceny in the Eternal City." Zeke raised his glass with a grin that was equal parts charm and mischief. "Because I've done some questionable things in my considerable years, but breakin' into the Vatican ranks somewhere between 'bold' and 'Lord have mercy.'"

"The Pope doesn't know what's in his own vaults," Lucan said. "And if these cardinals have their way, he never will."

Cori accepted a glass from Zeke. "How do we know the Nail is still there?"

"Marco confirmed it. It's in a sub-vault beneath the main archives. Warded. Locked. Guarded by security protocols that that make a Swiss bank vault look weak. There are regular intervals of surveillance. Physical, electronic, and magical."

"Which means they're predictable," I said.

"Exactly."

We drank in silence for a moment. The wine was simple but good, the kind Romans bought by the liter at corner shops. Outside, someone called to a friend across the courtyard. A door slammed. Life continuing, ordinary, and oblivious.

Lucan set down his glass. "Marco will brief us on the security layout. After that, we have three days to plan and execute. Four would be safer, but Charlie's monitoring shows increased activity at multiple guardian sites. We're running out of time."

"Three days," Cori repeated. "Day one for intel, day two for setup, day three for execution."

"Like plannin' a wedding," Zeke said, settling into a chair with the ease of a man completely at home in dangerous situations. "Except instead of flowers and cake, we're stealin' holy relics from armed guards in a buildin' that's been practicin' security since before most countries figured out which end of a sword was sharp."

"When you put it that way," I said, "it sounds almost reasonable."

Zeke's smile widened. "Hoss, nothin' about this is reasonable. But I've learned that reasonable rarely saves the world, and unreasonable makes for far better stories."

Bishop Marco Forino arrived exactly on time.

He came through the back entrance. Medium height, silver hair combed neatly back, dressed in a simple black suit with a clerical collar. Wire-rimmed glasses. Hands that looked more suited to turning pages than wielding weapons.

But his eyes were sharp. Alert.

Lucan met him at the door. They embraced briefly, the greeting of old friends who had not seen each other in too long.

"Bishop Marco," Lucan said warmly. "Thank you for coming."

"Lucan." Marco stepped back and studied him. "You look tired."

"We all do."

Marco's gaze swept the room, taking in each of us with quick assessment.

When his eyes met mine, he paused.

"James Crable," he said quietly. "I've read the historical accounts. Damascus. Jerusalem. Bram."

"Don't believe everything you read," I said.

"I believe enough." He moved to the table and set down a worn leather satchel. "Lucan tells me you need access to materials that certain people would prefer remained hidden."

"The Nail," I said. "From the True Cross."

Marco nodded slowly. "One of our holiest relics. It's kept in Vault Seven, three levels below the main archive floor. The official record lists it as 'Relic 447-C: Iron spike, provenance uncertain, historical significance moderate.'"

"Moderate?" Cori asked, giving a puzzled look.

"Vatican understatement," Marco replied. "The truth is it's one of the most carefully guarded items in the collection. I've been watching access patterns for months. What I've seen troubles me deeply."

He opened his satchel and pulled out a folder.

"I should tell you," Marco said, meeting each of our eyes, "I still have faith in the Church. In what it represents. In the good it has done for two thousand years. A few renegade cardinals don't undo centuries of light just because they've chosen darkness. But that's exactly why this matters. The Church survives because good men stand against corruption, even when it comes from within."

"The Watch understood that at one time," Lucan said quietly.

"Yes. I never knew the Watch personally, of course. It was disbanded long before my time. But the archives remember. The records speak of an order that served something greater than politics or power. That protected against things most people don't even know exist." Marco spread documents across the table. Floor plans. Security schedules. Ward diagrams sketched in careful detail. "When I saw these cardinals studying Watch protocols, accessing files about ritual objects used in ancient ceremonies, I knew something was wrong. The Church may have disbanded the Watch, but it should never have corrupted what the Watch stood for."

He laid out photographs taken from angles that suggested considerable risk.

Cori leaned forward, studying the layouts with professional focus. "These are current?"

"As of three days ago. The security rotation hasn't changed in eighteen months. They're creatures of habit."

"Habits can be exploited," I said.

Marco nodded. "The main challenge is the ward. It's not just a lock. It's a living barrier, maintained by three separate sigil arrays. Break one and the other two compensate. You need to neutralize all three simultaneously, or the alarm triggers."

"Can it be done remotely?" Cori asked.

"Theoretically. But you'd need someone who understands the geometric structure well enough to identify the load-bearing nodes and disrupt them in sequence."

"We have two people," I said. "Charlie Mitchell and Rabbi Eliyahu Ben Ami. They're in Jerusalem working together with the Keepers. If anyone can crack Vatican sigils, it's them."

Bishop Marco's eyebrows rose. "The Keepers of Eternal Earth are involved?"

"They're as concerned as we are. Charlie's been studying guardian ward structures with them. Rabbi Eliyahu has access to millennia of sacred geometry knowledge."

"Then you have a chance." Bishop Marco pulled out another sheet. "This is the guard rotation. Eight men on the archive level. Two stationed near Vault Seven's access corridor. They change shifts at midnight, six AM, noon, and six PM. The changeover takes approximately four minutes. That's your window."

Lucan traced the corridor on the map. "Four minutes to bypass three levels of security."

"If you're fast and lucky," Marco said. "But there's another problem. Three cardinals have been visiting the vault regularly. Cardinal Rossetti, Cardinal De Luca, and Cardinal Parisi. They've been accessing materials related to ancient rituals and sacred objects."

"How often?" I asked.

"Twice a week for the past three months. Their visits are logged but not questioned. They have authority."

"And they're the ones asking about the Nail," Cori said.

"Among other things. But yes, the Nail comes up frequently in their research requests."

The room fell silent. Outside, evening was settling over Rome. Church bells rang in the distance, calling the faithful to vespers.

Marco straightened. "There's something else you should know. Two weeks ago, I saw Cardinal Rossetti meeting with two visitors in the Cortile della Pigna. A man and a woman. I didn't recognize them, but the way they moved..." He paused. "They didn't belong. And Rossetti looked afraid."

"Describe them," I said, though I already suspected.

"The man was tall. Early to mid-forties, perhaps. Dark hair, strong features. Military bearing. The woman was younger. Black hair, pale skin. She wore a coat with silver clasps shaped like butterflies."

My stomach dropped.

"Arnaut," Lucan said quietly.

"And Dina," I finished.

Cori's hands stilled on the tablet. "They're already here."

"They've been here," Marco said. "And whatever they're planning, it involves the cardinals and the archives. I don't know what they want, but I know it's dangerous."

Zeke set down his wine glass with deliberate care. "Well now, that makes this more interestin' than a poker game with marked cards. We got corrupted cardinals, evil butterfly ladies, and your old friend with the military posture all wanderin' around the Pope's backyard like they own the place."

"It makes it more urgent," I said. "If Arnaut and Dina are working with the cardinals, we need to move before they realize we're here."

Marco gathered the documents back into his folder. "I can help with the initial access. Get you past the outer security. But once you're in the vault corridor, you're on your own. If you're caught, I can't protect you."

"We understand," Lucan said.

I looked Marco in his eyes. "Why are you doing this?"

Marco's expression softened. "Because I took an oath. Not to Rome. To something older. To the idea that truth matters more than power. That some things are worth protecting even when the institutions we serve have forgotten why they matter." He looked at each of us in turn. "The Watch was disbanded, but its purpose endures. If these cardinals are corrupting that purpose, someone needs to stop them. Even if it costs me everything."

Lucan placed a hand on Marco's shoulder. "Thank you, Bishop."

Marco nodded once, then stood. "I'll send you the final security updates tomorrow morning. After that, we execute on day three. Wednesday night. Midnight changeover."

"We'll be ready," I said.

Marco moved toward the door, then paused. "One more thing. Cardinal Rossetti keeps a private office in the Apostolic Palace. He stores research materials there that don't go into the official archives. If you want to understand what they're planning, that office might tell you more than the vault will."

"Can you get us in?" Cori asked.

"Not directly. But there's a reception tomorrow night. Patrons of the Vatican Library. Black tie, invitation only. Security will be focused on the public areas. If someone attended who had... appropriate credentials..." He looked at Cori. "The aristocracy still opens doors in Rome."

Cori smiled, small and dangerous. "I can manage an invitation."

Marco nodded. "Then I'll see you there. Wear something memorable. It helps with the distractions."

He slipped out the back door as quietly as he had arrived.

For a long moment, none of us spoke.

Then Zeke stood and moved to the window, looking out over the darkening courtyard.

"We're really doin' this," he said, voice carrying that distinctive Texas rhythm that made danger sound like an adventure.

"Yes," I replied.

"Vatican heist. Corrupted cardinals. Ancient evil in butterfly buckles wanderin' around like they're on a sightseein' tour." He turned back to us with a grin. "You know, when I signed up for immortality, I thought it'd involve more beaches, better whiskey, and considerably less breakin' into the holiest real estate in Christendom."

"The beaches come later," Cori said. "After we save the world."

"Well now, I'm holdin' you to that promise, ma'am. And I expect white sand, clear water, and a distinct lack of angry cardinals."

The next day began before sunrise.

Charlie and Rabbi Eliyahu appeared on the video call at five AM Rome time, both looking like they'd been awake for hours. Charlie sat in the Keeper compound with his laptop and three monitors visible behind him. Eliyahu stood beside him, hands folded, expression grave.

"Morning," Charlie said. "Or whatever time it is for you."

"Too early," Zeke muttered from the couch, though he was already dressed and alert. "Y'all are worse than roosters with insomnia."

"We've been analyzing the ward diagrams Bishop Marco sent," Charlie continued. "Rabbi Eliyahu brought records from the Keeper archives. Turns out the Vatican borrowed heavily from guardian ward structures when they designed their vault security."

Eliyahu leaned into frame. "The sigil arrays follow sacred geometry principles we've used for millennia. Triple-redundant configurations in rotating prime sequences. Whoever designed this understood the deep structure of reality."

"Can you break it?" I asked.

Charlie and Eliyahu exchanged a look.

"We can suppress it temporarily," Charlie said. "The arrays anchor to physical markers in the vault corridor. If you can identify the markers and feed us real-time positioning, we can calculate the disruption sequence together. Rabbi Eliyahu will handle the geometric calculations while I manage the technical feed."

"What's the window?" Cori asked.

"Ninety seconds," Eliyahu said. "Maybe less. These wards were built to resist exactly this kind of intrusion. They'll compensate rapidly once they detect interference."

"Ninety seconds before alarms start screaming," Charlie added. "After that, you'll have maybe two minutes before armed response arrives."

"We need to be fast," I said.

"And precise. Jimmy, you'll need to wear a camera. Something small that can transmit clearly in low light. We need to see the ward markers to time the disruption correctly."

"I can get one," Lucan said. "There's a specialty shop near Campo de' Fiori that handles that sort of equipment. I have used them before."

"Good. And I'll need David to hack into Vatican satellite feeds. Erin's already working on the bandwidth to handle simultaneous data streams."

"They're fully on board?" I asked.

"Are you kidding? When I told them we were robbing the Vatican, Erin said it was the best use of company resources she could imagine. David's been grinning for twelve hours."

Despite the tension, I smiled. "Tell them we appreciate the support."

"Tell them yourself when this is over." Charlie sipped his coffee. "Rabbi Eliyahu sends his regards, by the way. He's fascinated by the Vatican ward structure. Wants copies of everything for comparison with Keeper defenses."

Eliyahu nodded on screen. "The Church learned from us centuries ago. It's only fitting we learn from them now. Though I wish the circumstances were different."

"If we survive, I'll get you copies," I said.

"When you survive," Charlie corrected. "I didn't design all these sensor networks just to watch you die in an Italian vault."

"Appreciate the confidence."

"Just don't make me regret it." Charlie's expression sobered. "One more thing. The monitoring network picked up another spike two hours ago. France, near Lombrives. Whatever's happening, it's accelerating."

"We know," I said. "We'll move as fast as we can."

"Fast and careful, hoss," Zeke called from the couch. "Those two things ain't always compatible, but I have faith in your ability to make the impossible look routine."

"Do your best anyway." Charlie ended the call.

Lucan stood. "I'll get the camera equipment. Cori, you should start making calls about tomorrow's reception. The better your credentials, the less questions anyone will ask."

"Already on it," Cori said. "I have an old friend in Milan whose family has been patronizing the Vatican since the Renaissance. One phone call and I'll have an invitation."

"And I'll play the part of wealthy American philanthropist," Zeke said, standing and stretching. "Loud, generous, slightly overwhelmed by all this glorious history, and extremely distractin'. Basically myself, but with better shoes."

We had a plan, but like Mike Tyson once said, "Everyone has a plan until they get punched in the face."

13

Silk, Honors, and the Vault (Rome, Present)

The second day in Rome arrived with winter sunshine that made the city look almost innocent.

Cori left the safe house at three PM. Her dress and presence made everyone else in the room fall silent.

The gown was midnight blue, cut to suggest elegance rather than announce it. Her dark hair was pulled back in a style that showed the precise angles of her face. Minimal jewelry. Diamond earrings that caught the light. Heels that added height without compromising her natural grace.

She paused at the door and looked back at us.

"How do I look?" she asked.

"Like trouble wrapped in silk," Zeke said with appreciation. "The kind that makes cardinals forget their vows and monsignors forget their own names."

"Like someone cardinals will want to impress," Lucan added.

"Like you belong," I said.

Her smile was brief, but it reflected in her eyes. "Then let's hope they're paying attention."

She left in a car Lucan had arranged, heading toward the Vatican through streets already clogged with evening traffic.

Zeke and I followed an hour later in separate vehicles. Zeke wore an expertly tailored tuxedo that still managed to look American, complete with a bolo tie that he insisted was "high-class Texas formal." He carried an invitation

Marco had procured through channels I didn't ask about.

I stayed outside the reception entirely, positioned in a café across the piazza where I could monitor communications and provide backup if needed.

Bishop Marco had spent the day in the Vatican Secret Archives, mapping guard routes and timing for us. He sent updates every thirty minutes via encrypted text on a cell phone that Lucan gave him.

North corridor guard change 14:47. Exactly on schedule.

Vault Seven access visible from reading room three. Two guards, no variation from pattern.

Cardinal Rossetti in private office. Door closed. Assistant stationed outside.

At seven PM, Cori's voice came through my earpiece.

"I'm in. The receiving line is moving slowly, but I've made contact with Cardinal De Luca's assistant. She's very interested in my family's art collection."

"Keep her interested," I replied quietly.

Twenty minutes later: "I've been introduced to Cardinal Parisi. He's exactly as the Bishop described. Nervous. Eager to please. Currently boring me with stories about medieval manuscripts that I suspect he's embellishing for effect."

"Can you keep him occupied?"

"For hours if necessary. He clearly doesn't get much attention from women."

Zeke's voice cut in, louder and warmer than before. "Ladies and gentlemen, the American has arrived. And I brought my checkbook and best intentions. Now who wants to talk about restorin' frescoes and makin' history beautiful again?"

I heard laughter in the background. Multiple voices responding warmly. Zeke was already working the room.

"There's a monsignor here who is positively delighted to show me the Raphael Rooms," Zeke continued. "I may have mentioned that my dear late aunt collected Renaissance art and would've wept with joy at the preservation work y'all are doin'."

"Your great-aunt would have been dead for over two-hundred years" I said.

"Hoss, I don't even have a late aunt. But this monsignor doesn't know that, and his enthusiasm for my fictional family's philanthropic history is downright heartwarmin'. He's already shown me three brochures and promised a private tour if I'm serious about donations."

Two hours passed. The reception continued in the background of my earpiece, a blur of polite conversation and clinking glasses. Cori kept Cardinal Parisi engaged. Zeke charmed his way through three separate groups, dropping hints about generous donations and family oil money, and foundations that existed only in his imagination.

At nine fifteen, Cori's voice changed slightly.

"James. Cardinal Rossetti just left his office. He's heading toward the reception."

"Can you intercept?"

"Already moving. Stand by."

Five minutes later: "I've engaged him in conversation about restoration funding. He's very pleased to meet a potential patron. This could take a while."

"Take as long as you need."

Lucan's text arrived.

Rossetti's office is empty. Assistant went to reception. Window is open.

I texted back

Can you reach it?

He responded.

Not without being seen. Need a distraction.

I relayed this to Zeke.

"Oh, I can make a distraction," Zeke said, and I could hear the grin in his voice. "Give me two minutes to position myself strategically near somethin' expensive and fragile."

Ninety seconds later, I heard a tremendous crash through the earpiece. Glass shattering. Multiple voices raised in alarm.

"Oh Lord, oh no, oh I am so profoundly sorry!" Zeke's voice, absolutely mortified, but still charming. "Is that Venetian glass? Please tell me that wasn't irreplaceable Venetian glass! Ma'am, sir, I will personally fund a restoration team from Venice itself if that's what it takes to make this right! Actually, make that two restoration teams. And a historian. Do y'all need a historian? I feel like we might need a historian!"

More chaos. People rushing toward the sound. Security moving to assess. Zeke apologizing profusely while making the situation worse by trying to help clean up while also offering increasingly generous donations to cover the damage.

Lucan's text.

Moving now.

Three minutes of silence.

Inside Rossetti's office. Searching.

Another two minutes.

Found something. Documents referencing ceremonial protocols. Multiple mentions of "corruption integration" and "binding amplification." Photographs of the Nail. Notes in margins about "controllable degradation."

My blood went cold.

They weren't just studying the corruption. They were refining it. Learning to control it. To weaponize it.

I typed quickly.

Get out. Now!

The response seemed longer than it was.

Copying. Need 30 seconds.

Through the earpiece, I heard the commotion dying down. Zeke still apologizing profusely. Someone saying it was fine, accidents happen, the insurance would cover it. Security returning to their posts.

20 seconds.

Lucan, you need to move.

10 seconds.

Then.

Out. Returning to the reading room.

I exhaled slowly.

"Zeke, you can stop apologizing now."

"You sure? Because I am on a roll here. I think I've convinced them I'm a wealthy idiot who's going to donate a fortune out of guilt. The monsignor just offered me a personal blessing and a certificate of appreciation. I don't even know what that is, but apparently I'm gettin' one."

"Congratulations on the honors."

"I do my best work under pressure, hoss. Always have."

Cori's voice came through, "Rossetti is asking about my family's connection to the Medici. I think I'm making progress. He's mentioned a private tour of restricted collections."

"String him along as long as you can."

"Trust me, he's not going anywhere. He just ordered champagne."

The reception continued for another hour. By the time it ended, Cori had secured promises of private tours from two cardinals and a monsignor. Zeke had committed to a donation that would make his fictional great-aunt proud. And Lucan had copied enough documents to keep us reading for days.

We regrouped at the safe house near midnight.

Lucan spread the copied documents across the table. Photographs of the Nail from multiple angles. Close-ups showing dark veins spreading through the metal like infection. Notes describing "progressive corruption protocols" and "binding resonance amplification."

"They're experimenting," Lucan said quietly. "Testing how far they can push corruption into sacred objects without destroying their ritual effectiveness. This looks like the medieval era corruptions have been fixed and enhanced."

Cori leaned over the documents, face pale. "This is methodical. Scientific. They're treating corruption like a tool to be calibrated."

"Which means they've been working on this for years," I said. "Long before Arnaut attacked Grant Park. This goes deeper."

Zeke picked up one of the photographs, his usual humor completely absent. "So, we steal the Nail tomorrow night before they can corrupt it any further."

"Tomorrow night," I confirmed. "Before they finish whatever they're planning."

"And before Arnaut and Dina realize we're here," Cori added.

Lucan gathered the documents. "I'll send these to Charlie and Rabbi Eliyahu. They need to see the corruption progression. It might help them understand the ward structure better."

I stood and moved to the window. Below, Rome slept, or pretended to. Cats prowled between parked cars. A couple walked past, holding hands, laughing at something private.

Somewhere in this city, Arnaut was planning. Dina was hunting. And three cardinals were refining corruption like it was a science project.

We spent the rest of the evening planning, marking maps, and coordinating timing.

Tomorrow night, we would walk into the heart of Vatican security and steal from their most protected vault.

Nothing about that was reasonable. But we had run out of reasonable options.

Early on the third day in Rome we awoke with a nervous energy.

The final security briefing came from Charlie and Rabbi Eliyahu at nine AM.

Both men appeared on the laptop screen. Charlie looked like he hadn't slept. Eliyahu looked troubled.

"I've analyzed the ward structure forty-seven different ways," Charlie said. "The key is simultaneity. You need to disrupt all three sigil arrays within a one-point-three second window. Any longer and the compensatory wards activate. Any shorter and you won't complete the sequence."

"One-point-three seconds," I repeated.

"Plus or minus point-two," Eliyahu added. "The geometric structure is elegant but unforgiving. Charlie will guide you through the physical positioning. I'll calculate the disruption sequence in real time based on what we see."

"But Jimmy," Charlie continued, "you need to be positioned exactly where I tell you. Centimeter precision matters here."

"No pressure then."

"The camera feed is critical. We need clean visuals on each ward marker. Any interference and we're working blind."

"The equipment Lucan acquired is top quality," I said. "Military grade. It'll hold."

"It better. Because if this goes wrong, the entire Vatican security apparatus comes down on your ass."

"Again, no pressure."

David's face appeared beside Charlie's on the screen looking exceedingly proud. "I've hacked into their security feeds. Erin's coordinating the data streams. We'll have real-time monitoring of guard positions and movement patterns. If anyone deviates from their schedule, we'll know immediately."

"How illegal is what you're doing?" Zeke asked curiously.

David grinned. "Illegal only if you get caught. But Erin's new position gives us legitimate access to enough systems that we can bury the illegal parts in layers of corporate research authorization. If anyone asks, we're penetration testing surveillance systems as part of routine reviews."

"And they'll believe that?"

"They'll believe the paperwork. My firm does it for dozens of companies and organizations. No one reads the details."

Charlie pulled up a schematic. "Here's the timing. Midnight changeover begins at 23:58. The guards move from their posts at 23:59:30. You have exactly three minutes and forty seconds before the new guards arrive at Vault Seven's corridor. That's your window."

"What about the cardinals?" Cori asked. "If they're visiting regularly, they might be there."

"Marco's monitoring their schedules," Lucan said. "As of this morning, none of them are logged for vault access tonight. But that could change."

"We need to move fast and hope for luck," I said.

"And make our own luck when we need to," Zeke added. "Which, given our track record, is a work in progress."

The plan was simple in concept, complex in execution.

Lucan would use researcher credentials to allow him to stay late in the archives, ostensibly finishing work on a manuscript. His presence would seem normal, unremarkable. At 11:45 PM, he would position himself in Reading Room Three, which offered sight lines to multiple hallways.

Cori would create a diversion in the main archive entrance at eleven fifty-five PM. A lost patron, aristocratic and insistent, demanding access to materials she'd been promised by Cardinal Parisi. Security would respond because ignoring wealthy patrons was bad politics.

Zeke would stage a medical emergency in the Cortile della Pigna at eleven fifty-seven PM. Nothing serious, just dramatic enough to pull additional guards away from interior posts. An American patron, perhaps having consumed too much wine at dinner, requiring assistance.

I would enter through a service corridor the Bishop had identified, moving during the guard changeover when coverage was weakest. Charlie and Eliyahu would guide me through the ward markers. I'd have less than four minutes to reach the vault, suppress the wards, bypass the locks, retrieve the Nail, and exit before the new guards arrived.

Four minutes to complete a task that should take twenty. Assuming it was possible at all.

"This is insane," Cori said, studying the timeline.

"Completely," Lucan agreed.

"I love it," Zeke said with a grin. "It's got all the elements of a good plan: impossible timing, insufficient backup, and a healthy dose of 'what could possibly go wrong?' Those are my favorite kind."

The night came too quickly and not fast enough.

I dressed in maintenance coveralls Bishop Marco had provided, complete with Vatican service badges that would pass casual inspection. The tiny camera was mounted on my collar, barely visible. An earpiece connected me to Charlie and Eliyahu. A second earpiece connected me to the team.

My sword stayed at the safe house. Too obvious. Too hard to explain. Instead, I carried tools that could pass as maintenance equipment but could be weaponized if necessary.

Cori dressed in another elegant outfit, this one suggesting confused patronage rather than calculated seduction. Pearls. Modest heels. A designer bag that probably cost more than most Romans made in a month.

Zeke put on his American philanthropist costume again, adding a slight unsteadiness to his walk as he feigned too much wine. "I'm channelin' my Uncle Pete after Thanksgiving," he said. "Well-meanin', slightly tipsy, and absolutely convinced everyone wants to hear his opinions on European architecture."

Lucan was already at the archives, having entered at six PM for his so-called legitimate research.

At eleven-thirty, we left the safe house separately.

Rome at night was different from Rome in daylight. The tourist crowds had thinned. The streets belonged more to locals and less to cameras. Street lamps cast yellow halos. Scooters buzzed past, their riders helmetless and confident. In the distance, the dome of St. Peter's rose against the dark sky, lit from below like a monument to permanence.

I reached the service entrance at eleven forty-two. Bishop Marco was waiting inside.

"This is as far as I can go," he said quietly. "Once you're past this door, you're in the restricted corridor. If anyone asks, you're here to check humidity sensors in the vault levels. The work order is logged. You have until twelve fifteen before anyone questions why you haven't reported back."

"Thank you," I said.

"Don't thank me yet. Thank me when you're out safely." He handed me a small plastic card. "Access key for the service elevator. You need to get to Level Three."

I pocketed the card. "We'll get you out if this goes wrong."

"Don't worry about me. Just stop whatever they're planning." He opened the door. "Go. And James? Be careful. These people have corrupted more than objects. They've corrupted faith itself. That makes them more dangerous than you know."

I stepped through the door into a hallway that smelled of old stone and floor polish.

Behind me, the door closed with a soft click.

"Charlie, Eliyahu," I said quietly. "I'm in."

"Copy that," Charlie replied. "Feed is clear. I'm seeing the corridor. Proceed to the elevator, twenty meters ahead on your right."

I moved.

The hall was narrow, lit by fluorescent tubes that buzzed faintly. Concrete floor. Pipes running along the ceiling. Space that existed in every large building, necessary but invisible.

The elevator was exactly where Charlie said it would be. I used Marco's key card. The doors opened with a pneumatic hiss.

"James." Lucan's voice through the other earpiece. "I'm in position. Two guards in the main archive corridor. They're watching the entrance, not the interior. You should be clear."

"Copy."

The elevator descended. Level One. Level Two. Level Three.

The doors opened onto another hallway, colder than the one above. Stone walls instead of concrete. Older. This level predated the modern archive expansion by centuries.

"Okay," Charlie said. "You're now below the main archive floor. Vault Seven is forty meters ahead, then left down a secondary corridor. There should be two guards at the intersection."

I checked my watch. Eleven fifty-four.

"Cori," I said. "You're up."

"On it."

Through the earpiece, I heard her voice change. Imperious. Slightly frustrated.

"I don't care what the schedule says. Cardinal Parisi promised me access to the Barberini manuscripts tonight. Tonight. Do you understand? I've come all the way from Milan for this specific purpose."

A male voice, apologetic but firm: "Signora, I'm very sorry, but the archives are closed. If you could return tomorrow..."

"Tomorrow? Tomorrow I'll be in Firenze! This is completely unacceptable! Do you have any idea who my family is?"

The guard's voice shifted to his radio: "Command, we have a situation at the main entrance. Patron insisting on immediate access. Requesting supervisor."

"Copy. Sending supervisor now."

Charlie's voice: "Guard movement detected. Two personnel moving toward main entrance. You're clear to approach the intersection."

I moved quickly but carefully. The stone floor was worn smooth by centuries of use. My footsteps echoed softly despite my efforts.

The intersection appeared ahead. A T-junction where the corridor split left and right. The vault should be down the left branch.

Empty.

Both guards had responded to Cori's diversion.

"I'm at the intersection," I whispered. "No guards."

"Zeke," I said. "Medical emergency."

"Way ahead of you, hoss. Watch this."

Through the other earpiece, I heard Zeke's voice, strained and concerned but still maintaining that Texas charm even in crisis.

"Hey! Hey, somebody help! This gentleman just collapsed! I think he's havin' a heart attack! Somebody who knows CPR, please! I'd do it myself but I only know the version they taught us in Texas and I'm pretty sure that ain't up to European medical standards!"

Multiple voices. Footsteps running. Radio chatter increasing.

"Command, medical emergency in the Cortile della Pigna. Civilian down. Requesting medical response and additional security."

"Copy. Diverting units now."

Charlie's voice: "Three more guards moving away from your position. Vault corridor should be completely clear. Move now."

I turned left and ran.

The corridor stretched ahead, dimly lit by small lamps set into the walls at intervals. The air was cooler here, climate-controlled to preserve whatever was stored in the vaults below.

Vault Seven's door appeared at the end of the left corridor, large and unwelcoming. Heavy. Metal-reinforced wood. Three separate locking mechanisms visible on the surface.

Above the door, carved into the stone lintel, were three sigil arrays. Geometric patterns that looked like decorative elements to the untrained eye. To anyone who understood sacred geometry, they were sophisticated ward structures.

"I'm at the vault," I said.

"Feed is clear," Charlie replied. "Rabbi Eliyahu, you seeing this?"

Eliyahu's voice came through, calm and focused. "Yes. The arrays are as we predicted. First is upper left. Second is upper right. Third is centered above the door frame."

"Each one needs to be disrupted in sequence," Charlie added, "but the timing has to be exact."

"How exact?"

"I need you to touch specific points on each array when I tell you. One-point-three seconds total. If you're off by even a fraction, the compensatory wards trigger and alarms sound."

I looked at my watch. Eleven fifty-eight.

"Guards change in ninety seconds," I said.

"Then we do this fast," Eliyahu said. "Position yourself directly in front of the door. Arms raised. Left hand will touch the first array, right hand the second, then left hand moves to the third."

I raised my arms.

"Camera steady. I need clean visuals on each marker," Charlie said.

The earpiece went quiet except for their breathing. I could hear the faint click of keys as Charlie worked, Eliyahu murmuring calculations in Hebrew.

"Okay," Charlie said. "Rabbi Eliyahu has the sequence. There are three nodes on each array. You need to touch them in order: left array node two, right array node one, center array node three. One point three seconds. On my mark."

My heart hammered.

"Three."

I focused on the left array. Found node two with my eyes.

"Two."

Steady breathing. Centuries of training. Precision over speed.

"One."

The world narrowed.

"Mark."

I moved.

Left hand to node two. The stone was cool under my fingers. A faint vibration ran through it.

Right hand to node one. The vibration intensified. The arrays were connected, responding to contact.

Left hand to node three. The center array flared with brief light, visible only to someone who knew to look for it.

"Done," I said.

For a heartbeat, nothing happened.

Then the arrays dimmed. The faint hum of active magic faded. The wards dropped.

"Ninety seconds," Charlie said. "Go."

The three locks were mechanical, not magical. Vatican security had learned centuries ago that physical barriers were harder to circumvent than arcane ones.

I pulled out the tools Lucan had provided. Lock picks inside humidity sensors. I worked the first lock in twenty seconds. The second took thirty. The third resisted for forty-five seconds before finally giving way.

The vault door swung open with a low groan.

Inside was a small chamber, maybe three meters square. Shelves lined the walls, holding items wrapped in cloth, sealed in boxes, labeled with codes that meant nothing to me.

In the center, on a stone pedestal, sat a silver reliquary.

The Nail.

I approached carefully. The reliquary was beautiful, worked silver depicting scenes from the Crucifixion. Angels wept at the corners. Latin script ran around the base: *Sanguis Christi, fortis nos.*

The blood of Christ strengthens us.

I opened the reliquary's glass cover.

The Nail lay inside on red velvet.

It was perhaps four inches long. Iron, darkened by age and something else. Dark veins spread through the metal like infection, pulsing faintly with wrongness. The corruption was visible, undeniable, a stain that radiated outward from the Nail's core.

This was what they had used in Watch initiations for centuries. A relic from the True Cross, representing sacrifice and redemption, systematically corrupted into something that carried darkness instead of light.

I reached for it.

"Jimmy." Charlie's voice, urgent. "The compensatory wards are activating. You have maybe thirty seconds before alarms sound."

I pulled out a lead-lined pouch Marco had provided. Grabbed the Nail without touching it directly. Dropped it into the pouch. Sealed it.

"Got it. Moving."

I turned toward the door.

And stopped.

Three figures stood in the doorway outside the vault.

Arnaut. Dark hair gray at the temples. Military bearing still sharp despite the centuries. His eyes met mine, and recognition flickered there.

Dina. Black coat. Butterfly buckles gleaming. Smile already in place.

And between them, a bishop I didn't recognize. Older. Frightened. Clearly not here by choice.

"James," Arnaut said. His voice was steady and controlled. "I wondered when I would see you again."

"Arnaut."

"I believe you owe me a debt, after the park."

"My debt was paid when I let you leave."

Dina laughed, delighted. "Oh, this is wonderful! A reunion! How touching! And here I thought tonight would be boring."

The bishop tried to step back. Arnaut's hand caught his shoulder, held him in place.

"Don't run, Bishop Torrini," Arnaut said quietly. "You're part of this as much as we all are."

Through my earpiece, chaos erupted.

"Jimmy, guards are responding!" Charlie's voice. "Multiple units converging on your position!"

"James, what's happening?" Lucan.

"We have a problem," I said.

Arnaut smiled. It didn't reach his eyes. "You always were good at understatement."

Dina stepped forward, head tilted, studying me like a cat watching a bird. "Did you really think you could waltz into the Vatican and steal from us without anyone noticing? We've been watching you since you arrived in Rome. Well, since Jerusalem really. You're not as subtle as you think James."

"Then you know I'm leaving with this," I said, hand tight on the pouch.

"Oh, I doubt that very much," Dina replied, her Spanish accent thick, smile widening. "But I'm willing to be entertained while you try."

The corridor behind them filled with footsteps. Voices. Radio chatter.

Security was coming.

Arnaut's expression didn't change. "You can surrender the Nail and I'll let you walk away as a debt repaid. Or you can fight, and die here. Your choice."

"Those aren't the only options," I said.

"No?" Arnaut raised an eyebrow. "Then enlighten me."

I pulled power from the old disciplines. Clean magic, refined through centuries of practice. Light gathered in my free hand, subtle but present.

"I run," I said. "And you try to stop me."

Then I released the power in a bright flash that filled the corridor with blinding light.

The burst cost more than it should have. Even though I had closed my eyes, my vision tunneled for half a heartbeat, and the air tasted like iron.

I didn't wait to see their reaction.

I barreled through them as they recovered their sight and I ran.

Behind me, Dina's laughter echoed off the stone walls.

"Oh, he runs! How delightful! Arnaut, let's give chase! It's been so long since I had a proper hunt!"

14

Bullets, Police, and the Chase (Rome, Present)

The chase began in the vault corridor and exploded into the main archives within seconds. Up one level, then across into the public stacks, the corridors widening just long enough to make you think you understood them.

I hit the intersection at full speed, boots skidding on polished stone. Guards were running toward me from the main entrance. Lucan's voice crackled in my earpiece.

"Jimmy, north corridor! Reading Room Three! I'll meet you there!"

I turned hard, shoulder slamming into the wall for balance. Behind me, footsteps pounded. Not just guards. Faster. More purposeful.

Arnaut and Dina were coming.

"Charlie, I need exit routes!" I said, breathing hard.

"Working on it! David's pulling up building schematics now!"

Reading Room Three appeared ahead. Lucan stepped out, already moving, falling into stride beside me without breaking pace.

"Where are Cori and Zeke?" I asked.

"Extracting. They heard the commotion." He glanced back. "How many?"

"All of them."

We burst through a door into a corridor lined with filing cabinets. Older part of the archives. Pre-digital. Paper files stacked floor to ceiling.

Behind us, the door crashed open.

"Stop!" A guard's voice. Italian, heavily accented. "Stop now or we'll shoot!"

"They're bluffing," Lucan said. "They won't risk gunfire around the documents."

"You sure about that?"

"Reasonably."

A gunshot cracked.

The bullet struck a filing cabinet two meters ahead, punching through metal with a sound like a hammer on a bell.

"They're not bluffing!" I said.

We turned another corner. Stairs appeared, descending. We took them three at a time, hands on the railings, momentum carrying us downward in controlled falls.

Level Four. Deeper into the archives. Older manuscripts. Environmental controls humming. The air tasted of parchment and preservation chemicals.

"David!" Charlie's voice. "Where does this level exit?"

"Service tunnel!" David's reply, distant but clear. "East side. Maintenance corridor under the Apostolic Palace. Leads to a delivery entrance on Via della Stamperia!"

"Can you reach it?" Charlie asked me.

"Working on it!"

I ran through corridors that twisted like a maze. Left. Right. Straight. Past rooms filled with manuscripts in climate-controlled cases. Past restoration labs sealed behind glass. Past security checkpoints that had been abandoned when the guards responded to the alarm.

Behind us, the pursuit continued. Multiple sets of footsteps now. Radios crackling. Voices calling directions.

And above it all, Dina's laughter.

"James Crable! Playing hard to get! I thought we were friends! This is no way to treat an old acquaintance!"

We burst into a wider corridor. Windows on one side looked out into an interior courtyard. Lucan grabbed my arm and pulled me toward a door marked *Autorizzato Personale Solo.*

"This way!"

The door opened into a service stairwell. Metal stairs, concrete walls, harsh fluorescent lighting. We went down.

Two flights. Three. The sounds of pursuit echoed above us, magnified by the narrow space.

Four flights. Five.

We hit the bottom level. A heavy door marked *Tunnel di Servizio.*

Lucan shoved it open.

The tunnel stretched ahead, dimly lit by emergency lights spaced at intervals. Pipes ran along the ceiling. Cable conduits lined the walls. The floor was concrete, slick with condensation.

"This leads to the delivery entrance?" I asked.

"Should."

"Should?"

"The maps were last updated in 1987. Things change. But it's our best option right now."

We ran.

The tunnel curved gently, following the foundations of the Vatican buildings above. Water dripped somewhere. Our footsteps echoed hollowly.

Behind us, the stairwell door crashed open.

"They're persistent," Lucan said.

"That's one word for it."

The tunnel branched. Left or right.

"Charlie?" I said.

"Left! According to the schematics, left leads to the exit!"

We went left.

Fifty meters ahead, a door. Metal. Marked with faded yellow paint. Beyond it, the tunnel continued into darkness.

We hit the door at full speed.

It was locked.

"Damn it," Lucan muttered, already pulling out lock picks.

Footsteps behind us. Close now. Maybe thirty seconds.

Lucan worked the lock. His hands were steady, professional. But it was a good lock, designed to keep people out.

Twenty seconds.

"Lucan..."

"I know. Almost there."

"Screw it, stand back," I ordered Lucan and threw a blast of pure energy at the door handle. It flew open and made a loud clang as it struck the wall behind it.

We stumbled through into cold night air.

We were in an alley. Narrow. Trash bins against one wall. Delivery entrance for one of the Vatican service buildings. Above us, Rome's lights turned the night sky orange.

"Which way?" Lucan asked.

"Forward," I said.

We ran. I removed my coveralls as best I could at speed and then caught up to Lucan.

The alley opened onto Via della Stamperia. Traffic. People. Normal Roman nightlife continuing, completely unaware that two men had just fled from the Vatican with a stolen relic.

"Cori!" I said into the earpiece. "Where are you?"

"Piazza Navona. Zeke's with me. What's your position?"

"Via della Stamperia, heading... which way are we heading?"

"South," Lucan said. "Toward the river."

"South toward the river. Can you intercept?"

"We'll try. Keep moving."

We plunged into the side streets. Rome after midnight was a different city. Quieter. The tourists had mostly retreated to hotels. The Romans who remained moved with purpose, heading to late dinners or early bars or home from shifts that ended when most people slept.

We tried to blend in. Two men walking briskly but not running. Breathing hard but not panicked. Just two guys out late, nothing to see.

Behind us, sirens began to wail.

"They've called the police," Lucan said.

"Of course they have. We robbed the Vatican."

"Technically we'll save many lives."

"Try explaining that to the polizia."

We turned onto a larger street. Corso Vittorio Emanuele II. More people here. More cover.

Charlie came through on the earpiece. "Vatican security is coordinating with Roman police. They're setting up checkpoints. Avoid major streets."

"Side streets it is," I said.

We cut through an alley between buildings, emerging onto a quieter lane. Residential here. Shuttered windows. Balconies with laundry hung to dry. A cat watched us from a doorway, supremely unconcerned.

"Charlie," I said. "Are they tracking us?"

"Can't tell. Vatican cameras don't cover the full city. But if they get police drones up, you're exposed."

"How long until that happens?"

"Minutes. Maybe less."

"David," I said. "Can you do anything about that?"

"I can try to create interference. Make the feeds glitchy. But it's not my specialty and I can't guarantee how long it'll last."

"Do what you can."

We kept moving. Turned left. Then right. Following Lucan's instincts more than any plan. He knew Rome better than I did, knew which streets led where, which neighborhoods were safe at night and which weren't.

We crossed a small piazza. A fountain in the center, water trickling. A few people sitting on benches, smoking, talking quietly.

And then I sensed it.

That familiar pressure. That sense of wrongness in the air.

Corrupted magic.

"Lucan..."

He felt it too. His hand went to his coat, reaching for the weapon he'd concealed there.

Dina stepped out from behind the fountain.

She looked completely unhurried. Coat perfect. Hair perfect. Smile in place.

"Did you really think you could lose me in a city this small?" she asked pleasantly. "I've been hunting in Rome for decades, cariño. I know every alley. Every rooftop. Every little place someone might run when they're desperate and running out of options."

We backed up slowly.

She matched our pace, staying exactly the same distance away.

"I have made tracking prey a sport. I've seen every trick. Every desperate gambit. I've watched men run themselves to death thinking running would save them."

"Then you know we're desperate enough to fight," I said.

"Oh, I'm counting on it. That's when things get interesting."

Power gathered around her. Dark. Oily. The corruption was stronger than it had been in Jerusalem. She'd been feeding it. Refining it.

Lucan spoke quietly. "James. Get the Nail to safety. If she gets past me, she gets to that pouch. I'll hold her."

"You can't hold her alone."

"I can try."

"Lucan..."

"Go!"

He released his power in a controlled burst. Clean magic, disciplined, shaped into a barrier between us and Dina.

She smiled and walked through it like it was smoke.

"How sweet," she said. "Sacrifice. I do love watching people throw themselves away for nothing."

Her hand moved. Darkness lashed out.

Lucan met it with light. The clash lit the piazza in flashes of white and black, like lightning and shadow battling for dominance.

I ran.

Behind me, I heard Lucan shout. Heard the sound of stone cracking. Heard Dina laugh.

"Charlie!" I said. "I need Cori's position now!"

"She's moving toward you! Two streets north! Piazza San Salvatore in

Lauro!"

I sprinted through another alley. My lungs burned. The pouch with the Nail bounced against my side.

The piazza appeared ahead. Small. A church on one side. Closed shops on the others.

A car screeched to a stop at the corner.

Cori leaned out the passenger window. "Get in!"

I dove into the back seat. Zeke was driving. He punched the accelerator before my door was fully closed.

"Where's Lucan?" Cori asked.

"Fighting Dina. We have to go back..."

"No time," Zeke said, voice serious for once. "Look."

In the rearview mirror, police cars appeared. Lights flashing. Multiple vehicles.

"They've got the streets blocked ahead," Zeke continued. "Charlie's guidin' me through gaps but it's gettin' tighter than a tick on a hound dog."

The car slalomed through narrow streets. Zeke drove like someone who had learned to drive on roads that didn't believe in lane markers or traffic laws. Which, given he was from the American South, was probably accurate.

"Charlie," I said. "Can you see Lucan?"

"Negative. I lost his signal two minutes ago."

My stomach dropped. "Lost it how?"

"Could be interference. Could be... I don't know. Just lost it."

Cori twisted in her seat to look at me. "We'll come back for him."

"If he's still alive," I said.

"He's survived worse than Dina."

"Has he?"

She didn't answer.

Zeke turned hard, tires screaming. We shot down a street barely wider than the car. Walls on both sides. Scooters parked in alcoves that we missed by centimeters.

"This is insane!" I said.

"Well now, that depends on your definition of insane!" Zeke replied, completely focused. "Personally, I think insanity is doin' the same thing and expectin' different results. This here is improvisation, and improvisation requires a certain faith in physics, the Lord Almighty, and superior German engineering!"

We burst out onto a larger street. Lungotevere. The Tiber River on our left, dark water reflecting city lights.

Behind us, sirens. Close.

Zeke accelerated. The car hit ninety kilometers per hour on a road designed for fifty.

"Charlie, where are the police?" Cori asked, voice remarkably calm given the circumstances.

"Everywhere. They've got the bridges blocked. You need to cross before they close the net."

"Which bridge?"

"Ponte Sant'Angelo is closest but it's crawling with cops. Try Ponte Principe Amedeo Savoia. Two kilometers south. Less surveillance."

Zeke guided the car through traffic that shouldn't have existed at this hour. A taxi honked. A delivery truck swerved. Someone shouted in Italian that probably wasn't complimentary.

"There!" Charlie said. "The bridge!"

Ponte Principe Amedeo Savoia appeared ahead. A simple bridge, functional rather than beautiful. And blessedly empty.

Zeke hit it at full speed.

Halfway across, blue lights appeared behind us.

"They're on us," Cori said.

"I see 'em. Hold tight."

We reached the far side of the river. Trastevere sprawled ahead, the medieval heart of Rome, a warren of streets that predated city planning by a thousand years.

Zeke plunged into it without hesitation.

Left. Right. Straight through a piazza where late-night diners scattered. Down a street so narrow the mirrors scraped the walls.

The police cars tried to follow. One got stuck. Another gave up. But two kept coming.

"David!" Charlie's voice. "Can you kill their GPS?"

"No idea!"

Another turn. We shot past the Basilica di Santa Maria. The church was lit from below, golden and eternal. We were going so fast it blurred.

Zeke took us deeper into Trastevere's maze. Streets that turned back on themselves. Alleys that barely deserved the name. Past restaurants closing for the night. Past bars where people spilled onto sidewalks. Past centuries of history compressed into stone and shadow.

Finally, after what seemed like hours but was probably ten minutes, Zeke pulled into a parking garage. Three levels down. Dim lighting. Half empty.

He killed the engine.

For a moment, none of us moved. Just sat there, breathing hard, adrenaline still screaming through our veins.

"Everyone okay?" Zeke asked, his Texas drawl reassuring even now.

"Define okay," I said.

"Alive. Uninjured. Not currently on fire or under arrest."

"Then yes."

Cori opened her door and stepped out on shaking legs. "That was the most reckless driving I've ever experienced. And now that it's over I want to hug you."

"Why thank you, ma'am," Zeke said with a slight bow of his head. "I'll take that as a compliment since you're still breathin' and we ain't in handcuffs."

I pulled out the pouch. The Nail was still inside, still sealed. Mission accomplished.

Except Lucan was missing.

And somewhere in Rome, Arnaut and Dina knew exactly what we'd done.

"We need to get back to the safe house," Cori said. "Regroup. Figure out our next move."

"And Lucan?" I asked.

"We'll find him." Her voice was firm. "But not tonight. Let's see if he can make it back to us. Tonight we need to disappear. The entire Roman police force will be out looking for us."

She was right. I hated that she was right, but she was.

We left the car and moved through Trastevere on foot. Separately. Taking different routes. Meeting two blocks from the safe house to make sure no one was following.

The apartment was dark and quiet when we finally arrived.

Inside, I set the pouch on the table. The Nail sat inside, corruption pulsing faintly even through the lead lining.

"Charlie," I said. "We're clear. For now."

"Copy that. I'm sending the extraction coordinates to your phone. There's a private airfield forty kilometers outside Rome. A plane will be waiting at six AM. Can you make it?"

"We'll make it."

"Good. Because the Vatican just issued a statement. They're calling it a theft of irreplaceable religious artifacts. The Italian government's treating it as an attack on sovereign territory. You're officially wanted criminals."

"Wonderful," Zeke said, pouring himself a drink with steady hands.

"It gets better. They've released security footage. Not clear enough to identify faces, but enough to give descriptions. Male, early forties, athletic build, six and a half feet. Female, thirties, dark hair, five-eight to five-ten. Male, six-six to six-eight, blonde, American accent."

"They got us on camera?" Cori asked.

"Partial. David's working on scrubbing what he can, but the Vatican's security is better than we thought."

I looked at the Nail. We'd stolen from the heart of the Catholic Church. Made enemies of powerful cardinals. Lost Lucan. And branded ourselves as criminals in the process.

All for a corrupted piece of metal that shouldn't exist.

"Was it worth it?" Zeke asked quietly, the humor gone from his voice.

I thought about that. About what the Nail represented. About centuries of Watch initiations, of sacred oaths taken while holding a relic from the True Cross. About how that sanctity had been systematically corrupted, turned into a weapon.

"Yes," I said. "It was worth it."

"Then let's hope Lucan thinks so too," Cori said. "When we find him."

If we found him.

But I didn't say that out loud.

We left the safe house one by one in the dark and made our way to Charlie's extraction point. Eliyahu had called in some favors to get us a flight out of Italy quietly. The long journey back to Jerusalem was quiet and solemn. Even Zeke had nothing to say.

Two days later, Bishop Marco Forino was found dead in his apartment.

The news reached us through Lucan, who finally made contact forty-eight hours after the chase.

He'd escaped Dina, barely. Spent the night in a seedy hotel in Monti. Waited until the immediate search cooled before making his way out of the city.

When he called, his voice was tight with grief.

"Bishop Marco's dead," he said without preamble. "They made it look like natural causes. Heart attack. But I think we can guess the real story."

"I brought him into this. They knew he helped us. This was punishment."

Cori closed her eyes. "I'm sorry."

"He knew the risks," Lucan said. "He told me as much. Said some things were worth dying for. That the Church he believed in was worth protecting from those who would corrupt it. That doesn't make it any easier. He was a good man."

"He was," I replied. The sense of sorrow and loss sitting inside me as I thought of my friends that I dragged into this.

Silence on the line. The weight of choices made. Of consequences paid.

"The relic?" Lucan asked.

"Safe. We're analyzing it with Charlie and the Keepers. Trying to understand the corruption process."

"Good. That's good. At least his death wasn't for nothing."

"Where are you now?"

"Somewhere safe."

"Lucan..."

"I need time, James. Time to process this. Time to make sure I wasn't followed. Just... give me a day or two."

"All right. Be careful."

"You too."

The call ended.

I set down the phone and looked at Cori and Zeke.

"Bishop Marco's gone," I said.

"We heard," Zeke replied, all traces of his usual humor absent. "Damn good man. Deserved better than that."

Cori moved to the window of our rented apartment, looking out over Jerusalem. The city continued, beautiful and ancient and completely indifferent to our grief.

"He deserves better than a cover-up," she said quietly.

"He deserves justice," I agreed. "But first we need to survive long enough to deliver it."

The Nail sat on the table between us, wrapped in lead, radiating wrongness.

We'd stolen it from the Vatican. We'd made powerful enemies. We'd lost a good man.

But we had the Nail.

And with it, maybe we could start to understand how to fight the corruption that was spreading across the world.

15

Patterns, Lines, and the Architect
(Jerusalem, Present)

Charlie had been living in the Keeper compound for six days.

He had clearly sacrificed sleep for work. Eyes red, wrinkled shirt, three half-empty coffee cups scattered around his workspace. The exhaustion of learning things his brain wasn't built to process.

But he was smiling.

I found him in the lower chamber with Rabbi Eliyahu and two senior Keepers I had met briefly. The room was circular, carved from bedrock sometime before Rome existed. Sigils covered the walls in layers. Not painted. Cut into the stone with tools that probably predated iron.

Charlie sat at a table covered in laptops and monitoring equipment, his eyes fixed on cascading data streams. His fingers moved across the keyboard, isolating signals, filtering noise.

"There," he said quietly. "See that? The harmonic pattern in the background noise?"

Eliyahu leaned closer. "I see numbers. What do they tell you?"

"They tell me the guardian is there. Most people would miss it completely. It looks like statistical variance. Random fluctuation. But it's not random." Charlie pulled up another screen. "It's a signature. Distinct but subtle. Like a puzzle piece that locks into the picture, but most people only ever see the

159

picture, not the individual pieces."

One of the senior Keepers, an older man named Rabbi Yehuda, made a sound of wonder. He quoted something in Hebrew, then translated. "The Torah tells us, 'Turn it over and over, for everything is in it.' New tools show us what was always there."

"Exactly," Charlie said, excitement building in his voice. "The guardians have been generating this signature for millennia. We just never had instruments sensitive enough to detect it. But now that I know what to look for, I can track them across the entire network."

Eliyahu studied the screen with the intense focus I had seen him use on ancient texts. "This is remarkable. To see what we have only felt."

"It gets better," Charlie said. He pulled up another dataset. "Or worse, depending on how you look at it. Watch what happens when I overlay the anomaly data Erin's been sending."

The screen filled with new patterns. Bursts of activity at guardian sites. At first, they looked random, scattered across time and geography with no apparent connection except it was all happening at the same time.

"I thought it was just chaos at first," Charlie continued. "Attacks happening wherever the enemy found an opening. But then I remembered something from electrical engineering."

He zoomed in on one site's data, highlighting the burst patterns.

"This is resonant frequency degradation. In circuits, if you hit a component with pulses at specific intervals, you can degrade it over time. The individual pulses don't destroy it. They weaken the structure. Create microfractures. Eventually the whole thing fails, but I don't think they want to destroy it. They could have done that already at this scale."

"So, they aren't trying to destroy the guardian sites immediately," Eliyahu said, understanding dawning. "They are weakening them systematically."

"Yes. And the pattern isn't random. Look." Charlie pulled up a global view. "The bursts follow a sequence. Each one builds on the last. Creating resonance across the entire network."

Yehuda leaned in, fascinated. "In Talmud we study how small changes in foundation can shift entire structures. This is the same principle, yes?

Applied to the Veil itself."

"That's exactly what it is," Charlie said.

I moved closer to the screens. The patterns were becoming clearer. Intentional. Precise.

"How long until the sites fail?" I asked.

Charlie's smile faded. "Again, I don't think they're trying to make them fail. I think they're weakening them enough to recircuit them. Make them change."

Charlie rose and we followed him deeper into the compound, through corridors that were older the farther we went. The walls changed. Limestone gave way to harder rock. The sigils grew more complex.

We entered a room I had not seen before. Large. Circular. A stone table at the center covered in maps and papers. Candles and glowing sigils provided the only light.

The Nail sat on the table.

Still in its lead-lined pouch. Still radiating wrongness even sealed.

Around it, papers covered in Charlie's handwriting. Equations. Diagrams. Geometric patterns that hurt to look at directly.

"Studying the Nail gave us the key," Eliyahu said. "We could see the corruption's structure. How it works. How it bends natural flows without breaking them."

Charlie moved to the table and spread out three large sheets. Maps. The world, marked with dots and lines in different colors.

"The Nail showed us corruption at small scale," he said. "Individual object. Localized effect. But the principles scale. Once we understood how corruption reshapes flows in one relic, we could see the same patterns in Erin's global data."

He tapped the first map. Red dots scattered across continents.

"Every guardian site under pressure. Every anomaly. Every disturbance. As I said, at first it looked random. Chaos. But when I started connecting sites based on the geometric relationships Rabbi Eliyahu's been teaching me..."

He laid the second map over the first. Blue lines connected the dots. Not straight lines. Curves. Arcs that followed patterns I recognized from the sigils.

"Someone's drawing something," Charlie said quietly.

The third map showed the complete pattern. Lines intersecting at specific angles. Nodes where multiple flows converged. A structure so large it spanned the planet.

A sigil.

Enormous. Global. Still incomplete but clearly intentional.

"Sweet Christ," Zeke said from the doorway. I had not heard him enter. Cori was with him, both of them staring at the maps.

"It's like an architectural design," Yehuda said, tracing one of the lines with his finger. "Everything planned. Every angle calculated."

The word hit me like cold water.

Architectural.

"The Architect," I said.

Everyone turned.

"That's what the trow called it," I continued. "In Grant Park. It said it was surveying. That the Architect plans and they measure. I thought it meant one site. One attack."

I looked at the map. At the global pattern taking shape.

"This is what it meant."

"Who is this Architect?" Eliyahu asked.

"I don't know. None of us do. Just a name the trow used. But looking at this..." I gestured at the maps. "This level of planning. This scope. Whoever or whatever the Architect is, they've been working on this for a long time."

Cori studied the sigil pattern with the focus she brought to every threat assessment. "What does it do when it completes?"

Charlie pulled up more data on his laptop. "Based on the flow patterns and what we learned from the Nail's corruption structure, I don't think it destroys the Veil. I think it opens it."

"Opens it how?" I asked.

"Creates controlled access points. Permanent ones. Right now, the Veil is a barrier. Things can break through, but it's difficult. Near impossible when the Guardians are at full strength. What this sigil does is rearrange the flows. Turn barrier into doorway. Multiple doorways, positioned across the planet at these node points."

Eliyahu's face had gone pale. "Passages between worlds. Not breaches. Architecture."

"Exactly. They're not trying to tear down the wall. They're installing doors. And from the pattern, doors that can be opened from both sides. They are creating access points that they can control. It's not destruction its controlled access."

My phone buzzed. A text from Erin.

Conference in 5. Critical.

I showed Eliyahu. He nodded and gestured to a laptop already set up in the corner. Modern technology in a room that predated the printing press. The contrast was appropriate.

The screen came to life. Erin's face appeared, then David's beside her. Both looked like Charlie. Too much coffee, not enough sleep.

"You're looking at the maps?" Erin asked without preamble.

"Yes," I said.

"Then you see it. The global structure."

"Charlie thinks they're creating openings," I said. "Permanent access points between worlds."

David leaned into frame. "That matches our analysis. We've been running simulations based on the corruption progression data. If they complete this sigil, if all the nodes activate simultaneously, the Veil doesn't collapse. It transforms."

"Into what?" Cori asked.

"A membrane," Erin said. Her voice carried the certainty of someone who had checked their work a hundred times. "Permeable. Selective. Something that can be opened or closed at will by whoever controls the nodes."

The room went quiet.

Zeke broke the silence. "That sounds bad. That sounds real bad."

"It's worse than bad," Erin replied. "Think about what controlled access means. They could bring things through at will. Send things back. Use our world as a staging ground. Or theirs as a refuge. Complete control over the boundary between realities. Complete destruction would allow someone to go there and investigate, or try and stop them. This way it locks anyone on this side out unless they have permission to enter."

Charlie sat down heavily. "How close are they?"

Erin pulled up a new graph. "Based on current progression and assuming they maintain pace, maybe three weeks. Four at most. But that's if they don't accelerate."

"They'll accelerate," I said. "They know we're aware now. After Rome, after the Nail, they know we're active. They'll push harder."

David nodded. "That's our assessment too. Which is why I've been building redundancy into every system. Multiple data pipelines. Backup sensors. Distributed processing. If one node fluctuates, or goes down, we'll know immediately."

He looked exhausted. Excited too. The usual fidgeting and nervousness now lost to concentration and problem solving. He was clearly in his element.

"I'm staying in Tel Aviv," he continued. "Erin's running the company, but I need to be here. Close to the data. Close to the infrastructure. This is too important to remote manage. Charlie, send us any designs you have or data requests. I'll make sure the team here works overtime to get you what you need."

"David," I said gently. "You need to sleep."

"I'll sleep when this is over." He smiled, but it didn't reach his eyes. "We've got maybe a month to stop something that's been in planning for God knows how long. Sleep's negotiable. Success isn't."

Erin's expression tightened. She and David exchanged a look I could not quite read.

"We'll keep monitoring," she said. "Any change in the pattern, any acceleration, you'll know immediately."

"Send everything to Charlie," Eliyahu said. "He can now read the deeper structures. Between his instruments and our knowledge, perhaps we find the weak points."

"Already set up a secure feed," David replied. "Charlie should have access now. Send us what you need as you need it. We'll take it from here."

Charlie checked his laptop and nodded.

The call ended.

For a moment no one spoke. We stared at the maps. At the sigil taking shape across the planet. At the scale of what we faced.

Yehuda said something in Hebrew, then switched to English. "We have always known the Veil could be broken. But this. To reshape it entirely. This is ambition beyond anything in our records."

"Ambition that requires knowledge," Eliyahu added. "Deep knowledge of guardian mechanics and Veil structure. Whoever this Architect is, they understand more than we have learned in centuries."

Eliyahu arranged rooms for us in the compound, but that night I could not sleep.

I stood in the courtyard under the olive tree, watching Jerusalem's lights spread across the hills. The city was ancient and fragile all at once. So much history. So many layers. All of it resting on foundations that someone was systematically undermining.

Cori found me there an hour before dawn.

"You're brooding," she said.

"Thinking."

"Same thing with you."

She stood beside me, close enough that our shoulders almost touched. We watched the sky begin to lighten.

"What are you thinking about?" she asked finally.

"Arnaut."

"Of course."

I exhaled slowly. "I keep going back. Jerusalem. My sense of loss and guilt. The portal. How maybe I could have done more to prevent this. How when he came out, he was different. Changed."

"The trauma of being lost would change anyone."

"It wasn't trauma. Or not just trauma. It was something deeper. He experienced things there. Learned new paths. Even before that he was changing. More aggressive, less compassionate. The Church taught him new magic and it changed him. Like a seed planted. Waiting. And now…"

I turned to face her. "I keep asking myself if the seed was there before, why didn't I act. To help him. I feel like I ignored something that's sitting heavy with me all these years later."

"What do you mean?"

"During the Cathar Crusades," I said. "we saw Gerhard and Marko using corrupted magic. Arnaut was horrified. But he was also fascinated. I remember the way he watched them work. The questions he asked afterward. He wanted to understand it."

"I remember the two of them. Bastards. That doesn't mean he was compromised."

"No. They told us that they had been taught. Someone in the Church was teaching them these new methods. Arnaut mentioned in Anglsey that he was being taught that power as well. What if it wasn't just the Church that planted that seed. What if it was planned way back then, and only coming to fruition now?"

Cori was quiet for a long moment.

"You're asking questions that don't have good answers," she said finally. "Whether Arnaut was corrupted before Jerusalem or after, whether it was taught or chosen, none of that changes what he's become. Or what we have to do about it."

"I know. But, when I saw him in the Vatican, he offered to let me go as a kind of returned favor. What if there is still something of the old Arnaut in there?"

She took my hand. Her fingers were cool in the pre-dawn air.

"He was your friend," she said. "Maybe your best friend. Losing him to corruption doesn't erase that. But it also doesn't obligate you to save him if he can't be saved."

"What if he can be?"

"Then we find out. And if we can pull him back, we do. But James." She squeezed my hand. "You need to prepare yourself for the possibility that the Arnaut you knew is gone. That whoever is working with Dina now, whoever is part of this Architect's plan, they're not the man you lost at Jerusalem.

They're what grew in his place."

I knew she was right. I had known it for a while, but I wasn't yet fully convinced. Hearing it said out loud made it real in a way I had been avoiding, but that didn't erase the doubt, or the sliver of hope I was trying harder to bury.

The sun broke over the Mount of Olives. Light spilled across Jerusalem, turning stone gold.

"Storm's coming," I said.

"I know."

"Not just weather. Something bigger. I can feel it the way you feel pressure before lightning."

"We'll deal with it," Cori said. "We have before."

"This is different."

"Yes. But so are we. We're not alone this time. We have Lucan, Charlie. Erin. David. Casey. The Keepers. Even Zeke."

"Especially Zeke."

She smiled. "He does have a way of making impossible situations feel survivable."

We stood there as the city woke around us. Calls to prayer drifting from minarets. Church bells beginning their morning rounds. The smell of bread baking in ovens that had been tended by the same families for generations.

All of it resting on a Veil that someone was trying to rewrite.

Behind us, I heard movement in the compound. The Keepers beginning their day. Charlie probably already at his instruments, chasing patterns only he could see. Eliyahu preparing for morning prayers.

The work continued. The preparation. The analysis.

Because in a few short weeks, the Architect's sigil would complete.

And when it did, the world would learn what happened when you turned barriers into doorways.

I thought about David, exhausted but determined, building redundancy into systems he knew might fail.

About Charlie, pushing his mind past its limits to understand magic through mathematics.

About the Keepers, guarding knowledge that someone was using to reshape reality.

About Arnaut, corrupted by teachings he either chose or could not resist.

16

Artillery, Time, and the Choice (Constantinople, 1453)

The city was burning.

Not everywhere. Not yet. But enough that the smoke hung thick over Constantinople's domes and towers, turning the afternoon sky the color of old bronze. Fires scattered across the districts like stars fallen to earth. The Theodosian Walls, which had stood for a thousand years, had broken three hours ago at the Romanus Gate. Soldiers poured through the breach like water through cracked stone.

I ran through streets I'd walked for decades. The monastery of St. John Stoudios. The Church of the Holy Apostles. The forums and cisterns and ancient columns that marked a city older than Christianity itself. All of it dying around me.

Constantinople had been the jewel of Christendom for over a millennium. Capital of an empire that traced its roots to Rome itself. While Western Europe had stumbled through dark centuries, this city had preserved knowledge, maintained civilization, held the line between worlds. Libraries here held books that existed nowhere else. Churches contained relics that pilgrims crossed continents to see. The Hagia Sophia alone was worth more than most kingdoms.

And now the Ottomans were inside the walls.

Nikolaos was supposed to meet me an hour ago.

The plan had been simple. I'd been tracking a corrupted Byzantine cross for three weeks, following rumors and bribes through the city's underground networks. The Ottomans wanted everything of value. Gold. Relics. Knowledge. Anything that could be turned into leverage or power. Soldiers had been systematically searching churches and monasteries, followed by men who knew how to ask the right questions.

Nikolaos had found it first.

He was a monk at the Monastery of Stoudios, but calling him just a monk was like calling the Hagia Sophia just a church. Nikolaos was a scholar. He read Greek, Latin, Arabic, and Persian. He knew the city's hidden histories, the locations of forgotten cisterns and sealed chambers. He understood the old magic the way academics understood dusty manuscripts, not as power but as knowledge worth preserving.

We'd met thirty years ago when I'd needed help navigating the imperial court. He'd introduced me to other scholars, monks who kept records the Church in Rome had forgotten existed. Over the years, we'd shared meals and wine in monastery gardens. Long conversations about theology and magic and whether the world was getting better or worse. He'd shown me ancient texts, maps of the city's underground, chronicles that went back to Constantine himself.

He was careful. Methodical. The sort of man who checked his work twice and never took unnecessary risks.

Which is why when he'd sent word yesterday that he'd located the cross, I'd trusted him to retrieve it safely.

The message had been brief: Found it. Cistern under the Hippodrome. Will have it by midday tomorrow. Meet me at the palace complex, eastern courtyard.

That had been twenty hours ago, before the final assault. Before the walls broke. Before everything fell apart.

Now I was running through a dying city, hoping he'd made it out before the chaos started.

The streets near the Augustaion were packed with fleeing citizens and advancing soldiers. People fled in every direction, carrying what they could. A woman clutched an icon wrapped in silk. An old man dragged a chest that scraped against cobblestones worn smooth by centuries of feet. Children cried. Mothers screamed names into the smoke. Somewhere closer to the breach, steel rang against steel and men died on stones that had witnessed a thousand years of history.

Artillery boomed in the distance. The Ottomans were still shelling the inner districts, systematically breaking what remained of Byzantine resistance. Each impact sent tremors through the ground. Dust fell from buildings that had stood since before the Crusades.

The old palace complex sprawled across the southeastern corner of the city, overlooking the Marmara Sea. Centuries of Byzantine emperors had built and rebuilt here, adding halls and churches and baths until the whole thing became a maze. Most of it had been abandoned when the court moved to Blachernae, but the bones remained. Colonnades. Mosaics. Gardens gone wild.

I took a narrow passage between what had once been administrative buildings. The walls here showed layers of construction, brick on stone on older brick, each emperor adding to what came before. Windows with their glass long gone looked down like empty eyes. A mosaic of peacocks and pomegranates still decorated one wall, colors faded but patterns intact.

Another artillery strike, closer this time. The building to my right shuddered. Somewhere above, roof tiles slid and shattered against stone.

The passage opened into an interior courtyard.

And my stomach dropped.

The eastern wall had collapsed. Recent damage, artillery from the siege. Ottoman cannons had been targeting the palace complex for days, and one had finally found its mark. The rubble had spilled across the courtyard's floor, ancient marble and brick mixing with shattered roof tiles. What had once been a colonnade now lay in pieces.

And there, pinned beneath a fallen column, was Nikolaos.

He lay on his side, face pale, blood soaking through his brown monk's habit. The column had caught him across the legs. Not crushing completely, but heavy enough that he couldn't move. Dust covered his dark hair. His hands were scraped raw where he'd tried to shift the marble.

"Nikolaos."

His eyes found mine. Relief flooded his face, followed immediately by something else. Frustration. Anger at himself.

"James. Thank goodness."

I crossed the courtyard and knelt beside him. The column was marble, massive, easily a ton of carved stone. Part of the old palace's structure. It had stood for hundreds of years before Ottoman artillery brought it down. One end was still attached to the fallen colonnade, the other buried under brick and rubble.

I gripped the column and tested its weight, drawing on my strength, letting power flow into my muscles the way I'd learned centuries ago.

Even enhanced, the column barely shifted.

"How long have you been like this?" I asked, already knowing this was worse than it looked.

"An hour. Maybe more. Hard to tell." He tried to smile. Blood on his teeth. Internal bleeding. "I heard the walls break. Heard the bells stop ringing. That's when I knew we'd lost."

I assessed the situation quickly. The column wasn't just heavy. It was trapped. The far end was tangled in the collapsed colonnade. Moving it would require clearing the rubble first, then lifting from the right angle to avoid crushing Nikolaos further. Even with magic-enhanced strength, even working as fast as possible, it would take ten minutes. Maybe twenty. And I couldn't heal him until he was free. Healing magic would just knit flesh back together while the column was still pressing down, making the damage worse when I finally moved it.

"James." His hand caught my wrist. Surprisingly strong for someone losing so much blood. "The cross. I never made it."

My chest tightened.

"What happened?"

"The walls broke this morning. Earlier than anyone expected." He coughed, grimacing. "I was crossing this courtyard, heading for the cistern entrance. The artillery hit. The colonnade came down." He gestured weakly at the marble pinning him. "I have been here ever since."

"The cross is still there?" I asked. "In the cistern?"

"Yes. Right below us." His breathing was labored now. He swallowed hard, forcing the words out. "The entrance is through that archway." He pointed with his eyes toward the northern side of the courtyard. "Stairs descend to the Cistern of Philoxenos. The cross is in a sealed chamber, third column from the eastern wall. The wards are still active, but I know the sequence. I was going to bypass them this morning before..." He gestured at the fallen column.

Another boom. Closer. The walls around the courtyard trembled. Voices in the distance, speaking Turkish. The Ottomans were sweeping through the palace complex.

He told me the sequence quickly. A pattern of touches and words that would bypass protections laid down when Constantine himself ruled. Nikolaos had spent three days in the imperial archives researching it, cross-referencing chronicles and magical texts until he'd pieced together the method.

"The Turks know it's there," Nikolaos continued, each word costing him. "One of their men was asking questions near the Augustaion two days ago. They will figure out the location. Maybe already have." Blood flecked his lips as he coughed. "You have to get it first. Destroy it. Don't let them use it."

I looked at him. At the column. At the blood pooling beneath him on the ancient stone. At the rubble that would need to be cleared before I could even attempt to lift the marble safely.

"I'll get you out first," I said. "Then we'll both go."

"James." His voice hardened despite the pain. "Even if I was freed, I don't think I could walk. I can't feel my legs. Besides, you don't have time for both. It's just below us, but the wards will take time to bypass. If the Turks get here first..."

"They won't."

"You don't know that." He coughed again, worse this time. When he caught his breath, his voice was quieter. "This city is falling. We've lost. But that thing can't be used to make it worse. Can't be used to hurt more people."

His eyes locked on mine. "You know what corrupted relics do. You've seen it."

I had. Cities burned. People driven mad. Veil barriers torn open and things coming through that should never touch this world. I'd spent decades hunting such objects, destroying them before they could be weaponized.

And Nikolaos had helped me. Not because he had power himself, but because he understood the importance of the work. He'd risked his life more than once, diving into sealed archives, negotiating with paranoid scholars, mapping forgotten passages beneath the city.

He'd never asked for anything in return. Just good conversation and the satisfaction of knowing dangerous things were being kept out of dangerous hands.

Now he was bleeding out in a courtyard, and he was asking me to leave him.

"I can do both," I said. "Fifteen minutes. I'll secure the artifact and come back. I'll get you out."

Nikolaos studied my face. I could see him calculating. The distance. The wards. The complexity. He knew the situation and the choice that needed making.

Then he nodded slowly.

"Fifteen minutes," he repeated.

"I promise."

"I believe you." He tried to smile again. "I'm not going anywhere. Quite literally."

I stood. Looked down at him one more time. His brown eyes were calm despite the pain. Thirty years of friendship. Countless evenings discussing philosophy and magic and whether the Veil was humanity's blessing or its cage. He'd introduced me to his fellow monks, shared meals, laughed at my stories about dealing with Rome's bureaucracy.

A good man. A good friend.

"Fifteen minutes," I said again.

"Go." His voice was firm. "And James? Be careful with the wards. The third sequence requires you to trace the pattern counter-clockwise, not clockwise.

The chronicles were unclear, but I'm certain."

Even now, pinned and bleeding, he was still being careful. Still making sure I had the details right.

I ran toward the archway.

The sounds of the dying city followed me. Screams. Artillery. The roar of fires spreading through districts that had stood for a millennium. The clash of steel on steel as the last defenders made their stands in streets named after emperors who'd been dead for eight hundred years.

The entrance was exactly where he'd said. A doorway in the northern wall, half-hidden by vines that had grown over it during decades of abandonment. The door had been forced open recently. Nikolaos's work, probably early this morning before the artillery hit.

Stairs descended into darkness.

I conjured light. Clean, simple magic that wouldn't draw attention.

The stairs went down thirty feet before opening into the cistern.

It took my breath away despite the urgency.

The chamber was a forest of columns. Marble pillars rose from still water, each carved with intricate patterns, each topped with capitals that showed the craftsmanship of a lost age. The ceiling was brick vault work, ribs and arches that distributed weight the way Rome had taught a thousand years ago. The water was perfectly clear, reflecting the columns so that the chamber seemed to extend infinitely in all directions. Somewhere in the darkness, water dripped with a steady rhythm. The sound echoed off stone, multiplied, became something almost musical.

And it was silent.

Above, the city was dying. Here, the water didn't even ripple.

I moved carefully, stepping on stones that formed a path between the columns. The water was only knee-deep, but I didn't want to disturb it. Something about this place demanded quiet. The light from my hand cast strange shadows, making the columns seem to move, to shift position when I wasn't looking directly at them.

Third column from the eastern wall.

I found it. The column looked identical to the others at first glance.

Same marble. Same carved acanthus leaves spiraling up its length. Same Corinthian capital at the top. But when I looked closer, I could see faint marks near the base. Symbols. Old magic that predated empires and religions and still remembered the stones.

Above, muffled by thirty feet of earth and stone, I heard artillery fire. The boom echoed through the cistern, disturbed the water slightly. Ripples spread in perfect circles, breaking against the columns.

I touched the column in the sequence Nikolaos had given me. Counterclockwise, as he'd specified. The symbols in a precise order.

Nothing happened for a moment.

Then the stone shifted. A grinding sound, deep and low. The water around the column's base began to swirl, draining away through channels I hadn't noticed before. The column's base descended, revealing a hollow interior that went down another ten feet.

Steps led into the darkness.

I descended carefully, my light illuminating walls covered in more symbols. Byzantine Greek. Older scripts I didn't recognize. Protective wards layered on protective wards. Whoever had hidden the cross here hadn't wanted it found.

The passage ended in a small chamber. Barely ten feet across. The walls were smooth stone, unmarked except for a single large circle carved into the far wall. And within that circle, set into a niche, was the cross. It sat in a metal box, the lid already open like it was expecting me. I could see the glow emanating from the top, and feel the power reaching out across the chamber.

I leaned over it and looked inside. Byzantine workmanship. Gold and silver with precious stones set at the points. Rubies. Sapphires. Emeralds that caught my light and threw it back in fragmented colors. The craftsmanship was exquisite. Each line perfect. Each stone precisely cut and set. Beautiful.

But the beauty was like looking at a corpse dressed in fine clothes.

The corruption was obvious. A wrongness in the air around it. A smell like metal left too long in stagnant water. The shadows in the chamber seemed darker near the cross. Deeper. It gave the illusion it was pulling light into itself and giving nothing back.

I reached for it carefully, wrapping my hand in cloth before touching the metal box.

The moment I made contact, the corruption surged.

It wasn't an attack, but its presence was heavy. A weight. A voice. Not words but feeling. Offering certainty. Offering power. Offering simple answers to complicated questions. The same seductive pull I'd sensed in other corrupted objects. The promise that if I just accepted it, just used it, everything would be easier. Clearer. Better.

All I had to do was let it help.

I pulled my hand back.

This was worse than I'd thought. Not just corrupted. Actively malicious. This thing didn't want to be destroyed. It wanted to be used. It had been waiting down here in the dark for decades, maybe centuries, and it was hungry.

Above, another artillery strike. Closer. The chamber trembled. Dust fell from the ceiling. Voices echoed down from the cistern. Turkish. They'd found the courtyard. Would they find the entrance?

I'd need to contain the cross properly before trying to move it.

I pulled containment sigils from memory and began drawing them on the box with chalk. Precise angles. Specific geometry. Work that couldn't be rushed. Each line had to be exact. Each curve needed to follow mathematical relationships that trapped corrupted energy the way a cage trapped an animal.

Five minutes passed.

The voices above grew louder. They were in the cistern now. I could hear them calling to each other, the sound echoing off the columns. Searching.

Ten minutes.

The sigils needed to be perfect. A flaw would mean the corruption leaked through. I checked each line twice, made corrections, reinforced weak points. My hands were steady despite the urgency. This had to be done right. Once drawn, the sigils would lock onto the metal despite the impermanence of chalk.

Fifteen minutes.

Almost done. Just needed to seal the final containment layer. Then I could safely take the cross and destroy it.

Above, footsteps on the stairs leading down to my chamber. They'd found the opened column. Turkish voices, excited. They knew what they were looking for.

Twenty minutes.

The seal completed. I wrapped the box in sanctified cloth, bound it with cords marked with protective symbols. The corruption was contained. Angry, pushing against the barriers like something living trying to break free, but held.

The footsteps were halfway down the stairs.

I lifted the bundle carefully. It was heavier than it should have been. The corruption had weight of its own. And it was fighting me, making the cloth slip, making my grip uncertain.

The first Turkish soldier appeared at the bottom of the stairs. He saw me. Shouted.

I extinguished my light and ran.

Not up the stairs. That way was blocked. But Nikolaos had mentioned secondary passages. Drainage channels that led to other parts of the cistern, to other exits. I followed the wall, feeling for openings in the darkness. Behind me, more soldiers descended. Their torches turned the chamber orange.

My hand found an opening. Narrow. Barely wide enough for a man. A drainage channel cut through the stone, heading north.

I squeezed through, the bundled cross making it awkward. Tight. The corruption seemed to resist, making the cloth heavier, the passage narrower. But I forced it through and followed.

The channel ran for maybe fifty feet before opening into another section of the cistern. Different columns here. Older. The water was deeper. I waded through it quickly, heading for stairs I could see on the far side.

Behind me, the soldiers were trying to follow through the narrow passage. One got stuck. Others shouted. The delay would buy me minutes. Maybe.

I climbed the stairs and emerged into another section of the palace complex.

A hallway lined with empty niches where statues had once stood. Daylight at the far end.

Thirty minutes had passed.

I ran toward the light, toward the courtyard where Nikolaos waited.

The sounds of war were louder now. Closer. Screams. The clash of weapons. Buildings burning. The crackle and roar of fire consuming wood that had been dry for centuries. Artillery boomed again, and somewhere to the west, another ancient structure collapsed.

I burst into the courtyard.

And froze.

Nikolaos was still there.

Still pinned beneath the column.

Still facing the archway I'd used.

But his eyes weren't moving.

I crossed the space between us, my legs suddenly heavy.

"Nikolaos."

No response.

I dropped beside him and touched his neck. No pulse. His skin was already cooling in the afternoon heat.

I looked at his hands. They were scraped worse than before, worse than when I'd left him. He'd kept trying to free himself. Kept fighting. The stones around him were marked where he'd tried to dig himself out, tried to shift the rubble, tried to do anything that might help.

And his face was turned toward the archway I'd used.

Waiting.

He'd held on as long as he could. Then a little longer. Then longer still. Until he couldn't anymore.

And I hadn't been there.

I knelt there in the blood and dust, holding his hand, and something broke in my chest.

Fifteen minutes. I'd promised fifteen minutes.

It had been thirty.

Twice what I'd said. Twice what he'd needed me to be.

"I'm sorry," I whispered. "God, Nikolaos, I'm so sorry."

But sorry didn't matter. Sorry didn't bring him back. Sorry was just noise I made to myself to pretend I felt something other than the crushing weight of knowing I'd made a choice and this was the cost.

The artifact had mattered. That was true. Getting it away from the Ottomans had probably saved lives. The containment had needed to be perfect. Each delay had been justified. Necessary. The right call.

But Nikolaos was dead.

And I'd let it happen. I thought of Arnaut. Of others. Of the pattern I never seemed to break. My actions had cost yet another life.

I could have worked faster. Could have taken risks with the containment. Could have grabbed the cross and run, consequences be damned. Could have prioritized the friend over the mission, the person over the strategic objective, the life in my hands over the hypothetical lives the artifact might endanger.

But I hadn't.

I'd made the professional choice. The correct choice. The choice that saved more people. But the choice that would take the more personal toll.

And Nikolaos had died alone, watching an empty archway, waiting for me to keep my word.

I sat there, holding his hand, listening to Constantinople fall around me.

Had I been right? Was the artifact worth this? Would it truly have caused more deaths if the Ottomans had taken it? Or was I just telling myself that to justify what I'd done?

I'd thought I could do both. Thought I had enough time. Thought the math worked out.

I'd been wrong. Again. Another friend dead because of their connection to me.

The voices were getting closer. Ottoman soldiers, sweeping through the palace complex. I needed to move. Needed to leave before this became my grave too. Needed to survive so this wouldn't be for nothing.

But first I had to get Nikolaos out.

I couldn't leave him here. Couldn't let him be left for scavengers or simply forgotten in a courtyard while the city changed hands.

I drew on my strength again, letting power flow through me. Gripped the column.

The work was slow. Careful. The rubble had to be cleared first. Stone by stone. Brick by brick. Creating enough space to angle the column correctly. Each piece I removed might shift the weight wrong, might crush him further even though he was already dead.

It took ten minutes to clear enough rubble.

Ten minutes I hadn't had when he was alive.

Then I lifted. The column rose slowly. My muscles burned even with magic reinforcing them. The marble was massive, unwieldy. But I got it high enough to pull him free.

I laid him out carefully on the courtyard stones, away from the blood and rubble. Straightened his robes. Closed his eyes.

His face was peaceful despite how he'd died. Maybe he'd believed until the end that I was coming back. That I'd keep my promise.

That made it worse.

I lifted his body and carried it through the palace complex, away from the advancing soldiers. Found a small chapel in an abandoned wing, dedicated to some saint whose name had worn off the wall. The altar was still there, marble and gold leaf tarnished but intact.

I laid him before it.

I pulled out my dagger and carved his name into the altar:

Nikolaos. Monk of Constantinople. Scholar. Friend.

MCCCCLIII

The day the city fell.

That day I was reminded that doing the right thing and doing the good thing weren't always the same.

That day I learned that some choices, once made, carved themselves into you and never healed.

Then I left through a passage that led down toward the sea walls.

The cross didn't leave Constantinople with me.

I destroyed it before nightfall, burned the corruption out of it with magic and flame until the gold ran like wax. I did it alone, with shaking hands, because I could not risk it surviving the city's fall. I could not risk it being found again. I could not risk my own mind deciding, in some future moment of exhaustion, that I could use it just once.

The relic was gone.

The weight of the choice remained with me always.

Constantinople fell that day, but it had been dying for decades. Everyone knew it was coming. The walls would break. The city would be conquered. An age would end.

What surprised me was how personal it felt.

I'd thought I had time.

I thought I could do both.

I was wrong.

Thirty minutes. Fifteen more than I'd promised. Small delays that seemed reasonable at the time. Necessary choices. Correct priorities. The containment had to be perfect. The corruption had to be sealed properly. Each decision justified in the moment.

And my friend died alone, watching an empty archway, waiting for me to keep my word.

Was it worth it? I've asked myself that question for centuries. Asked it in a hundred different ways, from a thousand different angles, and I still don't know the answer.

The artifact was dangerous. I was right about that. Containing it properly probably did save lives. The strategic choice was sound.

But Nikolaos is still dead.

And he died because I chose the mission over the person. Because I decided that fifteen minutes could become twenty could become thirty. Because I thought I knew better than the promise I'd made.

I carried that weight out of Constantinople even after the corruption was gone.

I carry it still.

Some promises, once broken, can never be repaid.

Some choices, once made, become part of you.

17

Rain, Blades, and the Cost (Jaffa, Present)

The rain started just after we left the restaurant.

Not the violent kind. The steady Mediterranean drizzle that turned cobblestones slick and made the old port lights blur into halos. January in Jaffa was like autumn anywhere else. Cool without being cold. Wet without being miserable.

Fog rolled in with the rain, drifting up from the water in slow banks that softened the edges of everything. The old stone buildings seemed to float in it, their walls darkened by moisture, their windows glowing like lanterns suspended in gray air. Somewhere a church bell rang, muffled and distant. Closer, I could hear the slap of waves against the harbor walls and the creak of boat rigging.

Cori and I returned to Tel Aviv to check in with David, Casey, and Erin. We'd needed this. One night away from the compound. Away from maps and data and the weight of knowing the world was three weeks from catastrophe.

Just dinner. Just people.

The restaurant had been Erin's choice. A small place tucked into the old city where stone arches framed doorways and narrow alleys twisted back on themselves like a maze designed by someone who'd never heard of right angles. The kind tourists walked past without noticing. Low ceiling. Tables so close together you could hear your neighbor's conversation. The food was good. Traditional. Cooking that came from recipes passed down rather than written.

David had been excited the entire meal.

Not nervous excited. The old David would have been fidgeting, checking his phone, adjusting his glasses. This David leaned back in his chair and gestured while he talked, explaining the new data pipeline architecture he'd built with the enthusiasm of someone who finally understood their own worth.

"The redundancy is beautiful," he said, fork pointing at nothing. "Triple backup. Distributed processing. If Tel Aviv goes dark, the system reroutes through Dayton automatically. If Jerusalem fails, it kicks to the cloud servers in three separate continents."

"You're very pleased with yourself," Erin said, but she was smiling.

"I am. This is good work. Real work. It matters."

Casey reached over and squeezed his shoulder. "You've come a long way from the guy who nearly had a panic attack after the fetchling appeared in Crable's backyard."

"That guy was smart," David replied. "He knew enough to be terrified. But he also knew enough to get involved."

I watched them across the table. Casey in a jacket she'd borrowed from Erin. David with his hair still damp from earlier rain. Erin looking more relaxed than I'd seen her since taking over as CEO.

Cori sat beside me, close enough that our shoulders touched. She'd been quiet most of dinner, content to listen and observe. But I caught her smiling at David's enthusiasm.

"What are you thinking?" I asked quietly.

"That he's found his place. That's rare. Most people spend their whole lives looking."

"He's lucky."

"No. He's brave. There's a difference."

The conversation drifted. Erin talked about navigating board politics. Casey told a story about having to mediate between two managers who'd gotten into a screaming match over whose department got the corner office, which escalated to one of them barricading themselves inside with a filing cabinet while the other called facilities to have the door removed. David asked Cori about her time in France, which led to a discussion of wine regions, and I even learned a thing or two.

Normal. Human. Real.

For two hours, we weren't fighting to save the world. We were just people sharing a meal.

Then the check came, and reality returned with it.

"We should head back," Erin said, checking her phone. "Charlie texted. He and Eliyahu found something in the pattern analysis. Wants us back by ten."

We paid and stepped outside into the rain and fog.

Jaffa at night was beautiful. It made you forget about the politics and the history of the land. The old port stretched below us, boats rocking gently in their slips, their masts disappearing into the mist. Lights reflected on wet pavement, fractured into a thousand pieces by the rain. The smell of the sea mixed with spices from a restaurant still cooking somewhere nearby, cardamom and cumin and coffee strong enough to taste in the air.

A cat watched us from a doorway, its eyes reflecting green in the lamplight. Music drifted from an open window above, a song in Arabic that I didn't recognize but seemed appropriate. The fog thickened as we walked, turning the ancient streets into something dreamlike and strange.

"Let's walk back along the Promenade," David said. "It's not far back to our apartments and I need to move after that meal."

"It's raining," Casey pointed out.

"It's drizzling. There's a difference."

We walked.

The streets were narrow and winding, following patterns laid down when cities grew organically rather than by plan. Stone buildings pressed close on either side, their walls so old the mortar had darkened to match the stone itself. We passed closed shops with signs in Arabic, Hebrew, and English and lit windows where families sat around tables finishing late dinners. Small courtyards opened unexpectedly between buildings, their fountains still trickling despite the rain, orange trees heavy with fruit standing guard in corners.

The fog wrapped around us like something alive, condensing on metal railings and making the cobblestones gleam. Our footsteps echoed off the stone, multiplied by the mist until it sounded like more people walked these streets than just the five of us.

David and Casey walked ahead, arguing about something that made them both laugh. Erin followed, checking her phone periodically. Cori and I brought up the rear.

"You're tense," she said quietly.

"Am I?"

"You're scanning rooftops. Reading the street like a battlefield."

"Old habits."

"Or good instincts."

She wasn't wrong. Something was off. Nothing I could name. Just that pressure at the base of the skull that came from centuries of surviving things that wanted me dead. The fog made it worse, turning familiar streets into uncertain terrain.

"Maybe we should grab a cab," I said.

"Probably."

But we kept walking.

The street opened into a small square. Closed shops formed three sides, their shutters drawn, their windows dark. The fourth opened toward the waterfront, though the fog was thick enough now that the water was invisible, just a presence you sensed rather than saw. The sound echoed strangely in the enclosed space.

Empty. Quiet.

Too quiet.

I stopped walking.

"Cori."

She'd already sensed it. Her hand moved instinctively to where a weapon would be, found nothing, and settled for a defensive stance instead.

"David," I called. "Casey. Erin. Get behind us. Now."

They turned. David opened his mouth to ask why.

That's when Dina stepped out of the fog.

She looked exactly as she had in Rome. Black dress. Butterfly buckle gleaming even in the dim light. Hair pulled back severe and perfect. She smiled like she'd been waiting for this exact moment and was delighted we'd finally arrived.

The fog seemed to part around her, or maybe gather closer. It was hard to tell.

"James Crable," she said with feigned warmth. "And friends. What a lovely evening for a walk."

Arnaut appeared beside her, materializing from the mist like something conjured.

He looked tired. Older than he should. Exhaustion that came from carrying weight too long. His eyes found mine and held.

"James," he said. Just my name. Nothing else.

I stepped forward, putting myself between them and the others. Cori moved with me.

"Run," I said to David. To Casey. To Erin. "Back to the restaurant. Call Charlie. Go."

"Crable..." Casey started.

"Go!"

They ran. I heard their footsteps on wet stone, moving away, swallowed quickly by the fog. Good. That was good.

Dina watched them leave with amusement. "How noble. The shepherd sending away the sheep from the wolves. But really, James. We're not here for them."

"What are you here for?" I asked.

Arnaut stepped forward. "To talk. James, just talk. I need you to listen to what's being planned. What's possible. You don't understand the scope of..."

"I understand enough," I cut him off. "I understand you're working with people who killed two of Eliyahu's men. Who are systematically attacking guardian sites across the planet. Who want to reshape the Veil into something controllable."

"To make it better," Arnaut said. His voice carried conviction. Real belief. "The Veil as it exists is faulty. Imperfect. We're offering a solution. Structure. Control. Access when it's needed, barriers when it's not."

"Under whose authority?"

"Under someone with a true vision for the future. Someone who understands what they're doing."

Dina sighed dramatically. "This is boring. Arnaut, we didn't come here for philosophical debate. We came to retrieve him. One way or another."

She raised her hand. Darkness gathered around her fingers, coiling like smoke.

Arnaut turned to her sharply. "That wasn't the plan. I said we talk first."

"Plans change, cariño." Her smile widened. "And I'm so very tired of talking."

She moved.

Fast. Faster than she should have been able to. Dark magic coiled around her hands, lashing out like whips.

Cori met her with nothing but magic and momentum.

She deflected the first strike with a barrier of pure force, then drove forward, hands glowing with focused power. Their collision lit the fog from within, turning the square into something out of a fever dream. Shadows and light warring against each other while the mist swirled around them.

I released my power.

Clean light. Disciplined force. Centuries of training compressed into instinct. It struck Arnaut before he could react, driving him back across the wet stones.

He caught himself, hands extended, and I could sense his magic rise to meet mine.

Corrupted. Oily. But still recognizable underneath. Still the same foundation we had learned back when the world was younger and we thought we understood what we were fighting for.

"I don't want to hurt you," Arnaut said.

"Then stop."

"I can't. Not until you listen. Not until you understand."

Behind us, Cori and Dina fought in a blur of motion and shadow. Magic against dark magic. Precision against raw power. They were matched in a way that would have been beautiful if it wasn't terrifying. The fog twisted around them, moved by forces it wasn't meant to contain.

I hit Arnaut again. Harder this time. He deflected most of it but the edge caught him, spinning him sideways.

"I'm trying to save you," he said, recovering. "All of you. The Veil is dying, James. It's been dying for centuries. We're offering a way to preserve what matters while letting the rest evolve."

"By corrupting it? By turning guardians into tools?"

"By understanding what the Veil actually is intended for instead of just guarding it blindly!"

His power lashed out. I raised a barrier and the impact rattled through my bones. Rain hissed where it touched the corrupted magic, steam rising in thin coils that added to the fog.

Cori shouted something. I glanced over in time to see her score a hit across Dina's shoulder with a focused blade of pure force. Blood welled, dark and thick.

Dina laughed. Actually laughed.

"Oh, I like you," she said to Cori. "You have potential. Maybe after we're done with James, I'll teach you what real power looks like."

"I'd rather die."

"That can be arranged too."

Dark magic struck again, a whip of corrupted force. Cori barely deflected it. The impact drove her back three steps. She was tiring. We both were. This was a holding action at best. The amount of power we were throwing around was immense and unsustainable.

I needed to end this.

I gathered power, drawing deeper than I should. Reaching for the reserves I kept locked away because using them hurt. Because they carried weight and consequence and exhaustion that lasted days.

But David and Casey and Erin were running through dark streets. And Cori was being driven back step by step. And Arnaut stood across from me with belief in his eyes and corruption in his hands.

And so I reached.

The power came. Clean and bright and strong enough to make the rain evaporate in a perfect circle around me. Strong enough that even the fog retreated. Strong enough that Arnaut's eyes widened.

"James, wait..."

I released it.

The blast caught him square in the chest and threw him backward into the fountain. Water exploded outward. Stone cracked. He went under and came up coughing, magic scattered, defenses broken.

I moved toward him, power still burning in my hands. One more strike. One more and I could end this. Put him down before he hurt anyone else. Before whatever he'd become finished consuming what he'd been.

That's when I heard the footsteps.

Running. Fast. Coming from the direction David and the others had fled.

"No," I said, now distracted. "No, go back..."

David burst into the square.

He was breathing hard. Rain plastered his hair to his forehead. His glasses were fogged and crooked. The fog parted around him as he ran.

"I saw her," he gasped. "I saw what she was doing to Cori. You need..."

"Get out of here!" I shouted.

But it was too late.

Dina had driven Cori back. Pressed her advantage. Forced Cori's guard wide.

And then she turned. Saw me. Saw my power raised toward Arnaut.

Saw the opening.

Darkness gathered in her hand, coalescing into something solid. A thin black blade materialized.

It came around in an arc meant to take my head.

I started to raise a defense. Started to redirect the power. Started to do a dozen things that might have worked if I'd had another second.

David moved faster.

He crossed the distance between us in three running steps. No hesitation.

No calculation. Just momentum and desperation and courage that came from deciding what mattered.

He hit Dina from the side.

Tackled her.

Not cleanly. Not with any skill. Just threw his body at hers with enough force to knock her off balance.

They went down together in a tangle of limbs and rain and magic that was still active, still seeking a target.

The black dagger was between them.

I heard the sound it made going in. Wet. Final. A sound that I had heard too many times on battlefields. Sound you never forget because your brain knows instantly what it means.

David gasped.

Dina pulled the blade free and stepped back.

David fell.

I was moving before he hit the ground. Crossing the wet stone. Dropping beside him. My hands found the wound immediately.

High on the left side. Between ribs. The blade had gone deep.

"No," I said. "No, no, no."

I pressed my hand against it. Reached for magic. For healing. For anything that might close a wound and pull someone back from the edge.

The magic touched the wound and recoiled.

The blade had been corrupted. Anti-magic. Poisoned. Whatever healing I tried slid off like oil on water.

"David. Stay with me. Look at me."

His eyes found mine. Unfocused. Already distant.

"Did I..." he started. Coughed. Blood on his lips. "Did I help?"

"Yes. You helped. You saved me. But you need to stay awake. We're going to get you to a hospital. We're going to..."

"Liar." He smiled faintly and gave a soft chuckle. "You're a terrible liar, Crable."

"David..."

"Tell Charlie... tell him the designs... it's good work..."

"You're going to tell him yourself."

But he wasn't. I could feel it. The way his breath came shallower. The way his hand went slack in mine.

"I'm sorry," I said, fighting back tears. "God, David, I'm so sorry."

"Not your fault." His voice was barely a whisper now. "My choice." He looked me straight in the eyes. "Listen to me, this is *not* your fault."

Then his eyes went still and my heart broke.

I knelt there in the rain and fog, holding a dead man, while my magic burned uselessly in my hands.

Behind me, Dina laughed.

"Well. That was unexpected." Her voice was bright, amused. "He just jumped right in, didn't he? How delightfully stupid."

I turned.

She was examining the blade, turning it over in her hand like she was inspecting it for damage. Not a trace of concern. Not a hint of regret.

"Shame about the civilian," she continued conversationally. "But he really should have stayed away. This is what happens when amateurs interfere with..."

Arnaut hit her like a freight train.

No words. No warning. Just pure momentum and rage.

His shoulder drove into her ribs. Power exploded around him, wild and uncontrolled, as he grabbed her arm and pulled.

A portal tore open behind them. Jagged. Unstable. The edges screamed.

Dina's eyes went wide. "What are you..."

They went through together.

The blade tumbled from Dina's grip, clattering on wet stone as Arnaut dragged her into the portal.

I caught a glimpse of her face. Shock. Fury.

Then the portal collapsed.

Silence.

Just rain and the fountain and Cori's ragged breathing behind me. The fog drifted back in, softer now, covering everything like a shroud.

And David. Dead. Because he'd been brave enough to come back. Because he'd seen Dina attacking and acted without thinking.

Because of me.

Footsteps. Running. Coming fast.

Casey and Erin burst into the square, their forms indistinct in the mist until they were almost on top of us.

They saw me. Saw David.

Casey made a sound I'd never heard from her before. Grief doesn't have words sometimes. Just noise. Raw and animal and completely human.

She dropped beside me. Beside David. Her hands found his face.

"No. David. David, wake up. Come on. This isn't funny. Katz!"

"Casey," Erin said quietly.

"He's fine. He's going to be fine. We just need to get him to…"

"Casey."

Erin knelt beside her. Put her arms around her. Casey fought it for a second, then collapsed into the embrace.

She sobbed. Crying that shook your whole body. That came from somewhere so deep you couldn't control it or stop it or do anything but let it run its course.

Cori moved to stand beside me. Her hand found my shoulder. She didn't say anything. There wasn't anything to say.

Rain fell. The fog drifted. Casey wept. David lay still.

And I knelt there in the square, covered in his blood, knowing I'd failed him. Failed all of them.

After a while, Casey's sobs quieted to shaking breaths.

She pulled back from Erin slightly. Wiped her face with shaking hands.

Then her eyes landed on something across the wet stones.

The black blade. Still lying where it had fallen. The fog seemed to avoid it, leaving a clear space around it on the cobblestones.

She stared at it. Something shifted in her expression. Recognition. Or maybe just exhaustion. Or maybe something else entirely.

She stood. Walked over to it.

"Casey, don't…" I started.

She picked it up.

The blade didn't react to her touch the way it had to mine when I'd tried to heal David. It just lay in her palm. Inert. Waiting.

She looked at it for a long moment.

Then she opened her purse and slid the blade inside.

"Casey," Erin said carefully. "That thing killed David. We should…"

"I know what it did." Her voice was flat. Empty. "That's why I'm keeping it."

She looked at me. Her eyes were red but dry now. Hard.

"We're calling the police. We're telling them it was a robbery. Random violence. They won't believe it but they'll write it down anyway." She glanced at David's body. "And then we're all going back to Jerusalem. And we're going to finish what they started. Because that's what he'd want."

"Casey."

"Don't." She held up a hand. "Not now. Just… not now."

She was right. There wasn't anything to say that would help.

We called the police. Told the story Casey invented. They took statements. They looked skeptical but wrote it down anyway. Random violence in Jaffa. Tragic. They'd investigate. They wouldn't find anything.

By the time we got back to the compound, it was past midnight.

Charlie was waiting in the courtyard. He saw our faces and knew immediately.

"Where's David?" he asked.

Erin told him.

I watched his face while she spoke. Watched him process it. Watched the moment the words became real and hit him like a physical blow.

He sat down hard on the bench beneath the olive tree.

"He was excited," Charlie said finally. " About the work. He texted me during dinner. Said it was the best meal he'd had in months."

"I know," Erin said quietly.

"Did he…" Charlie looked up. "Did he suffer?"

"No," I said. "It was fast."

Charlie nodded. Stared at his hands.

"What do we do now?" he asked.

"We finish it," Casey said. Her voice was still flat. Still empty. "We finish what he started. We stop these people. And we make sure David didn't die for nothing."

She walked inside without waiting for a response.

The blade went with her. Hidden in her purse.

And I stood in the courtyard, covered in rain and blood that wasn't mine, knowing everything had just changed.

<h1 style="text-align:center">18</h1>

Maps, Timelines, and the Call (Jerusalem, Present)

Morning came gray and unwelcome.

I'd slept maybe two hours. Every time I closed my eyes, I saw David's face. The rain. The blade going in. His hand going slack in mine.

I gave up trying to sleep and found Charlie already in the lower chamber with Eliyahu. Neither had changed clothes. Coffee cups scattered around Charlie's workspace were evidence of a long night. The air smelled stale, recycled through too many hours without windows.

Charlie sat hunched over his laptop, data streams flowing across multiple screens. Erin's feeds from Emetrix. Global sensor data. Frequency patterns. His fingers moved with precision, isolating signals, filtering noise, chasing patterns through numbers that most people would see as random static.

Eliyahu stood behind him, watching. His face was drawn but calm. A calm that came from long experience with grief.

"How long have you been at this?" I asked quietly.

Charlie didn't look up. "Since you got back. The team at Emetrix sent the updated data sets an hour ago. Erin had them working all night. There's something here. Something in the pattern. I just need to..."

He trailed off, eyes fixed on cascading numbers.

I pulled up a chair. Watched the screens. The data meant nothing to me,

196

but Charlie saw stories in it. Structure. Mathematics that revealed what magic tried to hide.

His voice sharpened suddenly. "I found it."

Eliyahu leaned forward. Cori leaned in. She had entered without me hearing her.

"What is it?" I asked.

Charlie pulled up a visualization. The global map covered in red dots showing attacked guardian sites. Blue lines connected them now. Geometric curves following precise mathematical relationships.

"The data shows the corrupted frequencies propagate across the entire network," Charlie said. His fingers moved across the keyboard, highlighting specific nodes. "Each attacked site generates a corrupted resonance. Those frequencies don't just stay localized. They travel. Propagate along the ley lines like waves through a medium."

He zoomed in on one section. North America displayed the frequency waves spreading from one attacked site to another.

"I thought they were just degrading the sites. Weakening them. But that's not all that is happening. Look at the way it behaves at the far end of the system."

He overlaid another layer. The blue lines converged, following paths across continents. The angles were precise. Deliberate.

"They aren't just attacking randomly. They are creating a circuit. A massive geometric structure. Each node is positioned at a specific mathematical relationship to the others. The angles matter. The distances matter. It's like…" He paused, searching for the right analogy. "It's like they are building a massive antenna array, but for magical frequencies instead of radio waves. Once we saw the sigil pattern in the resonance fields, I started to look at the movement and not just the structure."

"An antenna transmitting what?" Cori asked.

"Not transmitting. Receiving. Or maybe channeling is the better word." Charlie pulled up more calculations. "In electrical engineering, you can use geometric arrays to focus energy. Direct it. Amplify it. This is the same principle, but applied to Veil frequencies instead of electromagnetic radiation.

I had the guys at Emetrix start to use AI models to look for things that a human may not pick up, and now we have the new feeds based on that data. We can now map not only the structure, but the movement of the frequencies."

He highlighted three points on the map. They glowed brighter than the others. A triangle spanning the globe.

"These are convergence points. Where multiple corrupted frequencies intersect at specific geometric angles. Central Europe. South America. Southeast Asia." His voice carried an edge of admiration despite the horror. "Whoever designed this understood harmonic resonance at a level I have never seen. The mathematics are beautiful. Terrifying, but beautiful."

"But they aren't endpoints," Eliyahu said, understanding. "They are relay stations."

"Exactly." Charlie zoomed the map further. Europe. Britain. Scotland. The Highlands.

A single red dot pulsed in the north.

"There," he said. "That's the final terminus. Where all the corrupted energy they've been generating channels into one location. Every attacked site, every corrupted frequency, every geometric relationship in this structure points to this one guardian site."

"What's at that location?" I asked.

Eliyahu was already pulling up records. Ancient texts. Guardian histories spanning centuries.

"The Glaistig's territory," he said quietly. "Scottish Highlands. Remote. One of the oldest guardian sites in the British Isles."

I knew the Glaistig. I had not visited the site, but I knew what she was. Half woman, half goat. Guardian of wild places. Protector of livestock and travelers. Keeper of boundaries between the human world and the places humans were not meant to go.

"Her connection to the Veil is strong," Eliyahu continued. "Exceptionally strong. She has maintained that site for over two thousand years. Maybe longer. And she has no warden to protect her."

"So, they can move and act with impunity. Have they attacked her directly?" Cori asked.

Charlie shook his head. "That's what is strange. They have hit sites across Europe, Asia, the Americas. But not Scotland. Not her."

"Because they don't need to," I said, understanding. "They are using her. Channeling the corrupted frequencies through her site without her knowledge. She becomes an unwilling conduit. And no one is there to protect her."

"Exactly." Charlie pulled up more calculations. "Her connection to the Veil is so strong that if they can route all this corrupted energy through her territory, they can amplify it exponentially. Use her strength against the entire network."

The room went quiet.

"When?" I asked.

Charlie checked the propagation models. "The corrupted frequencies are building toward a critical threshold. Based on current progression, they reach maximum resonance in two days. When the geometric alignment is perfect. That's when they activate it."

"Two days," I repeated.

"Maybe less if they accelerate."

Eliyahu moved to the maps. Studied the pattern. His fingers traced the lines connecting nodes.

"There are weaknesses," he said quietly. "Here. And here. Places where the geometric relationships aren't quite perfect. Small gaps in the structure."

"Can we exploit those?" Cori asked.

"I have some things I have been working on," Charlie answered.

We stood there looking at the maps. At the scale of what we faced. At two days that felt like no time at all.

Charlie swallowed hard, then spoke again, "As I said, I have been working on something. I have been in contact with the team at Emetrix, and we built something that may help."

Everyone turned.

"Built what?" Eliyahu asked.

Charlie pulled a fresh sheet of paper toward him and started sketching immediately. Not just circuit blocks. Sigil geometry too. Circles inside circles.

Angles. Containment lines. Shapes Eliyahu used when he taught sacred geometry, layered with the same structure Charlie used when he designed systems.

"It's not done yet, and it's just a prototype, but it's a small device," Charlie said. "Sigil based. But engineered. It would store power the way a capacitor stores charge, then release it all at once in a controlled burst."

Eliyahu leaned closer. "A vessel circle."

"Yes," Charlie said. "A containment lattice built from sigils. The geometry holds energy stable without bleeding into the Veil. Then a release pattern collapses the containment instantly and turns the stored energy into a pulse."

Cori's eyes narrowed. "A pulse of what?"

Charlie's pen tapped the paper once. "Interference."

My stomach tightened.

Charlie looked up. His face was drawn, but his eyes were sharp.

"It's basically an EMP," he said.

Eliyahu didn't flinch. He just studied the sketch harder.

"Electromagnetic pulse," Cori said.

"Yes, or at least the same principle," Charlie replied. "Different carrier. The Veil is a medium. Our data proves that. Energy propagates through it. Frequencies travel through it. Patterns move through it like signals. If the Architect is building a system that depends on synchronization, then we can disrupt synchronization."

He flipped to a clean page and drew a simple wave. Then another. Then a jagged spike cutting through them.

"In the real world, an EMP works because it overwhelms timing and structure. It does not need to understand the signal. It just floods the channel with a spike so violent that nothing coherent survives."

He tapped the spike again.

"And the way we do that magically is with sigils. A containment pattern to hold the charge. A release pattern to dump it instantly. A shaping pattern to spread the pulse across the right band of Veil frequencies."

Eliyahu nodded once. "And a grounding geometry so the pulse does not rebound into the lattice and tear it apart."

"Exactly," Charlie said, almost grateful. "Grounding. Containment. Release. Shape. It's engineering, just using sacred geometry and electro-magnetic design."

I looked at the global map again. The relay structure. The lines converging toward Scotland.

"And the risk?" I asked. "If we do this wrong, what happens to the Veil?"

Charlie didn't hesitate.

"It won't shut down the entire Veil," he said. "Not if we deploy it where it matters."

He pointed to the terminus point.

"The Architect's plan is to drive power through one site. A choke point. Everything they're building, every relay and convergence point, all of it routes into a final location so the signal becomes coherent enough to lock the whole structure into place."

"The Glaistig guardian site," Eliyahu said quietly.

"This site seems to be different than others," Charlie replied. "They are using this site as the throat of the pattern. They need that site because it's strong enough to carry the load."

Cori folded her arms. "Then we hit the throat."

"We hit the throat," Charlie confirmed. "Right at the activation window. We fire the pulse the moment they try to push the corrupted signal through. The signal breaks. The structure fails to synchronize. Their plan collapses before it can complete."

"And the rest of the Veil?" I asked.

"It stays intact...theoretically," Charlie said. "It might ripple. It might wobble locally. But the Veil is still a barrier. It's still anchored. We aren't tearing it down. We're jamming one transmission at one site."

Eliyahu's expression tightened. "And afterward?"

"Afterward," Charlie said, voice lower, "the Veil should recover. The Veil is resilient. It was designed to heal from stress. We have seen that with Grant Park. The Veil is not centralized like the Architect's design. We disrupt their global pattern, and temporarily halt only one Veil site. Theirs breaks, the Veil recovers. Again, theoretically."

The silence stretched.

"How long to build it?" Cori asked.

Charlie glanced at his sketches, already rewriting them as he spoke.

"That's the thing," he said, "it's already mostly built. I just need some help from Eliyahu on sigil design and placement."

"What's it made of?" I asked.

"Besides the electronics and housing, conductive metals," Charlie said. "Grounding components. Crystals that can hold charge without fracturing. And sigils. Lots of them. Layered correctly. Exact angles. Exact relationships. I need help with the last part."

Eliyahu nodded. "I will get my Keepers to assist with this right away. This has to be perfect."

Charlie's pen stilled. "No pressure."

I looked at the map one more time. Scotland pulsing at the edge of everything.

"The timeline is tight," I said. "We need to be in Scotland immediately."

Charlie didn't smile. He just nodded and went back to work like the decision had turned him into something harder.

Eliyahu moved beside him, already marking angles and arcs on the paper, turning ancient rules into something functional and lethal.

Because this was not just magic.

It was infrastructure.

And whoever the Architect was, he was not throwing magic at the world.

He was building a system meant to run forever.

Charlie went back to his sketches. Building something that might save us. Or break the Veil in ways we couldn't predict. But we were out of options, and more importantly out of time.

I had been studying the maps, and I looked over to where the Nail sat and had a thought.

"The weaknesses in the pattern. The gaps. What if we didn't just try to pause it? What if we tried to heal it? Not just the Veil, but the entire corruption."

Charlie looked strained. "That's the goal, Jimmy, but I am not sure I have any ideas at the moment."

"Oh, I know. That's priority one for sure." I said, and Cori looked at me, "but I was thinking about Anglesey. The tree cutting healed itself over time. By the time I gave it to Elaine, it was pure again. We simply have overlooked another tool in our arsenal. Druid magic."

Cori's eyes widened. "How did we miss that?"

"Too many things going on at once to deal with," I said. "Elaine and I had many talks while we worked to repair the park in Ohio. She would always tell me that if you understand what was damaged, you can restore it."

"But that was one site," Charlie said. "One localized corruption. This is global. Dozens of sites. Maybe hundreds."

"Let's solve one problem at a time," I said. "We need to focus everything on Scotland at the moment. However, we need to start thinking ahead and stop reacting."

Eliyahu nodded. "And if the druids can heal corruption, we can see if we can adapt our work to use healed frequencies as part of a counter resonance. Clean energy versus corrupted energy and feed it into our designs."

"I will call Elaine," I said. "See if the druids can help. Eliyahu, you work with Charlie on the device. I also need to speak with Erin to check on Casey."

"And Scotland?" Cori asked.

"We leave as soon as the device is ready," I said.

Charlie and Eliyahu bent over the paper again, sketching circles and angles like the right geometry could stop the end of the world.

As they started to lose themselves in their work, I was faced with two things weighing heavily in me. The Katz family and Casey.

"Excuse me, I need to call David's parents," I said quietly. Charlie's hands stilled, and he gave me a comforting look. I stepped into the hall and made the call. Told them their son was dead. Heard Mrs. Katz scream. Heard Mr. Katz's voice break when he said "Our boy." Arranged for them to fly to Tel Aviv tomorrow. The whole conversation lasted four minutes and destroyed a family.

After that, I decided to go check on Casey, but met Erin in the hallway.

"How is Casey?" I asked her.

"She needs time. Leave her be for the moment. She needs to process this. We all do really. She is sleeping now, finally. She was up all night crying."

"OK, let me know when she wakes up." Erin gave me a warm hug, and then moved on to find Charlie.

I pivoted, walked out to the courtyard, and pulled out my phone.

Elaine answered on the second ring.

"James. It's late. Everything alright?"

"No," I said. "I need to ask you something. I need your expertise on something."

A pause. Her voice shifted. Sharper.

"Tell me."

I looked out over the stone walls as Jerusalem woke up around us. The city moved like it always did. Old and busy and indifferent to whatever was coming.

"We recovered something in Europe," I said. "An object."

"What kind of object?" she asked.

"Old," I said. "Historical. Significant power. The kind that shouldn't exist in anyone's hands."

Elaine didn't interrupt. She just let me keep talking.

"It's corrupted," I added.

That got her attention.

"Corrupted how?"

"Same corruption as the tree cutting from Anglesey," I said. "We're seeing it in objects, people, and guardian sites."

Elaine was quiet for a beat.

"Alright," she said carefully. "What do you want from me?"

I hesitated, then said it straight.

"Remember the tree at Anglesey? The corruption in the cutting didn't clear because of a spell. It cleared because it sat on sacred ground for centuries, and the land did what it does when it's given enough time."

"Yes," Elaine said. "Nature can do wonders."

"We don't have centuries," I said. "We don't even have months."

Silence.

Then, "Go on."

"I want to know if what a sacred site does slowly can be replicated," I said. "Or accelerated. If your people can take that same kind of cleansing and do it with purpose. With intent."

Elaine didn't answer right away.

I kept going.

"It's not just objects," I said. "It's showing up in places. In the Veil system. And I've seen what it does to people when they carry it too long. When it gets into their thinking."

Her voice stayed calm. "You're asking if we can cleanse corruption the way the earth does, only faster."

"Exactly."

"And you want to know if it can be done more than once," she said. "If it can be applied broadly."

"Yes," I repeated. "Because if it can, it changes everything."

Another pause. Not hesitation. Consideration.

"I suppose it's possible," Elaine said. "But I need to ask around. It isn't something I have knowledge of, but some of my order will know more."

I tightened my grip on the phone.

"But if anyone can even tell me whether it's possible, it's the Druids."

Elaine exhaled softly. Thinking.

"Where is the object now?" she asked.

"Jerusalem," I said. "Contained. Secured."

"And you want us to come look at it."

"Yes," I said. "Not just look. Study it. Understand it. If there's a way to clean it, or even slow what it's doing, I want to know before we're out of time."

Elaine was quiet for a moment.

Then she said, "Alright."

Relief hit so hard it made my eyes sting.

"Once you speak with your order, we can arrange for a visit."

"I can't promise anything," she replied, and I could hear the faint smile in her voice. "What I can do is speak with some of my people and see what they think."

I nodded even though she couldn't see it.

"I need to speak to the Council of Groves," she continued. "They will know better than anyone. They have been working with the cutting already to see if it can be used to regrow our sacred trees to be more resistant to these corruptions."

"How long?"

"It's eleven PM here," she said. "The Council is in England, so they should be up. I'll call them immediately."

I let out a breath I hadn't realized I was holding.

"Thank you."

Elaine didn't soften her voice, but it wasn't cold either.

"James," she said.

"Yeah."

"If corruption is spreading through objects, places, and people the way you're describing, then you're right to take it seriously. That corruption nearly destroyed our order. I believe the Council will be eager to assist."

"That's why I called."

"I'll call you back," Elaine said.

The line went dead.

I stood in the courtyard for a long moment, phone still in my hand, listening to the city wake up.

The first seeds of hope crept into me.

It was something.

I stood in the courtyard watching Jerusalem wake. The city continuing around us. Unaware that in mere days, the boundary between worlds might reshape itself forever.

Cori found me there.

"The druids will help?" she asked.

"I think so. They are discussing it now, but I think they will help."

"So little time."

I nodded. "It's what we have."

We stood in silence for a moment. The city sounds grew louder. Traffic.

Voices. Life continuing.

"Scotland," she said. "Who is coming with us?"

"You, me, Lucan, Zeke. I'll ask Eliyahu."

"Charlie?" She asked.

"No."

"He won't like that," she said.

"He won't. We need him here though, working on the problem. Besides, I am not sure I am ready to put another friend in harm's way. You, me, and the others. We know what we're facing. They don't fully understand, despite their eagerness."

She nodded.

Cori watched me for a long moment.

"You need to stop blaming yourself for David," she said quietly.

"How can I not?" I answered, staring off into the distance.

Time was not on our side, but for the first time we had the beginning of a plan.

My phone vibrated in my hand.

Unknown number.

I stared at it for a moment too long. What now, I thought.

I answered.

"James," Arnaut said.

His voice was quiet. Controlled.

A long pause, and then a heavy sigh.

"I am sorry about your friend."

The words hit harder than they should have. Like a thumb pressed into a bruise.

"Don't," I said.

"I mean it," he replied. "I am sorry."

I didn't answer. I didn't trust myself to.

"I need to meet with you," Arnaut said. "To talk."

My grip tightened on the phone.

"What makes me think I won't just kill you?" I asked. I wondered how much I really meant it.

A pause.

"Maybe you do," Arnaut said. "And I know wanting to is tearing you apart."

Cori's eyes narrowed, the moment she realized who it was.

"We need to talk," Arnaut continued. "Not through intermediaries. You and me."

"What makes you think I will listen?"

"I think you will come," he said. "Because you need answers."

I swallowed.

"This afternoon," Arnaut said. "I'll come to Jerusalem. I assume you're with your Keeper friends? Don't worry, somewhere public. Somewhere open. You pick the place if you want. Noon."

Silence.

Arnaut exhaled once. "Please, James."

The line went dead.

I lowered the phone slowly, staring at the dark screen.

And the part of me that still believed Arnaut could be saved felt like a weakness I could not afford.

But the part of me that wanted him dead felt worse.

Because it didn't feel like rage.

It felt like relief.

<h1 style="text-align:center">19</h1>

Backgammon, Regrets, and the Anguish (Jerusalem, Present)

"You're not going alone," Cori said.

We were in the courtyard. Noon was forty-five minutes away. The sun beat down on Jerusalem's stone, turning everything the color of old parchment.

"I am," I replied.

"Arnaut killed two of Eliyahu's men. He's working with people who attacked guardian sites across the planet. He was there when David died."

"I know."

"Then you know going alone is stupid."

"Probably. But I'm going anyway."

Cori stepped closer. Her voice dropped. "James. This could be a trap. Dina could be waiting. Or worse, Arnaut himself could be the threat. Whatever he was, he's not that anymore. You said it yourself."

"I know what I said."

"Then why?"

I looked at her. At the concern in her eyes. The frustration.

"Because if there's any chance the old Arnaut is still in there, if there's any part of him that wants out, I need to know. And he won't talk if you're sitting at the next table watching."

"You risk everything on a maybe?"

"I've risked more on less."

She stared at me for a long moment. Then exhaled sharply.

"Fine. But you take this." She pulled a small blade from her belt. Guardian-made. Clean silver. "And if you're not back in two hours, I'm coming with everyone."

I took the blade. Slipped it into my jacket.

"Two hours," I agreed.

The walk to the Old City took fifteen minutes.

I entered through Jaffa Gate, passing under the Ottoman walls that had stood since Suleiman rebuilt them in the sixteenth century. The gate opened into a confusion of narrow streets that twisted back on themselves like the city had grown organically over millennia, which it had. Stone pressed against stone. Architecture layered on architecture. Romans built on Crusader foundations. Ottomans built on Mamluks. Everything compressed into a single square kilometer of humanity's stubborn refusal to let go of sacred ground.

The afternoon was cool, but the mid-day sun added a welcome layer of warmth. Tourists moved in clusters, following guides who held up umbrellas and flags. Their voices carried. English. Spanish. Mandarin. French. All of them here to see where prophets walked and empires fell.

I turned down the Via Dolorosa. The street was busy. Pilgrims stopped at the Stations of the Cross, touching the walls, praying. A group of nuns moved past in white habits, speaking quietly in Italian. Street vendors sold olive wood crosses and rosaries from small shops built into walls that predated their grandparents' grandparents.

The smell changed as I walked. Incense from the churches. Spices from the Arab quarter. Fresh bread from bakeries that had occupied the same locations for generations. Coffee. Always coffee. Strong and thick and brewed the way people had brewed it here for centuries.

I passed the Austrian Hospice, its entrance marked by the Habsburg coat of arms. A group of German pilgrims stood outside, consulting maps. Beyond them, the narrow street opened slightly where the Fourth Station chapel jutted out.

The café Arnaut had named was deeper into the Muslim Quarter. Al-Wad Street. A place called Jaffar's that had been there since before the Mandate.

The street narrowed as I went deeper. Buildings leaned close overhead, their upper floors almost touching across the gap. Laundry hung from balconies. Satellite dishes sprouted like mushrooms from ancient roofs. The stone underfoot was worn smooth by feet. Roman feet. Byzantine feet. Crusader feet. Ottoman feet. Israeli feet. All of them walking the same paths, leaving the same grooves.

A boy ran past, chasing a soccer ball. An old woman sat in a doorway, watching the street with eyes that had seen everything and been surprised by none of it.

Jaffar's occupied the ground floor of a building that might have been Mamluk originally. The entrance was small. Easy to miss if you didn't know it was there. Stone archway. Wooden door weathered gray by time. A hand-painted sign in Arabic and English.

I pushed open the door.

Inside was cool. Dim. The walls were old stone, interrupted by arched niches that might have held oil lamps once. Now they held brass coffee pots and photographs of Jerusalem from different eras. The floor was worn tile in geometric patterns. Blue and white. Cracked in places but clean.

Small tables filled the space. Four or five of them. Mismatched chairs. Furniture that had been collected over decades, piece by piece, as things broke and were replaced.

The smell hit immediately. Coffee. Cardamom. Tobacco smoke from a hookah in the corner where two old men sat playing backgammon. The pieces clicked against the wooden board. Steady. Rhythmic. They didn't look up when I entered.

Arnaut sat at the back table.

He'd chosen well. Back to the wall. Clear view of the entrance. Exit through the kitchen if needed. The position of someone who'd spent centuries learning not to be trapped.

Arnaut looked tired.

His posture was still military-straight. His clothes clean. Dark jacket. Simple shirt. Nothing that drew attention. But his eyes were tired. Exhaustion that came from carrying weight too long.

He saw me and modded once.

I walked to the table. Sat across from him.

For a moment, neither of us spoke.

A young man appeared from behind a curtain. The server. Maybe twenty. He set down two small cups of coffee without being asked. Turkish style. Thick and dark with grounds settling at the bottom.

Arnaut lifted his cup. Took a sip. Set it down carefully.

"Thank you for coming," he said quietly.

"You said you had something to tell me."

"I do. But first..." He paused. "I am sorry about your friend. Truly. I know you don't believe me, and I know sorry doesn't change anything. But I need you to know I meant it."

"Dina killed him."

"Yes."

"You could have stopped her."

Arnaut's jaw tightened. "Could I? By the time I realized what she was doing, your friend was already moving. Already throwing himself on her. By that time you had knocked me into the fountain."

I sighed, knowing he was right, but needing to find blame in anyone but me.

"You tackled her through a portal."

"I did."

"Why?"

Arnaut looked at his coffee, at the grounds swirling in the bottom.

"Because she was making it personal," he said. "David's death was unfortunate collateral. But Dina laughing? Mocking him? That's tactically stupid. It creates enemies we don't need."

"Collateral damage?" I fumed. "Is that what David was?"

"James, we're working toward something larger than individual vendettas, James. I learned that lesson at Grant Park. Push too hard, too visibly, before the structure is complete..." He shook his head. "Dina doesn't understand patience. She treats this like entertainment."

"And you don't?"

Arnaut shrugged. "You don't tear down supports while you're still building."

Outside, a scooter buzzed past. The backgammon pieces clicked. The hookah bubbled quietly.

"You hate her," I said.

"She is irredeemable. I've despised her since we started working together. She's a creature of pure appetite. No principles. No boundaries. Just hunger and cruelty wrapped in charm."

The word hung in the air between us. I didn't ask if he saw the mirror he was holding up to himself. Maybe he couldn't see it yet. Or maybe he could and that's what exhausted him.

"Then why work with her?" I asked.

Arnaut was quiet for a moment. Considering how much to say.

"Because the Architect wanted her involved," he said finally. "He said her talents were necessary. That her particular skills would be useful for certain aspects of the plan."

"What skills?"

"Corruption. She understands it in ways most people don't. Can shape it. Direct it. Use it like a tool instead of just a weapon."

"And you went along with that."

Arnaut looked at me. Something flickered in his expression. Not quite regret, and not quite doubt. Just... weariness.

"I did," he said. "Because the plan required it. Because I thought I understood the necessity. Because..." He stopped. "Because when you're certain you're right, you justify what needs justifying."

"That sounds like doubt."

"It sounds like experience." Pausing to take another sip of coffee. "You always had a gift for that, James. Seeing the complications. The gray areas. I envied that about you."

"Envied?"

"Everything was clear to me once," Arnaut said quietly. "Right action.

Wrong action. Good cause. Bad cause. The Church taught me that. For centuries, I knew exactly where I stood. What I experienced after the portal in Jerusalem cemented that certainty. The other side of the Veil is dangerous yes, but it is also harmony." He trailed off and stared at his coffee cup. I had questions, but gave him a moment; it was clear he wanted to say more.

"But since I have returned...things have been less certain."

He paused, collecting his thoughts. "The longer I am back on this side, the more questions I have. The more I remember the times with you, with Geoffrey, the early days in the Watch."

"What did you find?"

Arnaut held his cup for a moment without drinking. His gaze dropped to the grounds swirling at the bottom like a storm trapped in porcelain.

"Answers to questions I hadn't asked," he said.

He looked up at me again. And for the first time since we met those many years ago, his eyes didn't look like someone possessed of clarity. They looked like someone searching for it.

"When I came back, I was certain," he continued. "More certain than I'd ever been. No hesitation. No doubt. Just...belief."

"The Architect told you what needed to be done," I said.

He flinched, not at the words, but at what it implied.

"I have always found clarity in the mission," he said quietly. "The Oculi, the Church, the Watch, the Architect. I didn't have to think. Didn't have to question morality. Others carried that burden."

The dice rattled across the backgammon board. One of the old men muttered something in Arabic. The other laughed. Steady. Rhythmic.

"I crossed through the Wall thinking I was chasing a demon," Arnaut said. "I ran after it without thought, because that was our orders. Perhaps it was nothing more than arrogance."

His jaw tightened. The admission tasted bitter. He leaned forward slightly, and carefully formed what he said next.

"It was like stepping into the machinery behind the world," he said. "Not heaven or hell. Order and symmetry in balance with chaos. I wandered a long time before the Architect found me. He showed me how the chaos was contained, and the perfection of design."

"You learned patterns," I said.

A faint nod. Something in his eyes acknowledged that I understood more than most.

"Patterns," he echoed. "Geometry. Real relationships. The way force moves when it isn't constrained by our rules. The way intention becomes something you can trace. The Architect has been working for centuries to build a better world on both sides of the Veil."

He looked down at his hands, then back up.

Arnaut's expression tightened, but not with fear. With something more complicated. Respect, yes. Awe, maybe. And something that looked uncomfortably like gratitude.

"He was not confined there," Arnaut said. "He was not trapped like I was. He moved like he belonged. He could walk through the Veil the way you walk through a doorway."

My stomach turned.

"He can cross freely?" I asked.

Arnaut held my gaze.

"Yes," he said. "Not through weak points. Not through rifts. Not through cracks carved by despair or desperation. He crosses like he knows where the seams are. As if he can step between breaths."

A silence arose between us, heavy and immediate.

"He taught you," I said, and it wasn't a question.

"No," Arnaut said. "The Architect is ancient James. Far older than us. Perhaps older than history itself. That knowledge is his alone. He showed me what the Veil actually is, not what we thought it was. He showed me why it fails. Why it has always been failing. And he made me see the lie at the center of everything we've done."

"What lie?" I asked.

Arnaut's voice lowered.

"That we were in control," he said as he sat back, then rubbed his thumb against the edge of his cup like it grounded him.

"I believed him," he admitted. "Not because he promised me power or because he threatened me. What he said fit the shape of what I had always sensed but never dared to name. The way the world keeps repeating its mistakes. The way people keep burning each other in God's name. The way our work kept becoming maintenance of a system that demanded sacrifice forever."

The words landed with an old ache. Bram. The smoke. De Montfort saying burn them all. Arnaut watching two Watchmen murder a town with magic that should not exist.

"And the Vatican craft," I said carefully. "The magic they taught Gerhard and Marko. The corruption."

Arnaut's eyes flickered, and for a moment I saw him on that ridge above Bram, smelling the smoke and realizing something in the air was wrong.

"That was the first time I heard the song," he said.

"The song."

He nodded once, jaw tight.

"It lies underneath the old forms," he said. "It makes the magic we were taught feel slow. Small. It makes restraint feel like cowardice. I hated it when I first sensed it. I called it poison. I meant it." He swallowed. "But when I returned, I was offered to learn this new magic. I thought about what I could do with that power. How much more I could serve the cause. I spent years studying it with the Vatican mages. Over time, I learned its song. It changed me too. I was more confident, more certain. I think the Vatican knew that. Rome opened a door. I walked through it."

The confession was quiet, but honest. Worse than bravado.

"Rome never offered me that door." I said.

"Because of who you are," he said simply. "You were never truly the Church's man. You questioned authority, exercised free will, showed restraint. That didn't fit with the soldiers Rome desired."

"So, when you crossed over in Jerusalem that song got louder?" I asked.

"It did," Arnaut replied. "Because the other side rewards that part of you. The part that can stop thinking in terms of mercy. The part that can treat people like components."

He stared at his coffee.

"I came back with that voice in my head and called it purpose," he said. "I came back believing I had finally seen the world as it truly was."

"What changed?" I asked.

He was quiet for a moment.

Then he said, "Oh, I still believe in the purpose. It's the means to that end that troubles me. The Architect offers beauty and structure. I admire that. But I have seen too much chaos and destruction in how some of us have carried out the vision."

He said it like a burden.

"Dina." I said flatly.

"Her, and others. The Architect uses her as a weapon, like how the Church use the Watch. But she is pure chaos, pure corruption. The Architect says we need her, but it troubles me. I don't believe her goals and the Architect's are the same."

"But Grant Park, that was hardly order and symmetry," I rebutted.

"Grant Park was supposed to be clean," he continued. "Surgical. A demonstration. A proof of concept. Instead, it became... personal. Messy. Human."

His eyes lifted.

"And every action since then has been messier than the last," he said. "The certainty I came back with... it's harder to hold onto than I expected. The longer I am away from the other side, the more uncertain I become. Finding you again has only complicated that."

"You're losing faith in the plan?" I asked.

"No," Arnaut said immediately, then caught himself. His fingers tightened on the cup.

"The plan is sound," he said, slower now. "The vision is correct. But the execution..." He looked down at his hands. "I used to know how to proceed. Every step clear. After facing you, after seeing what you were willing to do to stop me, I find myself questioning the methods even while I'm committed to the outcome."

The backgammon pieces clicked again. One of the old men muttered something in Arabic. The other laughed.

"You came back corrupted," I said.

"I came back changed," Arnaut replied. "Perhaps corruption to you. I prefer evolution. It depends on your perspective."

"My perspective is that I have a friend dead, two keepers dead, a guardian severely injured."

Arnaut looked like he had been punched, but carried on. "The Veil is a barrier, James. It keeps things separate that maybe shouldn't be. What if opening it isn't destruction? What if it's progress?"

"Progress toward what?" I asked a bit too harshly, or perhaps not harsh enough.

Arnaut's hand tightened on his cup.

"A world where the boundaries between possible and impossible aren't dictated by ancient rules we were never taught and that we don't fully understand," he said. "Where power isn't locked behind walls maintained by guardians who've forgotten why they're guarding in the first place."

"Are you trying to convince me or yourself?" I asked.

He looked at me sharply. Then his expression softened. Almost smiled. Almost.

He gave a tired smile. "You see? That's the gift. You look at something and immediately see the complexity. The doubt."

"Then stop," I said. "Think about what you're really doing."

"Stop what?"

"Whatever this is. Whatever the Architect is planning. Walk away from it."

Arnaut shook his head slowly.

"I won't."

"Why not?"

"Because I've gone too far," he said. "I believe what I do is to make a better world. Even if I wanted to stop, even if I..." He paused. "There's no walking away from this now."

"There's always a choice."

"That's naive, James," Arnaut said, but there was no bite in it. Just fatigue. "Some choices close doors. Some actions can't be undone."

He leaned forward slightly and my mind went to David.

"I attacked Grant Park because I believed," he said. "No doubts. No hesitation. I was certain."

"And now?"

He was quiet for a long moment.

"Now I understand why you hesitated so often," he said. "Why you questioned every decision. It's not weakness. It's seeing the whole picture instead of just the parts you want to see. I am finding it harder to find any clarity, and clarity was something I took pride in."

"If you see the whole picture," I said carefully, "then you know what happens if the Architect succeeds. The Veil doesn't just open. It reshapes. And whatever comes through those new doors won't be controlled by anyone, but him."

"The Architect can control that," Arnaut said, but the words sounded like he was reciting them from memory. "He will better our world. Make people see what is possible."

"Do you truly believe that? How many more Dina's are there out there Arnaut?"

Arnaut's expression tightened.

"I believe the current system is failing," he said. "I believe people need something more to believe in. It's not just my lack of clarity. It's the world around us too."

"That's not an answer."

"It's the only answer I have."

The server appeared. Set down a plate of dates and almonds. Disappeared again.

"Why am I here, Arnaut?" I asked. "What do you actually want?"

He looked at me. Really looked at me. And for a moment, I saw something in his eyes that reminded me of the old Arnaut. The one before Jerusalem. Before Anglesey. Before Bram. Before the corruption had found a home in his thinking.

"I wanted to warn you," he said quietly.

I didn't move.

"I wanted to warn you before more people die," Arnaut continued. "Because Dina is... uncontrolled. Because she treats this like sport. I don't believe she cares about the vision. And because the more blood she spills, the more enemies we create that we don't need."

"You said that already," I replied.

Arnaut's jaw tightened.

"You dragged her through the portal," I said.

"I did."

"Why?"

Arnaut's eyes flickered toward the door like he expected Dina to step through it any second.

"Because I meant what I told you," he said, voice low, "we were sent for you. To bring you back to the Architect. So he could share what he plans. I had already failed; Dina didn't even try. That's twice she changed the plan on me. In Rome, and now in Jaffa."

He let the silence sit there. Let me understand what that meant. The break. The line crossed. The Architect's careful coalition splintering from the inside.

"You hate her," I said.

"She is dangerous," Arnaut replied. "Perhaps I have gained a little insight on how you felt about me for many years." His voice tightened. "She has a personal interest in you. Personal gets sloppy. Sloppy gets noticed. Noticed gets stopped."

"And you don't want to be stopped yet," I said.

Arnaut's mouth twitched.

"Of course not," he admitted.

Outside, children's voices rose in play. A woman called out in Arabic. Someone laughed.

We were going around in circles, so I changed the subject. "Scotland," I said.

Arnaut's eyes flickered. Surprise, then something else. Maybe concern or worry.

"So, you know," he said, a statement, not a question. Just a fact he seemed to already be aware of.

"We figured it out," I replied, "the pattern, the convergence, the terminus."

Arnaut nodded once.

"Of course you did," he said.

"Tell me what happens there."

Arnaut was quiet for a moment, considering. Not whether to answer, but how.

"You keep saying Scotland like it's a destination," he said finally. "Like it's a problem with a pin in a map."

"It's where the lines go," I said.

"They do, and more." He paused again before continuing. "It's where they want you to go."

My stomach tightened.

"They want us there."

"Yes," Arnaut said. "Because Scotland is not just a terminus. It's bait."

He leaned forward again. His voice dropped low enough that the backgammon men couldn't have heard it even if they cared.

"The Architect does not fear you," he said. "He fears variables. Dina and I could not deliver you, so he is bringing you to him."

I didn't blink.

"You and your friends have become variables," Arnaut continued. "You improvise. You disrupt. You don't behave the way models predict. Scotland was, in part, designed to pull you into a place where the variables can be contained."

"A trap," I said.

"Scotland is not what you think it is," Arnaut said carefully. "The Architect doesn't build battlefields. He builds systems. And systems are designed to remove variables."

"You're telling me to stay away."

"I'm telling you that if you go, understand what you're walking into. The convergence point exists, yes. But the Architect has accounted for your interference. He's planned for it."

"How?"

Arnaut shook his head. "I've already said too much. Just... be careful. Dina will be there. And she won't show the restraint I have."

My hands curled against the edge of the table.

"That's the part you haven't accounted for," Arnaut said. " You think you can arrive, stop it, and leave. James, you won't get to choose when you leave."

My throat tightened.

"Why tell me any of this?" I asked. Arnaut's eyes held mine.

"Because I am tired," he said. "And because I don't want you to die for nothing."

"Nothing?"

"When the Architect's plan succeeds, the world changes regardless of whether you oppose it." He paused. "I would rather you survived to see which future we get. That feels like the last piece of honor I have left."

I didn't speak.

He glanced down at his hands again.

"The magic Rome taught me," he said quietly, "it does something to your thoughts. It changes what feels acceptable. It makes cruelty feel efficient. It makes restraint feel foolish."

He swallowed.

"And for a long time, I leaned into that," he admitted. "Because it made things easier. Cleaner. Because doubt is exhausting. It was for me long before that, but you know that."

His eyes lifted.

"But lately," he said, "I have moments where I can hear myself again. The part of me that used to care about honor. About the difference between necessary and convenient. Seeing you again, and the strength you have held onto over centuries. I remembered. I remembered what Geoffrey taught us. I remembered your convictions. I...remembered the things that I have done."

He exhaled slowly.

"Perhaps I have been able to separate the goal from the actions we're taking to achieve it," he said. "Perhaps I've just realized how tired I am, and that I'd forgotten a life I left behind long ago."

The backgammon game ended. One of the old men stood, stretched, left coins on the table. The other stayed behind, packing up the board.

"Why did you really drag Dina through that portal?" I asked.

Arnaut was quiet for a long moment.

"Because when I saw your face," he said slowly, "when I saw you kneeling there holding your friend while he died, I remembered something. Something I'd buried."

"What?"

"That I used to care," Arnaut said. "Not in theory. In practice. About what it costs to do the wrong thing for the right reason."

He stood.

"I should go," he said. "This has already been longer than wise."

"Arnaut."

He paused.

"You don't have to do this," I said. "Whatever the Architect promised you, whatever you think you owe him..."

"I owe him the truth," Arnaut cut in quietly. "I've been forbidden to come to Scotland. Dina convinced the Architect I'm compromised. That seeing you has made me unreliable."

"Has it?"

He didn't answer immediately. "I still believe in the vision. But I no longer trust how we're achieving it. That's not the same as betrayal. I know I can't talk you out of going, but know this. You're stepping into a trap. I don't think Dina will restrain herself, even in the Architect's company. You cannot stop this now, so consider this a warning and a small debt repaid. The Architect has planned all of this. I don't want you to get yourself killed fighting the inevitable."

"So, this warning," I said carefully, "is you trying to save me from a battle you think I've already lost."

Arnaut's silence was answer enough.

He pulled some shekels from his pocket. Set them on the table.

"For what it's worth," he said, "I don't want to see you killed because of a madwoman's whims."

He hesitated at the edge of the room, then looked back.

He turned, and then he was gone.

I sat there alone. The coffee going cold.

The server appeared. Looked at the empty chair. At me.

"Your friend has left?" he asked in accented English.

"Yes, he's gone." The word *friend* turned over in my head. Could he ever be again after all that has happened between us?

I left the café and walked back through the Old City. The afternoon was cool and comfortable. It gave me the opportunity to think as I walked back to the compound.

By the time I reached Jaffa Gate, I'd made my decision.

We'd go to Scotland. We'd place Charlie's device. We'd stop the Architect's plan.

And if Arnaut was lying to me and he was there when it happened, if he was standing between us and that terminus point, I'd do what needed doing. I hoped that he wouldn't. I hoped that there was something left in him to trust. But I was no fool, and I couldn't risk taking chances with my friend's lives.

Cori was waiting at the gate. She fell into step beside me without a word.

"Well?" she asked after a block.

"He warned me," I said. "Confirmed Scotland. And told me something else."

"What did he say?"

"That Scotland is a trap," I said, watching her for a reaction.

Cori's expression didn't change, but I saw her tense beside me, as if she'd been expecting that and still hated hearing it out loud.

"Why would he tell you that?" she asked.

"Because he's tired," I said. "Doubting. But still committed. It's like watching someone drown in slow motion while they tell you they chose to swim here."

"Do you believe him?"

I thought about Arnaut's face. The weariness. The brief flashes of something like disgust when he spoke about Dina. The way he said he could feel the fog lifting, like it surprised him.

"I don't know," I said. "Maybe. If we stop the plan. If we break whatever hold the Architect has on him. But Cori..."

"What?"

"He's gone too far," I said. "Done too much. Even if we save him from the Architect, I'm not sure we can save him from himself."

She nodded. We walked in silence.

Jerusalem continued around us. Ancient. Stubborn. Refusing to give up even after millennia of people breaking themselves against its stones.

Maybe there was a lesson in that.

Maybe endurance was its own kind of victory.

We'd find out in two days.

As we walked through the Keeper compound, we stopped short as a voice came from behind us. Sharp. Hurt.

"You went to meet Arnaut?"

We both turned.

Casey stood ten feet back. Her face was pale except for two spots of color high on her cheeks. Her hands were clenched at her sides. David's journal clutched in one fist.

I felt Cori's hand find my arm. Steady. Grounding.

"Casey..." I started.

"You went to meet Arnaut," she repeated. Not a question. An accusation wrapped in disbelief. "David has been dead for less than twenty-four hours and you went to have a conversation with one of the men who helped kill him."

I opened my mouth. Closed it. What could I say? She was right.

"He called me," I managed finally. "He wanted to talk."

"So what?" Casey crossed the distance between us in three strides. Cori's hand tightened on my arm but she didn't move away. "So what if he called you? You just go running? Like he's still your friend? Like he didn't help orchestrate everything that's happening?"

I took it. Let the words hit. Added them to everything else I was carrying.

"Casey, I..."

"David trusted you." Her voice cracked on his name. "He looked up to you.

He ran back into that square because he thought you needed help. And this is how you honor that? By sneaking off to meet the people who killed him?"

"I wasn't sneaking," I said quietly. "We need answers." It was true, but there was more to it, and Casey knew that.

"You didn't tell me. You didn't tell Charlie. You didn't tell Eliyahu." She was shaking now, tears streaming down her face. "Because you knew we'd try to stop you. Because you knew it was wrong."

I couldn't argue with that. She was right. I had known.

Cori's presence beside me was the only thing keeping me grounded.

"Do you know what I did today?" Casey asked. Her voice was quieter now but more intense. "I found his backpack. I spent three hours going through David's things. His books. His notes. His stupid collection of fountain pens he was so proud of."

She held up the journal.

"He kept a journal. Did you know that? Started it after Grant Park. Wrote about the work. About feeling useful for the first time. About being part of something that mattered."

Her hand was shaking so badly the journal trembled.

"The last entry was from yesterday morning. Before dinner. Before Jaffa." She swallowed hard. "He wrote about how excited he was about the acquisition. How proud he was of the work." Her voice broke completely. "How grateful he was that you gave him a chance to be part of this."

The words hit like physical blows. My chest tightened. Cori shifted slightly closer.

"And you repay that," Casey continued, "by running off to save the soul of one of the men who took him from us."

"I'm not trying to save..." I started, but she cut me off.

"Yes, you are!" She was crying openly now. "You're trying to save Arnaut. Trying to find some piece of your old friend. Trying to convince yourself that he can be redeemed. And I need you to stop. I need you to accept that he's gone. That the Arnaut you knew doesn't exist anymore. That the man you met today is the enemy. We have all risked our lives to stop him. He put us in the hospital, and David is dead."

I stood there taking it. All of it. The grief. The anger. The accusation. Another weight added to the pile I'd been carrying for nine hundred and sixty years.

"When you get to Scotland," Casey said, her voice steadier now, hard, "if Arnaut is there, if he's standing between us and stopping this, what are you going to do?"

The question hung in the air.

I felt Cori's hand on my arm. Felt her waiting. Felt Casey staring at me with David's journal still clutched in her hand.

"I'll do what needs to be done," I said quietly.

"Will you?" Casey's eyes were red but her gaze was steady. "Because from where I'm standing, you can't even stay away from him when he calls. How am I supposed to believe you'll do what's necessary when it matters?"

"Casey," Cori said gently, "that's not fair."

"Who are you to say that? You weren't there at the park. You barely know David. He was my friend." She said the last part in absolute tears. She looked up at both of us, eyes bloodshot and tears on her cheeks. She looked at Cori. "I know you care about him. I know you're trying to support him. But someone needs to make sure he's thinking clearly. Because right now, I'm not sure he is."

"Casey..." I implored, but it was too little too late. She turned and stormed back into the compound.

I watched her go in silence. My heart ached seeing her like that. The truth is, she was closer to being right than I wanted to admit. One more burden to bury for the moment. We had work to do and plans to make and I would have to defer my own pain once again.

20

Thunder, Trails, and the Lakota (Dakota Territory, 1867)

The Powder River Basin spread before me like an ocean of grass turned gold by summer heat. I'd been riding for three days through country that made you feel small. Big sky. Bigger land. Emptiness that wasn't empty at all if you knew how to look.

The message had reached me in Centerville a month earlier. A trader who knew someone who knew someone. The Lakota needed help. Would I come.

I came.

I'd visited them before, years back, when I was trying to understand the creature sleeping beneath Ohio. The Wendigo had been waking, thrashing in dreams I didn't understand. The Lakota had experience with beings like that. Creatures tied to land and season and the space between worlds. They'd taught me how to read its moods. How to calm it when winter made it restless. How to recognize when it needed to be left alone.

Practical knowledge. You couldn't find it in books.

When they asked for help, I didn't hesitate.

The camp sat in a valley where the river bent around a stand of cottonwoods. Maybe forty lodges spread in careful arrangement, each one positioned with the entrance facing east to greet the morning sun. The lodges were substantial, fifteen to twenty feet across, constructed from tanned buffalo hide stretched over lodgepole frames. Some had geometric designs painted near the smoke flaps. Others showed scenes of hunts or battles, the images faded by weather but still clear.

Smoke rose from cook fires scattered throughout the camp. The smell of roasting meat mixed with sage and sweetgrass. Drying racks stood between the lodges, laden with thin strips of buffalo meat turning dark in the sun. Nearby, women worked fresh hides staked to the ground, scraping them clean with tools made from bone and stone. Their hands moved with practiced efficiency, stretching and working the leather until it softened.

Children ran between the lodges, playing some game involving sticks and a great deal of shouting. A group of boys raced small hoops down a clear stretch of ground, using long poles to keep them rolling. Girls sat in the shade, working on beadwork under their mothers' watchful eyes.

Men gathered in small groups throughout the camp. Some sat on buffalo robes spread in the shade, talking, cleaning rifles and checking arrows. Others tended to horses in a large herd grazing near the river. Young warriors practiced with bows, shooting at targets set up in the tall grass beyond the lodges.

It looked peaceful.

It wasn't.

I could see it in the way the men sat. In how the women kept glancing toward the ridge. In the number of horses kept close and ready. This was a camp preparing for something.

A young man intercepted me before I reached the lodges. He was maybe twenty, rifle held easy across his saddle, posture relaxed but alert. He studied me for a moment, then nodded.

"James Crable," he said. Not a question.

"Yes."

"Akeechita. Red Cloud is expecting you. Follow me," he instructed me, using the Lakota honorific for soldier and protector.

We walked through the camp. People watched but didn't stare. A few nodded. One old woman said something in Lakota that made the young man smile.

"She says you haven't changed," he translated. "She remembers you from before. Says it's good you keep your word."

"Tell her I try."

The young man led me to a lodge larger than the others, perhaps twenty-five feet across. Painted designs circled the base, geometric patterns in red and black. The hide covering showed careful maintenance, patches sewn with precision, the whole structure tight and weatherproof.

He pulled back the entrance flap and gestured for me to enter.

Inside, four men sat around a small fire. The interior was cooler than outside, the hide walls filtering the harsh sunlight into a warm glow. Buffalo robes and woven blankets lined the floor. Weapons hung from the lodge poles. A pipe rested on a wooden stand near the fire.

I recognized Red Cloud immediately. Older now, lines deeper around his eyes, but the same intelligence and controlled intensity I remembered. The other three I didn't know, but their bearing said they were leaders. Men who made decisions that people lived or died by.

Red Cloud gestured to an empty place in the circle. I sat.

For a moment, no one spoke. The fire crackled softly. Outside, children's voices rose in laughter.

"You came quickly," Red Cloud said finally. His English was precise, barely accented. Better than half the officers I'd met in the Army.

"You asked. That's enough."

"The last time we met, you asked us about the Wendigo near your home in Ohio. We told you what we knew. Shared what our grandfathers taught us."

"You did. And it helped. The creature is calmed. Quiet now."

Red Cloud nodded. "You understand that some things must be protected. That there are places where the boundary grows thin. Where guardians keep watch."

"I understand."

One of the other men spoke. Older, gray in his braids, scars on his arms that spoke of old fights. "The Army is building a road. They call it the Bozeman Trail. It cuts through our hunting grounds on treaty land they swore to leave alone."

His voice was matter-of-fact. No anger. Just stating the situation.

"Promises are again broken, and we are left with no choice but to protect our people and land," another man added. Younger, hard-eyed. "Fetterman. We killed him and eighty men last winter. They keep coming anyway."

"They want the road for the gold fields in Montana," Red Cloud said. "Miners. Settlers. All heading north. The trail saves them time. The army says they need forts to protect the travelers."

"And the guardian?" I asked.

Red Cloud's expression didn't change, but something shifted in his eyes. "The trail they're building. The forts they're placing. They cut across sacred ground. Ground where the Thunderbird watches."

The hair on my arms lifted.

I'd heard stories about the Thunderbird during my last visit. Creature of storm and wind. Guardian tied to high places where sky met earth. Powerful enough that even mentioning it required care. The Lakota had spoken of it with the same practical reverence they used for the Wendigo in Ohio. Real. Present. Necessary to respect.

"Show me," I said.

We rode out an hour later. Red Cloud, two of his warriors, and me. North along the river, then up into the hills where pine trees grew thick and the air smelled of resin and stone.

The land changed as we climbed. Got quieter. Even the wind seemed to move more carefully here.

We reached a plateau where the grass grew short and tough. Rock formations jutted from the earth like broken teeth. Storm clouds gathered on the horizon, dark and heavy, though the sky above us stayed clear.

"There," Red Cloud said, pointing.

At first, I saw nothing. Then the light shifted and I caught it. A shimmer in the air. Not quite visible. Not quite hidden. Heat rising off stone in summer, but wrong. Deliberate.

The Veil seemed to be thinning here. I could sense it. Too many intrusions, too many broken promises.

And something massive moved on the other side.

I dismounted and walked closer. The pressure built with each step. Presence. Something vast and ancient and utterly focused.

The Thunderbird. I had seen guardians before, but this inspired awe. Even in me.

"It's been here longer than our people have stories," Red Cloud said quietly. He'd come to stand beside me. "Our grandfathers' grandfathers knew to respect this place. To leave offerings. To pass through quietly when passing was necessary."

"And the Army wants to build through here?"

"Not through. Next to. Close enough that it doesn't matter. The forts they're planning, one would sit right there." He pointed to a spot perhaps two hundred yards from where we stood. "Soldiers. Wagons. Noise. All of it pressing against the boundary."

I could see it. Feel it. The guardian site worked because of silence. Isolation. The Thunderbird held the Veil steady here because nothing disturbed it. Put a fort beside it and the structure would strain. Maybe hold. Maybe not.

"How long until they start building?" I asked.

"They've already started. Fort Phil Kearny is finished south of here. They're surveying for the next one now. Carrington commands the operation. But there's another officer. A colonel. He's the one pushing the specific routes."

"I'll speak with him and see if I can try diplomacy and logic."

Red Cloud looked at me. "You can try. We've tried. They don't listen, and so we fight. To them, this is empty land. They see grass and sky and imagine nothing underneath that matters."

"Maybe I can make them understand."

"Perhaps." Red Cloud didn't sound convinced. "The colonel is based in Fort Phil Kearny. Unlike most officers, he seems to be a kind man, but stubborn. He is set on his plan, and accepted no negotiation from us."

Fort Phil Kearny sat in a valley like a scar on the landscape. Raw timber walls. Buildings laid out in neat rows. The American flag snapping in the wind. Everything ordered and angular and completely convinced of its own permanence.

I approached in the early afternoon. Sentries challenged me from the walls. I gave my name and said I was there to speak with the commanding officer.

They made me wait an hour before opening the gates. It wasn't every day a lone man walked up to a frontier military outpost.

Inside, the fort smelled of fresh-cut pine and horses and men living too close together. Soldiers watched me with the wary curiosity men showed strangers in hostile territory. I didn't blame them. They'd lost eighty men to Red Cloud's ambush. They had every reason to be nervous.

An aide led me to the headquarters building. A long structure with a covered porch and narrow windows. Inside was cooler, dim after the bright sunlight.

Two officers waited. One was clearly in command, middle-aged, tired-looking, with the expression of a man carrying more responsibility than he wanted.

The other stood by the window.

He was younger. Maybe forty. Tall and lean. He moved with gracefulness that seemed more priest than warrior.

And he was pale.

Not sickly pale. Not sun-starved. Something else. His skin was the color of snow in moonlight. His hair was white, not gray, not blonde, but white like fresh snow, pulled back in a style twenty years out of fashion. His eyes were ice blue, crystalline in the dim light.

He smiled when he saw me. Warm. Genuine.

The older officer stood. "Mr. Crable. Colonel Henry Carrington. This is Colonel Lindgren."

Lindgren extended his hand. I shook it. His grip was firm, his palm dry despite the summer heat. His fingers long and thin. Hands too smooth for a frontier military officer.

"Well met, Mr. Crable," Lindgren said. His voice carried a faint accent, maybe Scandinavian heritage, but his English was perfect. "It's a pleasure to welcome you."

Carrington gestured to chairs. "I understand you want to discuss the trail route."

"I do. Specifically, the section north of here. The one that runs near the plateau with the rock formations."

Lindgren tilted his head slightly. "Interesting section. Challenging terrain. But necessary for proper alignment."

"Why that specific path?" I asked. "There are other ways north."

"Several," Lindgren agreed. "But, none as efficient. We need a grade that wagons can manage. Access to water at regular intervals. Clear sight lines for defense. The route we've surveyed meets all those requirements."

"It also runs very close to ground the Lakota consider sacred and are protected by treaty," I said.

Carrington sighed. "Mr. Crable, I respect native beliefs. Truly. But we have an obligation to protect travelers on this road. That requires forts at specific intervals. We can't choose locations based on spiritual concerns."

"This isn't spiritual. It's practical. That ground is unstable. Settling it would be dangerous."

Lindgren's eyebrows rose slightly. "Unstable how? We've had surveyors examine the plateau thoroughly. The ground is solid. Excellent drainage. No sign of seismic activity."

"Not unstable in that way. There are..." I paused, choosing words carefully, "there are natural phenomena in that area that react poorly to disruption. Building there would be unwise."

"What phenomena?" Carrington asked.

I couldn't explain the Veil. Couldn't describe the Thunderbird. They'd think I was insane or mocking them.

"Atmospheric disturbances," I said finally. "Severe storms form there with unusual frequency. Lightning strikes. High winds. Putting men and supplies in that location, would be asking for losses."

Lindgren smiled again. That same warm expression. "I appreciate your concern, Mr. Crable. But the army has experience building in difficult conditions. We can handle storms, I assure you. When the railroad comes, it won't present an issue."

"Not these storms."

"Then we'll find out." His tone stayed pleasant, but something in it suggested the conversation was over. "The route has been finalized.

Surveying is complete. The alignment is optimal. Construction begins next month."

"You could choose a different path," I said. "One mile east would avoid the worst of it."

"One mile east disrupts the entire alignment," Lindgren said before Carrington could answer. "It creates inefficiencies at three separate points along the route. The current path provides perfect geometric alignment with the terrain. Minimal grading required. Optimal sight lines. Everything positioned correctly for the railroad that will follow. We aren't just planning for today, you see. Our vision is one of the future."

He leaned forward slightly, enthusiasm creeping into his voice. "You see, Mr. Crable, it's not just about this fort. It's about the entire system: roads, rails, telegraph lines and so forth. All of it must align properly. One degree off here creates problems for miles in either direction. We've calculated the angles precisely. This route provides the correct alignment for everything that comes after."

Something about the way he said it made me pause. The focus on alignment. The precision. The certainty that everything had to be positioned perfectly.

But I was focused on the guardian site. On the Thunderbird. On the immediate threat.

"I'm asking you to reconsider," I said. "For everyone's safety and to honor the oaths bound by treaty."

Carrington spread his hands. "I can't, Mr. Crable. My orders come from Washington. The route is set. Colonel Lindgren has assured me the alignment is correct, and I trust his engineering expertise. But I appreciate you coming here. Shows good faith."

There was no point arguing further. They'd made their decision. Nothing I said would change it.

Lindgren walked me to the door.

"I understand your position," he said quietly. "Truly. But progress requires certain sacrifices. The railroad will follow this trail within a decade. Proper alignment now saves effort later. Everything must be positioned correctly. Alignment matters, Mr. Crable. Get them wrong and the entire structure suffers. Surely you see the logic."

"I see it," I said. "I just don't agree with it."

"Perhaps not. But history moves in one direction. We can work with it or be swept aside. I prefer to work with it. To align myself with what's coming rather than resist it. We plan in years, decades even. Not weeks or months."

He offered his hand again. I shook it. The same firm grip. The same dry palm.

"Safe travels, Mr. Crable. I hope we meet again under better circumstances."

I left Fort Phil Kearny, knowing I'd failed.

I rode back to Red Cloud's camp as the sun dropped toward the western hills. The shadows grew long. The air turned cool. By the time I reached the valley, stars were beginning to show.

Red Cloud listened to my report without interruption. When I finished, he nodded once.

"They won't change the route," I said. "I'm sorry."

"We didn't expect them to. But we needed to know for certain. Now we do."

One of the other men spoke in Lakota. Red Cloud responded. They went back and forth for a minute, their voices calm and measured despite whatever they were planning.

Finally Red Cloud turned back to me. "The fort construction starts next month. We'll be ready. Will you help?"

"Of course. I can't fight your war for you, but I can keep them away from the guardian site. Where should we start?"

"The guardian site specifically. That's where they'll strike first to try to establish position before we can react. If you can keep them away from the plateau, we can handle the rest."

"I'll keep them away."

"Good." Red Cloud stood. "Rest tonight. Eat. In the morning we'll show you the ground and explain the plan."

The attack came three weeks later.

The Army moved a construction detail north with an escort of forty soldiers.

Wagons loaded with timber and tools. Surveyors with their instruments. Engineers marking out where the new fort would stand.

They reached the plateau at midday.

Red Cloud's warriors were already waiting.

I won't pretend I understood all their tactics. The way they moved, appeared, and vanished, struck and withdrew. The coordination between different groups. The timing that came from years of fighting on this exact ground.

But I understood enough to stay out of their way.

My job was specific. Keep the soldiers away from the guardian site itself. From the place where the Veil ran thinnest and the Thunderbird watched.

The first soldiers who tried to establish position near the rock formations met me instead.

I didn't harm them. Didn't need to. Just made it impossible for them to stay. Rocks sliding under their feet. Tools breaking at crucial moments. Sudden winds that made their tents tear loose and scatter.

Small things. Irritating things. Things that made holding that specific ground more trouble than it was worth.

Meanwhile, Red Cloud's warriors tore into the main force. Hit them from three sides at once. Drove them back toward the tree line. Cut off their supply wagons.

It was over in two hours.

The Army retreated south, leaving tools and supplies scattered across the plateau. Fifteen men dead. Twenty wounded.

By evening, the construction detail was back at Fort Phil Kearny, and the new fort plan was officially under review.

Two weeks later, I heard they'd changed the route. Moved it east, away from the plateau. Added a few days to the journey time, but avoided the worst of the terrain.

Colonel Lindgren was reassigned. Sent back east. Carrington stayed another year before being replaced himself.

The Bozeman Trail continued operating for a while. Then the Army abandoned the forts entirely after more fighting. Too expensive. Too many losses. Not worth it.

Red Cloud's War, they called it later.

I stayed long enough to verify the guardian site was safe. I spoke with the elders and shared knowledge of the guardians and their safekeeping. The Thunderbird returned to its watch. The Veil remained stable.

Before I left, I met with Red Cloud one last time.

"Thank you," he said simply.

"You won this. I just helped with one piece."

"One important piece. Without it, the rest doesn't work."

We sat in silence for a moment, watching the sun set over the hills.

"The Army will come back," Red Cloud said finally. "Maybe not here. Maybe not soon. But they'll come. There will always be another trail. Another fort. Another reason why the land we protect doesn't matter to them."

"I know."

"But not today. Today we won. Today the guardian is safe. That's enough."

He was right.

It was enough.

I left the Powder River Basin a week later, riding south toward civilization and rail lines and cities where people lived without thinking about the boundaries between worlds.

The Thunderbird was safe.

Red Cloud had won his war.

The trail had been rerouted.

That was what mattered.

The Veil held for another day.

21

Comms, Fractures, and the Architect (Jerusalem and Scotland, Present)

"This is it," Charlie said, holding up the device.

We were gathered in the lower chamber of the Keeper compound in Jerusalem. Maps covered the tables. Data streams ran across Charlie's laptop. The device sat in the center of everything capturing the full attention of the room.

It was smaller than I'd expected. About the size of a thick paperback book. The casing was carbon fiber, black and matte. But the surface was covered in silver tracings, sigils etched into the material itself. They caught the light strangely, seeming to shift and move even when the device was perfectly still.

"The EMP," Charlie continued, "works by creating a localized interference pattern across Veil frequencies. When activated, it generates a pulse that disrupts magical synchronization within approximately a one-kilometer radius."

He set it down carefully.

"The sigils are the containment lattice. They hold the charge stable until release. When you press this," he indicated a recessed button on the side, "the lattice collapses. All the stored energy dumps at once. Think of it like... a magical flashbang. Everything in range gets scrambled."

"And the Architect's network?" Eliyahu asked.

"Should collapse. His whole system depends on precise geometric synchronization. If we hit the terminus point at the moment of activation, the interference should cascade back through the entire structure." Charlie pulled up the map of Scotland. "Here. This is where you need to be."

The location was marked in the Highlands. Remote. Nothing nearby for miles except mountains and lochs and old stone.

"The Glaistig's territory," Eliyahu said quietly.

"It's the only guardian site that hasn't been touched by the corruption yet. The Architect is using her node as the final convergence point," Charlie added. "All the corrupted frequencies from every attacked guardian location are channeling through her territory."

He pulled up another diagram, zooming in on the geometric pattern.

"The convergence has a structural weakness," Charlie continued. "Here." He pointed to a spot in the pattern. "The angles don't quite align. It's a tiny flaw, maybe point-three degrees off perfect, but that's where the whole structure is most vulnerable. That's where you activate the device."

"How do we find it?" Eliyahu asked.

"You'll feel it. The frequencies will be strongest there, but also... dissonant. Like a note that's almost right but not quite."

He handed the device to Eliyahu. He took it carefully, turning it over in his hands. The weight seemed to settle on him like responsibility made manifest.

"You need to reach the center of the convergence," Charlie said. "The exact geometric focal point. You'll sense it when you're close. Once you're in position, activate the device. The pulse will do the rest."

"What about us?" Cori asked. "What happens to anyone in the radius when it goes off?"

Charlie hesitated.

"I think you'll be fine," he said slowly. "The device is designed to target the Architect's corrupted network and the Veil structure itself. But I'm not entirely sure. You might feel disorientation. Nausea. Your own magic might scramble temporarily, disrupt your ability to use it for a short period. But you should recover."

"Should?" I asked.

"Should," Charlie confirmed. "I've never tested this. No one has. But theoretically, your magic operates on different frequencies. You'll feel the pulse, but it shouldn't do permanent damage."

"How long until we recover?" Lucan asked.

"Minutes. Maybe less. Maybe more. I don't know."

"And the Architect?"

"If he's there, if he's channeling corrupted power when the pulse hits..." Charlie shrugged. "Unknown. Best case, it breaks his concentration and disrupts his network. Worst case..." He trailed off.

Eliyahu carefully placed the device into a reinforced case.

"Communications," Charlie said, changing the subject. He pulled out a small case and opened it. Inside were eight earpieces. "Encrypted. Range is global as long as I'm at a terminal. You'll be able to reach me, and I can relay between you if needed."

He handed them out. Small. Discreet. I fitted mine into my ear. Charlie's voice came through immediately, testing the connection.

"Can you hear me?"

"Loud and clear," I replied.

The others nodded, adjusting their own pieces.

"Wait," Lucan said. "You call it an EMP. Won't that fry our comms gear?"

Charlie shook his head. "It's not a true electromagnetic pulse. It's tuned specifically to the magical frequencies the Architect is using and the Veil frequencies themselves. Your earpieces run on standard electronics. They'll be fine."

Rabbi Moshe, a Keeper Eliyahu had just introduced as part of the team, cleared his throat. He looked in his early thirties, with a close-trimmed beard and calm eyes. He wore simple clothes under his vest and carried himself like a man who had been trained to stand his ground. He had the quiet steadiness of someone who had learned discipline early and never let go of it.

Eliyahu glanced at him, the smallest nod of acknowledgment.

Moshe spoke softly, his Hebrew measured.

"Be strong and courageous," he said. "Do not be afraid."

He looked around the room, then met Eliyahu's eyes.

"We have faced worse," he added.

Eliyahu gave a faint smile. It was tired, but it was real.

Avraham, younger, maybe thirty if that, adjusted the straps on his vest. He carried himself like a soldier. Protective. Watchful. His eyes tracked the room constantly.

"The plan is sound," he said. "We get Eliyahu to the center. We hold the line. We activate the device. We leave." He looked at me. "Simple."

"Nothing about this is simple," I replied.

"Then we make it simple."

The third Keeper, Yael, nodded once. She was quiet and efficient. Her expression didn't change when she spoke.

"When do we leave?" she asked.

"Now," Eliyahu said. "The Architect's timeline is accelerating. If we wait, we lose the window."

We left within the hour.

The flight to Scotland was long. We flew in silence mostly, each of us preparing in our own way.

Cori sat beside me, her hand finding mine somewhere over England.

"You're thinking too much," she said quietly.

"I'm thinking the right amount."

"That's what worrying is."

"Then I'm worrying the right amount."

She squeezed my hand. "We'll be fine."

"You don't know that."

"I choose to believe it anyway."

We landed at a small airfield in Inverness. From there, a van took us north into the Highlands. The land changed as we drove. Gentler hills gave way to harder mountains. Trees thinned. Stone showed through like bones.

The sky was heavy. Gray clouds pressed down, turning the afternoon dim. Rain threatened but hadn't started yet.

"Ten kilometers," Charlie's voice came through the earpiece. "You're close."

The van stopped where the road ended. A dirt track continued, but not far. We'd walk the rest.

We geared up in silence. Light. Mobile. Nothing we couldn't carry or move with. The device went into a reinforced case on Eliyahu's back. The Keepers carried their own equipment. Weapons. Supplies. Sacred objects wrapped in cloth.

Lucan checked his sword.

"Stay close," I said. "Stay smart. If things go wrong, we scatter and regroup."

"Things will go wrong," Lucan replied. "They always do."

"Then we adapt."

We moved into the Highlands.

The landscape was beautiful in a harsh way. Mountains rose on either side of the glen, their peaks hidden in cloud. The ground was rough. Heather and rock and patches of bog that sucked at boots. A burn ran down the center of the valley, dark water moving fast over stones.

And ahead, maybe two kilometers distant, was the loch.

The loch sat in the valley like a wound.

The surrounding mountains leaned inward, their slopes dark with heather and broken stone. Mist clung to the surface, thick and low, refusing to burn off even under the gray afternoon light.

The air was wrong here. It was both too heavy and too quiet. Like the space between breaths before something terrible happens.

"The Glaistig's territory," Eliyahu said quietly.

I could feel the Veil here. Still strong. It was dense, stable, and hard. A reinforced boundary, layered and anchored into the earth. It was like standing beside a fortress wall. It didn't flex when the wind pushed. It didn't tremble under distant pressure. Whatever was happening elsewhere, whatever damage the Architect had done to other sites, this place still held.

That made it worse.

If he was using this as his convergence point, it was because he wanted the strongest structure available.

We moved carefully down the slope toward the water. The corruption

Charlie had mapped, all of it flowing toward this single point like water circling a drain.

The loch itself was maybe half a kilometer across. No boats. No buildings. No signs that humans had ever touched this place and survived the experience. Just black water and stone and the weight of something very old watching from the shadows.

"She's here," Eliyahu said quietly. "Watching."

I sensed it too. Old eyes. Patient. The Glaistig had guarded this territory for eons. Half woman, half goat, tied to the wild places humans feared to tread.

As we left the tree cover, we saw the figures on the far side of the loch. More than twenty of them standing in formation around a massive sigil carved into the stone. The geometry was precise and unnatural. It didn't look drawn. It looked engineered into the world.

And at the center, directing it all, was the Architect.

Tall. Thin. Snow-white hair hanging long and straight down his back. His face was sharp, almost too precise to be natural. But it was his eyes that locked me in place.

Ice blue.

Not cold with emotion. Cold with calculation.

For a heartbeat, the Highlands disappeared.

I was back in the Dakota Territory, a century and more ago, helping Red Cloud and his tribe protect the Thunderbird's land.

I remembered the man that greeted me inside Fort Phil Kearny. Colonel Lindgren. Hair that seemed out of place with the time. Eyes that watched the land like it was a diagram. He had spoken politely. Calmly. Like the wilderness was a classroom and he was simply waiting for the lesson to begin.

I had thought him harmless.

I had been wrong.

"That's the Architect," I said quietly.

Eliyahu turned his head slightly. "How do you know?"

I kept my eyes on the far shore.

"We have met before," I said. "A long time ago."

The Architect saw us at the same moment. He didn't react. He didn't raise an alarm. He simply watched as we approached. I had the feeling our arrival was part of the design.

We stopped maybe twenty meters from his position. Close enough to see the details. Far enough to move if we had to.

His followers were a mix. Sorcerers in dark robes. Creatures that looked human until they moved, until the angles of their bodies betrayed what they were. And Dina stood off to one side, her butterfly buckle gleaming even under the gray sky. She smiled when she saw me.

No Arnaut.

Part of me was relieved. Part of me felt the absence like a wound that had never closed properly.

The Architect stepped forward.

When he spoke, his voice carried without effort. Calm. Measured. Not a shout. Not a threat. Just certainty.

"Mister Crable," he said, "you have always been difficult to account for."

"You built this?" I asked.

"Isn't it beautiful?" he asked, spreading his hands to take in the construct.

He gestured to the sigil beneath his feet. The carved geometry seemed to catch the light wrong, lines shifting in my vision when I tried to focus on them too long.

"This took time," he continued. "Decades of small adjustments. Centuries of influence applied in the right places. You don't build a convergence by force. You build it by shaping what people already believe they want."

His gaze sharpened on me.

"And you have been an obstacle since before you understood what you were interfering with."

I didn't answer.

He took one slow step along the edge of the sigil.

"To you this seems very sudden, but I assure you, this is centuries in the making. Around the world I have toiled to get the symmetry just right. I suggested the right modifications at the right moments, at the right places, at the right times," he said. "Small changes. A shifted avenue in a city grid. A rotated axis on a rail line. A road intersection moved just enough to create the geometry I needed. People do the rest on their own. They call it planning. They call it vision. They never ask who benefits from the pattern once it exists."

He looked at me again.

"And then you ruined years of work by helping to shift the Bozeman Trail."

The words hit like a slap.

"You disrupted the line," the Architect said. "You broke the flow. You forced me to rebuild. It matters little. I have the time and the patience. One little setback is small in the grand design. I am a patient man, Mister Crable."

"You were manipulating routes," I said.

"I was guiding them," he replied. "There is a difference."

He lifted his hand, and the air around the sigil shimmered. The Veil frequencies were visible now, faint lines of force woven into the space above the stone.

"Select locations," he said, as if reading my thoughts. "Select nodes. Specific locations with specific purposes. You don't need the entire world to sing. You need the right notes, in the right places, at the right time."

Eliyahu stepped forward.

"So, you could reshape the Veil," he said.

"No! So I could perfect it," the Architect replied. His voice carried conviction. Real belief. "The Veil as it exists is flawed. Incomplete. It was never meant to be permanent. It's infrastructure from a forgotten age, maintained by guardians who inherited the work and forgot the reason."

"We have not forgotten," Eliyahu said.

"You have preserved fragments," the Architect replied. "You have maintained what you were taught to maintain. But you don't understand what it is. You don't understand what it could be."

Cori's hand tightened on her sword.

"By corrupting it," she said.

"By changing it," the Architect replied. "You call it corruption because you fear what you cannot control."

The wind picked up again. The loch rippled. The sigil beneath his feet held steady, unmoved by weather or time.

"You cannot stop this," he continued. "The network is aligned. The convergence is imminent. In minutes, the Veil will shift into its corrected form. Humanity will finally have access to what has been sealed away."

"Under your control," I said.

"Under my management and guidance," he replied. "Under structure. Under design."

Dina laughed.

"This is boring," she said. "Can we kill them now?"

The Architect didn't look at her. His eyes stayed on us.

"Not yet," he said. "They will witness what they tried to prevent."

Cori tensed beside me. Lucan shifted his footing. Zeke drew his sword, the blade dark against the gray light, and his grin widened like he had been waiting for permission.

"Charlie," I said quietly, knowing he could hear through the earpiece, "we're in position. Give us a countdown."

"Copy," Charlie replied. His voice was tight. Controlled. "Convergence reaches critical mass in approximately eight minutes. You need to reach the center and activate before then."

Eight minutes.

I looked at the Architect's position. At the carved geometry around the loch. At the forces arrayed between us and the convergence point.

"This is going to get messy," Lucan said.

"It always does," I replied.

I drew my power. Clean light. Centuries of discipline compressed into a single breath.

Beside me, Cori's hands began to glow.

Lucan raised his sword.

Zeke rolled his shoulders once and brought his blade up, stance loose, ready.

The Keepers formed up around Eliyahu. Rabbi Moshe began chanting in Hebrew. Avraham and Yael moved into position, blades ready, bodies angled to shield.

"For what it's worth," the Architect said, "I respect persistence. But persistence does not change outcome."

Then Dina moved.

She crossed the distance between us in seconds. Dark magic coiling around her hands. She hit Cori first, a whip of corrupted force aimed for her throat. Cori raised a barrier at the last instant, and the impact shoved her backward across the rock.

I hit Dina with everything I had. Clean power. Focused. Precise.

She deflected it and laughed.

"I've been waiting for this," she said with a smile.

Then the sorcerers attacked.

Dark bolts of energy. Corrupted fire. Force shaped into weapons that should not exist. They came at us from three sides, trying to pin us down, trying to separate us from Eliyahu.

The smell hit as the magic collided. Ozone and copper and something sweet and rotten underneath, like fruit left too long in the sun. Corrupted magic smelled wrong. Tasted wrong on the back of the tongue.

Lucan met the first wave with steel and light, his blade cutting through a bolt of shadow that should have torn him in half. The air around his sword flared white for an instant, then snapped back to gray.

Zeke moved like a man who had been told the world was ending and decided to enjoy himself. He met a creature head-on, his sword biting into flesh that felt wrong under the edge, like cutting through wet leather stretched over bone.

Cori surged forward again, her sword bright with power, her movements sharp and controlled. She drove a sorcerer back with three precise strikes, then slammed a palm out and sent a burst of clean force that shattered another man's barrier like glass.

The ground shook as magic hit stone. Each spell that landed sent vibrations through the rock. The loch's surface rippled with impacts. Birds fled from the surrounding peaks, their calls sharp and panicked. Corrupted fire splashed against the stone and hissed. Bolts of dark energy carved scars into the earth.

The air itself seemed bruised where dark magic had passed through it.

"Go," I shouted to Eliyahu. "We'll clear the path."

Eliyahu moved.

The Keepers went with him, Rabbi Moshe and Avraham tight on his flanks, Yael a half step behind, blade up, eyes scanning for the next strike.

We pushed forward in a wedge, driving into the space between the sorcerers. Every step was like walking into a storm.

A bolt of black force slammed into my chest. My wards weakened it, but pain flared across my ribs like a hammer blow.

I answered with light, a spear of power that punched through the air and slammed into the sorcerer who had cast it. He went down hard, smoke curling from his hands.

Dina laughed again and came for me.

She didn't carry a weapon. She didn't need one.

Her magic shaped itself into edges, into hooks, into invisible blades that cut when she gestured. She flicked her hand and something sliced across my shoulder, heat and pain and blood. Another motion, and the air itself snapped at my ribs, opening a line that burned like acid.

I drove at her anyway.

We collided in the space between the lines. Light against corruption. Discipline against hunger. She hit fast, each strike meant to break rhythm, to make me overcommit. I countered, keeping my feet under me, keeping my breath steady.

Cori joined for a heartbeat, her blade flashing between Dina and my throat. Dina twisted away and her laughter turned sharp.

"More friends," she said, and her magic flared outward like a wave. "An opportunity to finish what I started with your friend in Jaffa."

Cori's barrier took it and held, but it shoved her back, boots skidding on rock.

Lucan cut down a creature that had slipped around the flank, then pivoted and drove his sword through a sorcerer whose hands were already forming the next spell.

Zeke took a hit across the side, a dark lash that opened his shirt and painted his ribs red. He barely reacted. He just smiled wider and kept moving.

"Four minutes," Charlie said in my ear. His voice sounded distant, like he was speaking from the bottom of a well. "The frequencies are spiking."

Eliyahu and the Keepers were halfway to the center. The Architect's forces shifted with them, tightening the net, focusing their attacks, trying to stop them before they reached the focal point.

The Architect himself didn't move.

He watched.

As if the fight was noise.

As if the outcome was already written.

We drove forward anyway.

Magic struck from above, from the sides, from angles that should not exist. Corrupted fire rained down in sheets, forcing us to break formation. I threw up a ward and sensed it buckle under the pressure, the heat of it searing through the air.

Cori's voice cut through the chaos. Her power snapped into place, and a barrier rose, clean and hard, buying us seconds.

Lucan stepped into that gap and took three strikes meant for Eliyahu, his sword intercepting each one with a clang that vibrated through my bones.

Zeke moved to the other side, blade up, catching a creature that tried to slip behind us. He drove it back with brutal efficiency, then turned and cut down another that seemed to crawl out of the sigil itself.

The air shimmered as the Veil frequencies tightened. The convergence point pulled at everything. The magic around us didn't just move. It flowed, dragged toward the center like water down a drain.

That was when Yael went down.

A sorcerer hit her from the side with corrupted fire. It punched through her defense and burned. She hit the ground hard, breath knocked out of her.

Rabbi Moshe broke formation and moved to her without hesitation. All of it compressed into a single choice.

"Moshe, no!" Eliyahu shouted.

But the rabbi was already there, dragging Yael back, putting his body between her and the next strike, still chanting in Hebrew even as the creature closed the distance.

A creature moved in.

Fast. Wrong.

It hit Moshe before anyone could reach him.

The sound of impact carried across the water. Bone and stone.

The chanting stopped.

Moshe fell and did not rise.

Avraham screamed and surged forward. He met the creature with steel and rage. He drove it back and cut it down, but the act cost him. It pulled him out of position. It opened the line.

More sorcerers surged into the gap.

"Two minutes," Charlie said. His voice was shaking now. "Jimmy, you need to activate. The convergence is accelerating."

Eliyahu was close. Five meters, maybe less. But the air between him and the focal point was filled with spells, with bodies, with violence shaped into barriers.

I disengaged from Dina and ran toward Eliyahu.

"Lucan, Cori, Zeke," I shouted. "Defense. Around him. Now."

They understood instantly.

The shift was immediate.

We stopped trying to win the fight and started trying to hold the world in place.

Lucan moved to Eliyahu's right, sword raised, stance wide, braced against impact.

Cori took his left, her blade glowing, her free hand already drawing wards in the air.

Zeke slid behind, sword up, shoulders squared, guarding the rear with a grin that had gone sharp and empty.

I stepped in front.

Eliyahu pulled the device free, hands shaking, eyes fixed on the focal point.

We pooled our power.

Not separate strikes. Not individual attacks.

Combined defense.

A lattice of wards formed around Eliyahu, layered and reinforced, Cori's precision locking into my structure, Lucan's will anchoring it, Zeke's raw force adding weight, all of it wrapped around Eliyahu like armor made from light.

Spells hit us.

The wards flared.

Corrupted fire splashed and hissed and slid away.

Dark bolts slammed into the barrier and shattered into fragments of shadow that dissolved before they could reach him.

The air shook with impacts. The ground trembled. The loch behind the Architect churned now, ripples racing outward as the convergence pulled harder.

Avraham took one more step toward us, blood on his hands, trying to close the gap.

A sorcerer reached him first.

Corrupted magic touched his chest.

He went rigid. His eyes went wide. He fell.

Eliyahu reached the center.

I saw it clearly now. The exact geometric focal point where everything converged. The air shimmered there, dissonant, making my teeth ache just like Charlie had said. Reality looked too tight, pulled into alignment by forces it didn't want to obey.

Eliyahu raised the device.

"One minute," Charlie said. His voice was raw. "Activate now."

The Architect began to move.

Not rushing. Just walking. Calm. Certain.

"You're too late," he said.

Eliyahu pressed the button.

Nothing happened for a heartbeat.

Then the device began to vibrate and thrum. Low. Deep. A deep rumble that registered in my bones.

The sigils on its surface flared bright, painful to look at. The containment lattice was collapsing. The stored energy was preparing to release.

"Mister Crable," the Architect said, and his voice changed. The certainty cracked. Something else showed through. "You don't understand what you're doing."

"I understand enough," I said.

The hum grew louder. The air around Eliyahu distorted. Veil frequencies became visible. Waves of force radiated outward from the focal point.

The Architect's expression shifted. Understanding. Concern. A flash of something close to fear.

"That's not supposed to..." he began.

The device detonated.

The world froze in complete and utter silence.

A pulse of pure interference spread outward from Eliyahu's position. Expanding. Growing. A wave that scrambled everything in its path.

The impact hit like a fist to the chest and the skull at the same time. My magic scattered. My senses reeled. The world tilted.

Sound returned, and the Veil screamed.

Not metaphorically. Not poetically.

It screamed in frequencies my ears could not process but my mind could feel. Pain. Shock. Violation.

The Architect's sigil flared. All the corrupted energy he had been channeling suddenly had nowhere to go. The interference pulse cut off pathways and broke synchronization.

But instead of collapsing cleanly, the network locked.

The Veil locked.

Reality froze like a machine jamming under too much pressure. The barrier between worlds stopped.

Completely.

And in stopping, it fractured.

Cracks appeared in space itself. Not breaks. Not openings. Fractures. Like safety glass after impact. The Veil was still there. Still intact. But damaged. Frozen in a state that could not sustain itself.

"Charlie," I shouted, "what's happening?"

His voice came back panicked. "The Veil is locked. Not open. Not closed.

The resonance we have been tracking is frozen. James, this wasn't supposed to happen."

The fractures spread. The damage cascaded through the structure.

Then the Veil reacted.

It grabbed us.

All of us.

Not gently. Not with intention. It reacted like something wounded.

Reality tore.

The sensation hit of being pulled by forces I could not see or fight. The ground vanished. The sky vanished. Everything became chaos.

I tried to grab onto something. Anything.

I saw Cori reaching for me. Our hands almost touched.

Then she was gone.

Pulled away. Torn into a different current.

Lucan vanished. Eliyahu disappeared into the fractured space. Dina was pulled away mid-laugh, her expression shifting from amusement to shock. The sorcerers disappeared one by one, grabbed by different currents and scattered. Even the Architect's creatures twisted through the chaos before blinking out of existence.

The Architect himself fought it for a moment. I saw him trying to anchor himself to the sigil, power flaring around him, ice-blue eyes wide with effort. But the Veil's reaction was too violent. Even he couldn't resist.

His expression as he vanished wasn't anger.

It was shock.

Pure, complete shock that his perfect system had failed.

Everyone scattered.

Thrown.

Distributed across the Veil's network like debris in a hurricane.

No control. No choice. Only violent displacement.

Then I hit something.

Ground.

Solid.

Real.

I lay there for a long moment. Disoriented. Nauseous. Every sense scrambled. My magic felt distant, like a limb that no longer answered.

Slowly, the world came back.

Trees. Dense forest. Hot. Humid. The smell of earth and vegetation and something older beneath it.

I pushed myself up. Checked for injuries. Nothing serious. A few cuts and bruises, and shock.

"Cori," I called. "Lucan. Zeke."

No answer.

I was alone.

Completely alone.

The forest around me was thick. Jungle, not Highland. Somewhere tropical. Somewhere far from Scotland.

My earpiece crackled.

"James," Charlie's voice said. Frantic. Then relieved. "James, can you hear me?"

"I'm here," I managed. "Where am I?"

"I don't know," Charlie said, fingers typing in the background. "Your signal is unstable. Central America. Guatemala maybe. James, what happened? One second you were all in Scotland and then every signal scattered. Global distribution. Everyone is in different locations."

"The Veil locked," I said. "The device froze it. It threw us."

"It looks like cross guardian sites," Charlie said. More typing. "I'm seeing pings from everywhere. Cori is alive. I got a signal from Japan. Lucan is in Australia. Eliyahu is alive. South Africa. Zeke appears to be in Norway."

I sat heavily against a tree. The weight of it landed all at once.

We had stopped the Architect. We had prevented him from reshaping the Veil.

But we had broken something else instead.

The Veil was locked. Frozen. Fractured. Unstable.

And the team was scattered across the planet.

"Charlie," I said quietly, "how bad is it?"

"Bad," he replied. "The Veil is not broken, but it's not whole. It's frozen.

I don't know what that means. Right now, I am making sure everyone is alive."

I closed my eyes. Listened to the jungle around me. Insects. Birds. The distant sound of water.

I didn't even know if we had won the battle. If what we did was worse than the Architect planned. And the war was far from over.

"Start mapping everyone's locations," I said. "Get them to safety. Then we can figure out how we fix this."

"On it," Charlie said. Then, softer, "James. We'll figure this out."

I wanted to believe him.

But sitting in a jungle thousands of miles from where I was supposed to be, with Cori in Japan and the Veil fracturing around us, belief was like a luxury I could not afford.

I stood. Checked my bearings. Started walking.

There was work to do.

There was always work to do.

22

Epilogue – Grief, Guilt, and the Healing

PART 1

The cemetery was crowded.

I stood at the edge of the gathering, watching mourners file past the simple pine casket. The sun was too bright for this. The sky too blue. The world should have been gray.

David's funeral.

The body had been released by the Tel Aviv District police four days after Jaffa. Flown home to Centerville. To the small Jewish cemetery on the edge of town where his grandparents were buried.

The service had been brief. Traditional. The rabbi spoke about David's life. His work. His dedication to preserving what mattered. Words that were both true and insufficient.

Casey stood beside the casket with Erin. Her face was stone. She hadn't looked at me once since the service began.

David's parents stood on the other side. His father, Michael, leaned heavily on his mother, Ruth. Both looked smaller than I remembered. Diminished. Like grief had carved pieces away.

The mourners had torn black ribbons pinned to their clothes. Keriah. The visible symbol of a heart that had been rent.

I wore mine over my heart.

It felt appropriate.

The rabbi finished speaking and stepped back. The casket was lowered into the ground. The sound of wood settling into earth was too final and too permanent.

The first shovel of dirt hit the casket with a hollow thud.

Jewish tradition. The mourners help bury their dead. Don't leave the work to strangers. Face the reality of what's been lost.

I watched as people took turns. A shovelful of earth. Then another. The sound of dirt on wood filling the silence.

Casey's turn came. She gripped the shovel hard enough that her knuckles went white. Threw the dirt with force. Then again. And again. Each impact like an accusation.

When she finally stepped back, Erin took the shovel from her hands gently.

The line continued. Colleagues from David's company. Friends from graduate school. People who'd known him as family, as a friend, as a good person who'd died too young in a senseless act of violence.

That's what they'd been told. Random violence. Wrong place, wrong time.

They didn't know about Dina. About the Architect.

They didn't know their friend had died protecting something they'd never even heard of.

When it was my turn, I took the shovel.

The weight of it was like every choice I'd made may have been the wrong one. Nikolaos. The children of Anglesey. Arnaut. And now David. Every moment I'd hesitated or acted or tried to do the right thing and failed weighed on my conscience.

I shoveled dirt onto David's casket.

The sound echoed in my chest.

I handed the shovel to the next person and stepped back.

Cori moved beside me. Her hand found mine. Squeezed once.

I didn't deserve the comfort, but I held on anyway.

The burial continued until the grave was filled. The rabbi said Kaddish. The mourners' prayer. Words in Hebrew that had been said over the dead for thousands of years.

Yitgadal v'yitkadash sh'mei raba.

Magnified and sanctified be His great name.

The words washed over me. Ancient and worn smooth by grief.

When it finished, the mourners began to leave. Quiet conversations. Embraces. The slow dissolution of a community gathered to witness loss.

David's parents remained by the grave.

I knew I should leave. Should give them space. Should let them grieve without the weight of my presence.

But Ruth saw me. Her eyes met mine across the cemetery.

She gestured. A small motion. Come here.

I walked over slowly. Cori stayed back, giving us space.

"James," Ruth said. Her voice was rough. Raw from crying. "Thank you for coming."

"I'm so sorry," I managed. The words were pathetic. Insufficient. "I'm so sorry."

Michael looked at me. His eyes were red.

"He loved you," Michael said quietly. "Did you know that?"

The words hit like a fist.

"He talked about you all the time," Ruth added. "About the work you did together. About how much he learned from you. How honored he was to help."

I couldn't speak.

"He said you were doing important work," Michael continued. "That you were protecting things that mattered. He was proud to be part of it."

No. No, no, no.

"He shouldn't have been there," I said. My voice came out broken. "I should have sent him further away. Should have made sure he was safe."

Ruth reached out and took my hand.

"David made his own choices," she said gently. "He chose to help you. Chose to be there. He believed in what you were doing."

"That doesn't make it okay," I said. "That doesn't bring him back."

"No," Michael said. "It doesn't. But it means something that he died doing what he believed was right."

I stood there, holding Ruth's hand, and felt the weight of years of failure pressing down.

Jerusalem. Wales. Constantinople. Jaffa. The same pattern. The same choices. The same crushing guilt.

I thought I'd learned. Thought I'd changed.

But David was still dead.

And I was still the one left standing.

"Thank you," Ruth said again. "For being his friend. For giving him purpose. For caring about him."

They left. Walking slowly back toward the cars. Leaning on each other. Carrying a grief I couldn't take from them even if I offered.

I stood alone at the grave for a long moment.

The headstone wasn't up yet. Just the fresh earth. The flowers people had left despite Jewish tradition saying not to. The visible evidence that someone who mattered was gone.

I stared at the dirt until my eyes started to blur.

Then I sensed a presence beside me.

Casey.

I hadn't heard her approach. I only sensed the shift in the air, like a storm had stepped close.

She stood with her arms crossed tight over her chest, like she could hold herself together by force. Her eyes were fixed on the fresh earth. Not the flowers. Not the people. Just the dirt.

For a long moment, she didn't speak.

Then her voice came out low and rough.

"I can't do this," she said.

I didn't ask what she meant. I already knew.

She swallowed hard. Her throat worked like she was trying to force something down that wouldn't go.

"I keep waiting for it to feel real," she whispered. "And it won't. It's just stuck. Like my brain refuses to accept it."

Her hands clenched into fists, then loosened, then clenched again.

"And I'm so angry," she said, the words shaking now. "I'm angry at him. I'm angry at you. I'm angry at Dina and Arnaut. I'm angry at God, and I don't even know if I believe in God."

She let out a laugh that wasn't a laugh at all. Just air and pain.

"I'm angry at myself because I keep thinking maybe if I'd grabbed his arm harder, maybe if I'd yelled louder, maybe if I'd..." Her voice broke and she stopped, pressing her lips together like she could hold it back.

But she couldn't.

Her eyes filled and she turned away from me fast, wiping at her face with the heel of her hand like it offended her.

"I don't want to be this person," she said. "I don't want to be the one who falls apart in public. I don't want to be the one who screams or shakes or can't breathe."

She stared at the grave again.

"But I can't stop it," she admitted, quieter. "I can't stop seeing it. I close my eyes and I see him on the ground. And I keep thinking... if he can die, then any of us can."

Her shoulders rose with a breath that hitched halfway through.

"And that means I can die," she said. " Charlie can die. You can die. *Erin* can die."

As she said Erin's name more tears came out.

Then her voice sharpened, sudden and bright with rage.

"And you're still here."

The words weren't cruel on purpose. They were just honest. Honest grief that comes out when it has nowhere else to go.

I didn't flinch.

"I know," I said.

Casey stepped closer, and her anger had nowhere to land except the space between us.

"I hate that I don't know what to do with this," she said. "I hate that I can't fix it. I can't talk my way out of it. I can't work harder and make it go away. I can't be the one to make us all feel better."

Her eyes locked on mine.

"I can't even punish the right person," she said, and the bitterness in her voice made my stomach twist. "Because she's gone. And the people who did this are always gone. They always disappear. And all I'm left with is this."

She gestured at the grave with one sharp motion.

Then she shook her head, breathing hard now, like she was trying not to drown.

"I need it to be someone," she said. "I need it to be somebody's fault."

Her voice dropped again.

"And the worst part is I know David would have done it anyway, even if he knew the consequences."

She said his name like it was a bruise.

"I know he would have," she repeated. "And I hate him for it. And I love him for it. And I don't know how to hold both."

She blinked hard. Another tear escaped anyway. She wiped it away immediately, furious at herself for letting it happen.

Then she looked at me, and for the first time there was something under the anger.

Fear.

Raw and exposed.

"I don't want to lose anyone else," she said. "I can't do this again."

I nodded slowly.

"I won't ask you to," I said.

Her mouth tightened.

"You can't promise that," she said, and it wasn't an accusation. "We're involved now. Erin is involved now." It was a fact.

Casey stared at me for another second, and her expression flickered, the anger slipping just enough for something else to show through.

Not forgiveness.

Not peace.

Just the smallest thread of recognition that I was carrying my own version of the same weight.

"I don't hate you," she said, like the words cost her. "Not the way I want to. Not the way that would make this easier."

I didn't speak. I let her have it.

She took a breath, shaky and uneven.

"But I need space," she said. "And I need you to stop looking at me like you're waiting for me to say it's okay."

"I won't," I said.

She nodded once.

Then she turned away, shoulders squared again, forcing herself back into the shape of a person who could walk.

But her hands were trembling at her sides.

When she reached Erin, she didn't even try to stay upright.

She just fell into her.

And the sound that came out of her wasn't anger anymore.

It was everything underneath it.

Erin held her. Tight. Steady. Like she could keep Casey from coming apart completely if she just didn't let go.

Cori came back to my side. Her hand found mine again. Quiet. Present. Not trying to fix anything.

Charlie joined us a moment later. He looked uncomfortable in his suit. Like he wasn't sure what to do with his hands.

"His parents seem like good people," Charlie said quietly.

"They are," I replied.

"This wasn't your fault, Jimmy."

"I wish I believed that."

"No," Cori said firmly. "Dina killed David. The Architect's network put him in danger. You tried to protect him. He believed in doing the right thing, right up until the end."

"I didn't try hard enough."

"You can't protect everyone," Charlie said. "You can't control everything. You did what you could."

I looked at him. At Cori. At two people trying to help carry weight they couldn't possibly understand.

"I've been doing this for too long," I said. "Fighting threats. Protecting people. Trying to keep the world safe. And I keep losing people. Keep watching friends die because I made the wrong call or moved too slow or thought I had more time than I did."

"That's the work," Cori said gently. "It costs. It always costs. But that doesn't mean it's not worth doing."

"David would agree," Charlie added. "He knew the risks. He chose to help anyway."

I thought about David's last words. About him telling me it wasn't my fault. About him making a choice that cost him everything.

It didn't make his death hurt less.

But it meant something that he'd chosen it.

We stood in silence for a while. The three of us at the edge of a grave in a small Ohio cemetery.

Finally, I spoke.

"We need to move forward," I said. "Fix what's broken. The Veil. The way we work. All of it."

"We will," Charlie said. "The druids are helping with the Nail. Eliyahu is reaching out to other Keepers. Lucan is contacting the old Watch members he trusts."

"And you're building a network," Cori added. "Coordination. Shared knowledge. The thing the Watch should have been."

"It'll take time," Charlie said. "Money. Resources. We're talking about a global organization. Multiple groups working together. That's not something you build overnight."

"But it's something we can build," I said.

"Yes," Cori agreed. "It is."

I looked down at David's grave. At the fresh earth. At the space where a headstone would eventually stand.

"We're going to fix this," I said quietly. "All of it. The Veil. The Watch. Everything we let break. No more fighting alone. No more losing people because we didn't coordinate. Didn't trust each other. Didn't share what we knew."

I meant it as a vow. A promise to David. To Nikolaos. To every person I'd lost over centuries of trying to protect a world that didn't know it needed protecting.

"We'll do it together," Cori said. "All of us."

"The Keepers. The druids. Whomever answers the call," Charlie added. "Everyone who understands what's at stake."

I nodded slowly.

The work ahead was massive. Rebuilding trust between groups that had been separate for millennia. Fixing a Veil that was frozen and fractured. Finding the Architect before he tried again. Dealing with the corruption that still spread through guardian sites across the world.

And doing it all while carrying the weight of everyone we'd lost.

"Let's go," I said. "We have work to do."

We walked back through the cemetery together. Past headstones marking lives lived and lost. Past the visible evidence that everyone's time was finite.

Behind us, David's grave settled into the earth.

The work wasn't done.

It was never done.

PART 2

The Nail sat in the center of the table, sealed in its silver case.

We were gathered in the lower chamber of the Keeper compound in Jerusalem. The same room where Charlie had briefed us before Scotland. The same maps on the walls. But different people now. Different purpose.

The druid leadership had arrived three days ago.

Maeve sat across from me, her hands folded on the table, her expression calm but watchful. She led the Council of Groves and carried herself with the quiet authority of someone who didn't need to announce their power. Gray hair pulled back. Sharp eyes that missed nothing. She'd brought two others with her. Bryn, an older man with weathered features and the bearing of someone who'd spent decades working with the land, and Seren, younger, maybe forty, with the quiet intensity of someone who had spent years studying things most people didn't believe existed.

They'd come because I'd asked Elaine to reach out to them. Because the Nail was corrupted and we needed help understanding what had been done to it. Elaine had brought the request to the Council of Groves, and they'd agreed to send representatives.

Charlie sat beside Eliyahu, laptop open, data streams running.

Lucan stood near the wall, arms crossed, watching. Cori sat beside me.

Maeve reached forward slowly and placed her hand near the case. Not touching. Just close enough to sense what was inside.

Her expression tightened.

"May I?" she asked, gesturing to the case.

Eliyahu nodded. "Please."

Maeve opened the case carefully. The Nail lay inside, wrapped in cloth. She pulled the cloth back just enough to see the metal beneath.

The corruption was visible if you knew what to look for. A darkness in the iron that shouldn't exist. A wrongness that made the air around it feel heavy.

"This is deeply wrong," she said quietly.

"How bad?" Eliyahu asked.

She studied it for a long moment before answering.

"The corruption isn't surface damage. It's woven into the very essence of the metal. Into its nature. Whoever did this understood how to twist something pure into something poisonous."

Bryn leaned forward, studying the Nail without touching it.

"It reminds me of land that's been poisoned," he said. "When toxins seep into soil, into water, they change the fundamental character of the place. The earth remembers what it was, but the corruption has rewritten what it is."

"The base material is ordinary iron," Eliyahu said. "But something has been done to it. Changed it at a fundamental level. The corruption is stable but present. Like it's been locked into the metal itself."

"Can it be cleansed?" I asked.

Maeve looked at Bryn. The old druid studied the Nail for a long moment before speaking.

"Yes," he said finally. "But not easily. And not quickly."

Seren leaned forward.

"You were right to point out the cutting of the ancient oak that you returned to us," she said.

The clipping from the tree that the Romans felled when driving out the Druids from Wales. The piece of wood that the Church had corrupted that led to a massacre.

"The earth healed it over time," Seren said.

Bryn nodded.

"You buried it on sacred ground. Let it rest in a place where the natural power was strong and clean. Over time, the earth pushed the poison out. It took years, but the corruption faded."

"That took years, time we don't have now. Do you think you can expedite that process with the Nail?" I asked.

"I do," Bryn replied. "The principle is the same. Corruption is unnatural. It fights against the world's natural order."

Maeve carefully rewrapped the Nail and closed the case.

"The question is where," she said. "We need time to study it and work our magic. We need sacred earth to work from."

"If you are willing to perform the cleansing, we can host it here," Eliyahu said firmly. "In the compound. We have sacred ground beneath this site. Ground that's been protected for over two thousand years."

"That could work," Bryn said thoughtfully. "If the ground is strong enough. Old enough. The corruption in the Nail is severe. It would need to be buried in earth that has deep roots. Deep memory."

"The catacombs beneath the compound. The oldest sections. Some of those chambers go back to the Second Temple period," Eliyahu offered.

Seren spoke up.

"We'd need to prepare the site properly. Cleanse the chamber. Create the right conditions. The earth needs to be receptive, ready to do the work."

"The golem that lives below us can assist," Eliyahu said.

"How long would the preparation take?" I asked.

"Days," Seren replied. "Maybe a week. We'd need to work with the Keepers to understand the site. To make sure we're not disrupting other protections already in place."

Bryn stood and moved closer to the table, his eyes still on the case.

"The process itself is simple," he said. "We bury it in the sacred earth. Create a perimeter of natural protections. Rowan. Salt. Running water if possible. Then we work the land to speed the healing process. Our order will need unrestricted access to the chamber during preparations."

"And you're certain it will work?" Lucan asked from his position by the wall.

"No," Bryn said honestly. "The oak in Anglesey was living wood. This is iron. Worked metal. The principle should be the same, but..." He shrugged. "We've never tried this with something like this before."

"But it's the best chance we have," Maeve added. "Corruption this deep doesn't respond to just magic. Doesn't respond to force. It has to be coaxed out. Naturally."

Maeve looked around the table.

"So. We prepare a chamber in the catacombs. We work together, druids and Keepers, to create the right conditions. We bury the Nail and let the earth do its work. And we monitor it to see if the corruption fades."

"Yes," Eliyahu said.

"How long?" I asked.

"We won't know until we begin. Weeks? Months? It depends on how it responds."

I nodded.

"Then we have an agreement," Maeve replied. "The Council of Groves will provide the knowledge and the preparations. The Keepers will provide the site and the security."

She stood.

"We'll need to see the catacombs. Understand what we're working with. Begin the preparations."

Eliyahu rose as well.

"I'll take you down myself. The oldest chambers are restricted, but under the circumstances..." He glanced at me. "This is worth making an exception."

Maeve, Bryn, and Seren followed Eliyahu out of the chamber. Their voices faded as they descended deeper into the compound.

Charlie closed his laptop.

Cori looked at me.

"You think this will work? The cleansing?"

I thought about the oak cutting I buried in Anglesey.

"I don't know," I said honestly. "But it's better than keeping it sealed in a box forever. At least this way, there's a chance it can be cleansed."

Charlie stood.

Lucan pushed off from the wall.

"I'll talk to Eliyahu about security. Make sure the wards around the catacombs are as strong as they can be. We need to keep the site safe."

They left, leaving Cori and me alone in the chamber.

She looked at the table where the Nail had been.

"The druids seem trustworthy," she said quietly.

"They are," I replied.

"And if this works? If the Nail can be cleansed?"

I thought about that. About what it would mean. A corrupted artifact restored. Proof that even the deepest damage could be healed given time and the right conditions.

"If it works," I said slowly, "then maybe there's hope for other things too."

She understood what I meant. Arnaut. The corrupted guardians. Even the Veil itself, frozen and fractured.

"We should get some rest," Cori said. "Long day tomorrow."

"Always is," I replied.

We left the chamber together. Behind us, the lights went dark.

In the catacombs below, the druids and Keepers were preparing sacred ground, creating conditions that would hopefully cleanse the corruption.

It was a small thing. One artifact. One attempt.

But it was a start.

And sometimes, that was enough.

About the Author

Jack Calder grew up in Ohio, spent several years living in London, and now resides just outside Washington, DC, proof that he can thrive in everything from Midwestern winters to British drizzle to Beltway chaos. He spent most of his adult life in corporate strategy and M&A, with more than two decades of global experience, he has spent an impressive percentage of his life in airports. His work has taken him across Europe, the Middle East, and Asia, giving him a front-row seat to the cultures, histories, and odd coincidences that inevitably find their way into

his fiction.

A devoted world traveler and unapologetic lover of food and wine, Jack insists that every new setting in his stories should be researched thoroughly, which usually involves a good meal. When not writing or working abroad, he enjoys life with his wife, while their three college-aged children check in just often enough to remind him they still exist, usually when they need something.

You can connect with me on:

🌐 http://www.jackcalder.com